"MY NAME IS RAIDER. I'M AN OPERATIVE OF THE PINKERTON NATIONAL DETECTIVE AGENCY."

The lieutenant listened impassively, fingering his crossed cartridge belts, then asked, "You come to Mexico for what purpose?"

"I am trailing an American who stole his father's money," said Raider.

"I think you are under arrest," said the lieutenant.

"Why?" Raider was astounded.

The lieutenant shrugged. "I do not think you are a Pinkerton. I think you are an American shootist, come to hunt William Bridenbaugh like the rest of Mexico...."

J.D. HARDIN

SONS AND SINNERS

PLAYBOY
PAPERBACKS

CHAPTER ONE

Caleb Comstock tilted his chair back against the wall, pulled the cigar from his mouth, and lifted his glass of whiskey. "Yes, sir," he said in his raspy voice. "Callin' in the Pinkertons was the smartest thing we ever did." He tossed off his whiskey. "Smartest thing we ever did."

At his words, Doc and Raider looked at each other, eyebrows raised. John Swain, the sheriff of Valencia County, remained silent as well. He puffed sullenly on his own cigar and stared into the glass of whiskey before him on the table. He nodded as if he agreed with the banker, but Raider knew very well he did not agree. The bankers had hardly given him a vote of confidence when they called for the Pinkertons.

Caleb Comstock poured himself another glass of the cheap, raw whiskey with which he was favoring them. "You, Doctor?" he said to Doc. Without waiting for an answer, he poured Doc's glass full. "We are grateful, gentlemen," he said to Doc and Raider.

Doc smiled. "It's our business, Mr. Comstock," he said smoothly.

"Well, the whiskey is on me, the steaks are on me, and if you happen to want . . ." He pointed a finger toward the two sorry-looking whores at the bar and winked. "That's on me, too."

Raider looked at the two whores. Old and hard, they matched the quality of the whiskey. The steak dinner would likely be the same. Raider's stomach hurt. He took another swallow of the whiskey. It went down hot.

5

But Doc . . . Raider knew what he would say. He looked at him and silently formed the words he knew would issue out of Doc's mouth as soon as he smiled wide enough.

"Why, thank you, Mr. Comstock," Doc said. "It's very generous of you."

Bullshit. Doc was full of it. He had some kind of stupid saying about how more flies are caught with honey than with vinegar. And he was playing the honey tonight. He had bathed and had himself shaved. He was wearing one of his New York suits: three-button, light gray, with a pale yellow silk vest and a white silk shirt. He held a lighted cheroot between two fingers. He sipped Comstock's whiskey as if it were good, aged bourbon.

"You saved us the expense of a hanging, Mr. Raider," said Comstock.

"That was an accident," said Raider.

Comstock laughed. "Not hardly. He would have shot you down in cold blood if you hadn't been faster than him—shot you and Dr. Weatherbee, too. Or so I hear. It's what they say."

"We would have preferred bringing the boy to trial, Mr. Comstock," said Doc. "That's one of Mr. Pinkerton's principles—that we do not hunt men down and kill them; we bring them to justice."

"Justice was done in this case," rasped Comstock. "Tommy O'Connell killed a dozen men in the course of his robberies. Right, John? Isn't that right?"

The sheriff nodded. He was an old man, in his sixties, Raider judged. He was leathery, rawboned. He wore a five-day growth of white whiskers—probably because he had himself shaved just once a week—and his cigars had stained his bushy mustache. He was embarrassed. He had taken Raider for the bank robber and had thrown him in the Valencia County jail. He was embarrassed, too, because Raider had escaped.

"There wasn't a bank safe from Houston to Laredo,"

Comstock went on. "He was what they call a desperado. Yes, sir, a real desperado."

Comstock exaggerated, Raider knew. Tommy O'Connell had not killed a dozen men, but he wanted people to think he had. He had wanted them afraid. Some ways he had been smart. It was as if he knew the banking business—and maybe he had. He had hit those banks when they had the most money in them. He had hit when they least expected him. He had worked in disguise. He had walked the streets of towns where he had robbed banks, half an hour after the robbery, unrecognized and safe.

Doc had figured him out. One way the boy had been completely stupid. If you took a map, the way Doc had done, and laid it out and marked the towns where O'Connell had hit banks, with the dates when he hit them, you could figure out how he was moving across south Texas, and you could figure out where he would hit next. Doc had misjudged him twice, but they had finally caught up with him and followed him here, to Scottsville. He'd decided he was being followed, and on the road outside Scottsville he had tried to bushwhack them.

"Steaks'll be ready in ten minutes, gen'mens," the saloon keeper yelled from behind the bar.

"I'm looking forward to that," said Doc with a smile at Comstock. "I could eat a horse."

Which is probably what you'll get, was Raider's thought. "Ten minutes," he said to the sheriff. "Time enough for me to go down to your office and pick up my .44."

"Sure," said the sheriff. "Deputy'll give it to you."

"I'll be back in time for the steaks," Raider said to Doc.

The sheriff had taken his .44 Remington when he threw him in jail two weeks ago. Raider had resented being without it. He had carried Doc's .38 Diamondback, but he didn't like it. When Tommy O'Connell opened fire on them, he had shot him down with his Winchester.

Raider strode across the saloon toward the door. The two whores smiled invitations at him. A young woman sitting at a table with a cowboy—probably her husband —smiled shyly, too. He was accustomed to being noticed and appreciated by women. He enjoyed seeing them appraise him. He was tall. His deep black eyes caught their attention. His black mustache sometimes did, too. It amused him to see how often their eyes dropped to the bulge in the tight crotch of his denim pants. The cowboy's young wife checked him there. He jammed his black Stetson on his head and walked out without returning her smile. He didn't need a fight with the cowboy right now.

His horse was tethered outside the saloon, and he decided to ride the length of the town to the sheriff's office and jail. He had bruised his leg when he threw himself off the horse to duck Tommy O'Connell's bullets, and he was gimpy. "Ho, Dave," he muttered to the gray stallion to quiet it. He had no idea what someone else had called the stallion, but he had called it Dave the four months he'd had it, and it seemed to respond. He liked it. He didn't often care what horse he rode, but he had developed a liking for this big, ill-tempered gray. "Ho, Dave." He sat easily, and the horse carried him to the far end of the town's one street.

"Hey, deputy!" No one answered inside the weathered brick and adobe building. "Deputy!" Impatient, Raider gave the door a shove. It opened. He walked in. "Deputy! Goddammit!"

The sheriff's man was not there. All right. He knew where his .44 was, and he did not intend to make a second visit to pick it up. He opened the desk drawer where he had seen the sheriff put it. It was there, in his holster, with his belt wrapped around it. He pulled it out, circled his hips with the belt, and felt the familiar weight of the Remington on his leg. He drew it, checked it for ammunition. It was loaded. Satisfied, he was ready to leave.

"Who's out there?" A woman's voice. A woman's small voice, from the rear of the building, where the cells were. "Who is it?"

Frowning, reluctant, Raider opened the door to the rear. "Laura!"

"Raider . . ."

She was locked in one of the cells: Laura, the girl who had traveled with Tommy O'Connell. She had run when he shot Tommy, but men from the town had caught her on the road and brought her in. He had seen her with Tommy, before Tommy began to suspect they were Pinkerton operatives and that they were following him. She had been a part of Tommy's disguise. He had walked the streets of towns with her on his arm —after he had robbed a bank in that very town—playing the part of the young drummer and his young wife, or the part of the farmer and his wife. They stayed in hotels. Posses had chased him all over the dust of south Texas, while he sat in a comfortable hotel room with Laura and laughed.

He was sorry to see her in jail. She stood behind the bars of her cell, looking as defeated as he had ever seen a human being look. She was too pretty to be in there. Her hair and eyes were brown, and she was on the plump side. She wore a white shirtwaist and a straight black skirt. Even though the shirtwaist was modestly buttoned all the way to her throat, the big round tits he had stared at before strained against the white cotton. This was not the first time his cock had swelled, looking at Laura.

"Raider . . ." she whispered. "Raider, don't go. Stay and talk to me."

Raider shook his head. "I'm sorry about this, Laura. I'm sorry you're in here."

"You couldn't be as sorry as I am," she said. She sighed.

He thought she was going to cry. Her little fists were

closed tight around two bars. Her knuckles were white. "Raider!" she whispered urgently. "Let me out!"

"Oh God, Laura," he said. "I wish I could."

"You can. Why not?"

"Because you're a bank robber, goddammit. And I'm a Pinkerton. My partner and I put you in there. I can't let you go."

She shook her head. "I'm not a bank robber," she said. "I'm not charged with being a bank robber."

"Then why is the sheriff holding you?"

"Ask him," she said.

"I'm asking you."

She sighed. "There've been telegrams back and forth. All yesterday. All today. Nobody's charging me with any crime. The sheriff is holding me here till my husband comes to get me. And my father."

Raider nodded. "Anyway, you're not going to the penitentiary then."

"I'd rather," she said simply, quietly. "I'd be better off. I'll probably get a beatin' from them. Then I can go back to the ranch and take up where I left off—cookin' for the two of them, washin' the filth out of their clothes. He'll have me pregnant soon as he can, my husband. That's what he wants. I ran off with Tommy O'Connell. It wasn't because I liked Tommy so much. Hell, Raider, I'd have run off with Billy the Kid."

Raider shook his head. "I'm sorry, Laura," he said. "If things were some other way, I . . ." He turned and walked back into the sheriff's office.

"Raider!"

He glanced back. She was pulling open her buttons. She ripped away the last two and pulled the shirtwaist open, spilling those two big round tits out where he could see them. They were even better than he'd thought: big, yes, but solid, with big pink nipples pointing at him. They were like two melons. She thrust them between the cell bars.

"Raider!" she whispered hoarsely.

"Laura . . ." He shook his head. "What can I do?"

She was tugging at her skirt. It fell to the floor. She tugged at a petticoat the same way. It fell, and she stood naked.

His cock throbbed. He looked down at it. She laughed.

"Bring it here, Raider."

"Through the bars . . . ?" he asked.

"Bring it here."

He stepped back inside the jail. He stopped. On a thought, he closed the door between the office and the jail, and on another thought, he unbuckled his gunbelt and hung it on the doorknob.

"Raider . . ."

She had slipped down to her knees. My God! She had it in mind to . . . He stepped up to her. She put one hand behind him, on his butt, and pulled him closer. With the other she unbuttoned his pants. She reached inside and pulled out his cock. For a moment she looked at it thoughtfully. Most women did. It was big. Long and thick. Then, with sudden resolution, she opened her mouth and took it inside. She tightened her lips over it and pulled back. Her lips slid the length of it and popped. She licked it. Her tongue was wet and velvety and warm.

"Drop your pants," she whispered. "So I can kiss your balls."

He was breathless. His mouth was dry. He thought his cock might shoot right now, before he'd had half of what she meant to give him. He unbuckled the thin belt he wore under his gunbelt and let his pants fall down. As she'd said she would, she began to kiss, then to lick, his balls. She sucked each of his balls into her mouth, first right, then left. She held them up and licked their underside. He thought he would come then. She thought he might, too, and she grabbed his cock and pulled it into her mouth. She sucked hard. She got it all in. It had to be in the back of her throat. He hung on the cell bars, his head thrown back, and moaned. He came. His balls pumped the juice through his cock, squeezing it through in hard spasms. Laura gagged once, then began to swallow it. She kept on sucking and licking. He kept on coming. When finally it stopped, and she stopped, he hung limp on the cell bars. She looked up at him, smiling contentedly, her chin glistening with what had run out of her mouth.

He stepped back, but she grabbed his butt with both hands. "No!" she whispered. "More."

"Ma'am, there ain't no more," he laughed breathlessly.

"Oh yes there is, Raider," she whispered. "There's another time and maybe a third time. We're not going to leave a drop in you."

"Laura . . ."

" 'Cause you're goin' to let me out of here. Aren't you? Aren't you, Raider? And I'm going to make it worth whatever you think it's going to cost you."

The steaks were eaten when he sat down again at the table with Doc, the sheriff, and Caleb Comstock. He cut a piece of his own steak. It was as good cold as it had been hot: stringy and tough and tasteless.

"Sheriff," he said. "You've had another escape from your jail. Your deputy wasn't there. The jail's wide open. Whoever you had in there is gone. I looked around that end of town for the deputy, but he's gone, too. Who'd you have in there?"

"Goddam!" said the sheriff. He looked at Raider angrily and suspiciously. "Laura Sweeney, Tommy O'Connell's girlfriend."

Raider gnawed on his bite of steak. "Shit," he said. "You've let one of our bank robbers get away from you."

Doc sat at the table with Raider after Caleb Comstock and the sheriff had gone—the sheriff to look for his deputy, Comstock back to his bank. Raider continued to chew on the tough meat while he waited for the barkeep to fetch a plate of beans he had ordered as soon as Comstock was out the door. Doc had ordered

another bottle of whiskey, this one some decent bourbon.

"Was she any good?" Doc asked innocently.

Raider reached for the bottle. "Best I ever had."

"You can be more kinds of damn fool than any other
man I ever saw," said Doc.

"She wasn't charged with a crime," said Raider.

"The hell she wasn't. They meant to hang her as an
accessory to two or three of Tommy O'Connell's kill-
ings."

"Shit," said Raider.

Doc shrugged. "I have to admit, I hated to hear them
talk about what they were going to do with her."

"Well . . ." said Raider. "She escaped. Wasn't there
when I got there. Maybe the deputy . . ."

"Unless you were stupid some way, they don't have
any choice but to buy the story that she wasn't there
when you got there," said Doc. "But you took one hell
of a risk. I hope she was worth it."

Raider shook his head. "She wasn't."

"How do you mean?"

Raider leaned back and smiled faintly at Doc over
his glass of bourbon. "While I was gettin' my pants
straightened out and wipin' up what she'd spit on the
floor, the bitch ran out the door and rode off on Dave.
She stole my goddam horse, my goddam saddle, and my
goddam Winchester."

Doc bent forward, laughing so hard he had to put
his head down on his arms on the table.

CHAPTER TWO

Judith was an amiable creature, for a mule. Raider had
to admit that. She ambled along the rutted, dusty road,
pulling the Studebaker wagon at her own speed—in-
furiatingly slow, in Raider's judgment—while Doc
scribbled endlessly in his diary and the reins hung loose.
Doc had shed his coat at least. He sat with his writing
board on his lap, dipping his pen in the bottle and
scrawling an endless succession of words on light blue
paper. He still wore his derby and his yellow silk vest,
and his yellow spats covered his soft button-up shoes.

"Damn!"

Raider laughed. Judith had pulled one of the wheels
of the Studebaker over a rock in the road, and the lurch
had jerked Doc's pen across the paper, spilling out a
big blot of ink.

"Where's *your* diary?" Doc asked.

"Diary my ass," Raider snapped.

"What about your report?" Doc pressed him.

"Report, shit," grumbled Raider.

"Well, I guess you won't mind if I write and send the
report, then," said Doc. "And I guess you won't complain about what I say of your part in the O'Connell
case."

"I don't care what you say. We got the son of a bitch,
didn't we?"

Doc shrugged and looked again to his writing. Judith
ambled on. Raider sighed. It looked like at this rate
they'd sit behind Doc's stupid mule for a year, while

14

he used a gallon of ink and wrote all over a wagonload of paper. If the country wasn't so poor and rattlesnakes so likely, he'd get down and walk.

"Too poor to grow peas," said Raider.

"What?" Doc asked. He looked up from his writing.

"This country. Too poor to grow peas."

Doc shrugged and looked back to his diary.

"My granddaddy used to tell about friends of his, from when he was a young man, that pulled up stakes and went off to what they used to call 'The Texies.' If they'd seen their 'Texies,' they'd have stayed home in Arkansas."

"It's got a certain beauty about it," said Doc.

"Shit," said Raider.

There were mountain peaks to the north. Dark clouds over the mountains meant a possible rainstorm. Raider thought about a big summer rainstorm, building up, turning the day cool, then dumping rain on the fields, greening up everything. Things would smell better. Right here, all it smelled was dry—that is, it would if he could smell anything but Doc's cheroot. He tipped his hat down over his eyes and tried to sleep. A dead man couldn't have slept with the incessant *scratch-scratch-scratch* of Doc's pen in his ears.

"Ah," said Doc at last.

"Ah, what? You got it all wrote?"

"The wire," said Doc.

Raider lifted his Stetson. Another road, a better one, was coming in from the right and would cross this one just ahead. A single strand of telegraph wire followed the other road, strung along a line of poles that stood all along it like forlorn dead trees.

"We'll send our report to Chicago," said Doc. He picked up the reins and guided Judith off the road, to a stop beside one of the poles. "You want to hook us up?" he said.

"Hook yourself up," said Raider. He pushed his hat down over his eyes again.

"Raider, goddammit . . ."

"Goddammit yourself, Doc. Why'm I always the one that's got to shinny up? Why me? Why not you just once? Just one goddam time, Dr. Weatherbee."

Doc had climbed into the back of the wagon and was lifting the floorboards to expose his telegraph batteries, toolbox, and weapons. "Since you won't write a report and you can't telegraph a report, it seems to me the least you could do is climb the pole and hook up the wire." He opened the box and took out the telegraph key. "The least you can do," he repeated.

Raider jumped down from the wagon and watched Doc carry out the key and the looped wire. "You'd like to get some pay money, I expect," Doc said. "Well, you're not going to get it until our report gets to Wagner in Chicago. So climb the goddam pole, Raider."

Raider drew a breath. "With them shoes, I'd be surprised you could walk across the ground as far as that pole," he said scornfully, nodding at Doc's thin-soled, flimsy, spat-protected shoes. "And that silly goddam hat'd fall off your head."

"This silly hat's got the code in it, so we can send the report," said Doc.

Raider snatched the curled-brim gray derby from Doc's head. Doc's blond hair fluttered in the dusty wind. "I don't see a thing in it," he said.

"In my head, you illiterate ass," said Doc. "Not in my hat."

"Then you don't need the hat," said Raider. He tossed the derby to the ground and gave it a contemptuous kick.

Doc grabbed the black Stetson from Raider's head, slammed it on the ground, and planted a foot on it. Cocking his head and grinning at Raider defiantly, he twisted his foot and ground the Stetson in the dust.

"Well, I be goddam!" yelled Raider. "I never seen a man who'd do a thing like that to a good Stetson. You know what you are, Doc? You're *depraved* is what you are." He looked sadly at his hat, flattened and dusty. "I oughta do that to you, is what I oughta do."

Doc backed away, bent down and picked up his derby, and stood and set it carefully on his head. "Will you climb the pole, please," he said calmly. "So I can send the telegram."

It was irritating to see Doc sit there, tap-tapping away on that key, all absorbed in what he was doing and sort of vacant in the face; but he was talking to somebody a thousand miles off, and you couldn't help but admire it some way. Raider gathered some brush and built a small fire. He would make some coffee while Doc tap-tapped and while they waited for an answer from Chicago. They had left Scottsville before dawn and had been on the road about four hours. Unless orders from Chicago sent them somewhere else, they were on their way to Abilene. If Wagner would wire some expense money and back wages, he could pick up a horse and saddle—and a Winchester, too— and go on ahead. He didn't know if he could keep his sanity if he had to ride all the way to Abilene in Doc's apothecary wagon.

Doc had hung out the signs on the wagon again this morning: DOCTOR WEATHERBEE—HOMEOPATHIC MEDI- CINE. CONSULTATION AND PRESCRIPTION, FREE OF CHARGE. Squatting over the coffeepot, Raider smiled to himself, thinking of how Doc had drunked up a Baptist preacher with Weatherbee Golden Tonic. The stuff was supposed to have iron in it. It probably did—the rust from the still. And sometimes women let him rub on their first dose of bust-developer cream. It was a con- venient cover, playing doctor; and it brought Doc a lot of fun, too. Doc was smart. And conceited. And dandi- fied.

Doc drank a cup of coffee while he waited for a reply from Chicago. When the sounder began to click, he hurried back to it and sat copying the message onto paper. He took the message, acknowledged it, and signed off. He unhooked the key from the wire and gave Raider a sign to climb the pole and unhook from the line. When Raider returned to the wagon, the key and the neatly coiled wire were stowed under the false floor with the batteries once again, and the Studebaker reassumed the identity of an itinerant apothecary's wagon.

Doc handed him the message from Wagner:

GO TO BRIDENBAUGH RANCH NEAR ADENA TEXAS STOP OUR CLIENT JACOB BRIDENBAUGH STOP JACOB BRIDENBAUGH WILL EXPLAIN YOUR ASSIGNMENT STOP URGENT YOU ATTEND TO HIS MATTER STOP DO SO WITHOUT DELAY STOP ADENA MERCHANTS BANK AUTHORIZED TO PAY YOUR ARREARS IN SALARY PLUS ACCUMULATED EXPENSES NOT TO EXCEED FIFTY DOLLARS APIECE STOP WAGNER STOP

Raider liked Jacob Bridenbaugh. He could see that Doc liked him, too, though for different reasons. Bridenbaugh was in his sixties. He had come out to Texas from Virginia many years ago, and he still spoke with the broad accent of a Virginian. He spoke slowly, softly, with the air of a man who had complete confidence in himself and did not expect very often to be contradicted. His square face was clean-shaven. His once sandy red hair was gray. His blue eyes were surrounded with deep lines, and they looked out on the world with obvious patience, tolerance, and some amusement. He smoked a cigar as they sat on the long porch before his ranch house. The evening was close and hot, and he had put aside his fringed buckskin coat. He sat in his shirtsleeves, with his collar loose and his black string tie lying casually aside.

"Sam's been with me a long time, haven't you, Sam?"

Sam nodded. He was a Negro man, about the same age as Jacob Bridenbaugh. "Yes, Jacob," he agreed. "A long time." He sipped from the glass of whiskey Jacob had poured for him as soon as he came to the porch. He was foreman of the Bridenbaugh ranch. A gray Stetson covered his curly gray hair. His mustache was thick and gray. He wore denims like Raider's, with a blue cotton shirt, and he carried a .32 Smith & Wesson in a holster on his hip.

Doc probably liked Jacob Bridenbaugh for reasons very different from Raider's. He had seen the dining room being set up for their dinner as he and Raider had followed a man upstairs to the rooms assigned to them, and he had seen white linen, gleaming silver, and bottles of red wine open and breathing on the sideboard. Jacob Bridenbaugh served fine bourbon and offered his guests fine, aged Havana cigars. Doc had, of course, responded as Doc would: by bathing, shaving, slicking down his hair, and dressing in his latest New York style suit, a light brown with a darker brown stripe in the wool, silk vest, silk shirt, polished shoes, spotless spats. Raider thought he had seen Jacob's eyebrows rise slightly at the sight of Doc when he came down for their before-dinner whiskies on the porch.

They had discovered in Adena, before they came out to the ranch, that the Bridenbaugh Ranch was estimated to contain some 240,000 acres and occupied almost one quarter of the whole land area of Monroe County. Jacob Bridenbaugh was president of the Adena Merchants Bank, from which they had drawn their back pay this morning. He was president of the Bridenbaugh Artesian Well Company and of the Bridenbaugh Brokerage Company. Raider had bought a new Winchester in Adena and had discovered that the Monroe Harness & Equipment Company was another Bridenbaugh enterprise.

"I suppose there's not much in this part of the country I'm not involved in," said Jacob modestly. "When Sam and I came out here, there was nothin'. If you needed somethin', you had to build it yourself, and that included a house to put a roof over your head, a store, a bank, a saloon, a water company . . . anything. I do believe we're goin' to get a rainstorm."

"God allow us that," said the foreman.

From the porch of the long, low ranch house, you

could see for miles across the flat Texas countryside, to a chain of hills almost out of sight in the distance. Black clouds growing over those hills were flashing with red and white lightning.

"Sam, you're welcome to take dinner with us, as you know," said Jacob to his foreman.

"Thank you, Jacob," said Sam. He stood and gulped the last of his whiskey. "I think I'll have dinner at my house."

The tall, slender, aging black man swung astride his horse. He touched his hat and trotted down the lane toward the gate that kept the cattle out of the irrigated grove and lawns around the house.

"My father gave me Sam the day I left Virginia, more than thirty-five years ago," said Jacob Bridenbaugh. "As soon as we were out of sight of the house and my daddy couldn't hear it, I told Sam he was a free man and could come to Texas with me or stay at home, as he chose. He chose to come with me. I stopped at the first lawyer's office we came to and formally manumitted Sam. I'm glad you met him. You may want to talk with him tomorrow. I want you to know I'd trust my life and everything I own to that man, anytime. He's a witness to some of what I want you to look into."

"He has his own house?" Raider asked.

Jacob nodded. "Built it himself. He has a family. He married an Indian woman some twenty-five years ago. He's been a better stud than I've been. He has children and grandchildren all over. Some of them work for me. Some have moved on. Myself, I only had three children. It's one of them we have to talk about."

Dinner was served by two young Indian women who worked quietly and knowledgeably around the table. They served salad and soup and veal with vegetables, and they kept the wine glasses half full. They kept taking Raider's fork and knife and replacing them with others, at first to his annoyance, then to his embarrassment. Having laid out his place with more silverware than he needed in the first place, still they kept pulling it away and putting down more; and he noticed, shortly, that Doc and Jacob were using all of the variety of forks, knives, and spoons on the table, while he kept using the same kind and seeing them disappear and be replaced.

Doc and Jacob talked about the wine. Jacob Bridenbaugh had it shipped to Texas all the way from France. It had been in the bottle twenty years and more. Raider was curious about it. He found he liked it. He would have drunk two or three bottles of it, if they had poured fast enough.

"I had a piece of land over near Beaumont," said Jacob Bridenbaugh. "Some ten thousand acres. There's been a railroad company formed, called the San Antonio, Houston & New Orleans Railroad Company. They propose to build a railroad connecting south Texas to New Orleans. Naturally, they've been around, selling railroad stock to every rancher and banker in south Texas. Well, I'm for the railroad, of course. It would be a good thing for this country. But I'm not for putting a lot of money in a business other men are going to run. I made them a proposition—I'd sell them my Beaumont land cheap, and they could sell it now for a little profit or hold it until the tracks are laid and sell it for a big profit." Jacob stopped and smiled. "You see my point. Maybe I could make it more profitable for them to build the railroad than to run off with the investors' money.

"Anyway, they chose to buy the land. My price was $25,000 in gold, to be transferred to my account in the McMullen Bank in El Aguila. I chose that bank because they had an account there, too; and, besides, the bank is run by my old friend Jeffrey McMullen. The deal was made. I put the deed in escrow with Jeff McMullen, against the railroad boys depositing my $25,000 in gold with him. I wrote Jeff and told him I'd want my gold here and was sending some men to pick it up. They'd pick it up September 8."

Jacob Bridenbaugh turned in his chair and looked

out the window. The rainstorm promised by the hills was coming. Lightning was flashing hard outside.

"I sent my younger son, Bill, to El Aguila to pick up the gold. Sam and two hands—one of them Sam's son—went with him. Sam came riding back here two weeks ago with a sad story. The four of them arrived in El Aguila and went directly to the bank to make themselves known. Then they took a day or two to enjoy what you might call the joys of the town. On September 9 they picked up the gold, which Jeff Mc-Mullen delivered to them in a pair of locked saddle-bags. Out toward the edge of town as they rode away, Bill wanted to stop and pay his last respects to a little whore he'd grown fond of in the cathouse. He went in; Sam and the others waited outside. Next thing you know the little whore is dead and Bill is accused of murder. Bill lit out and hid while Sam tried to straighten the thing out; the town called him and his son niggers and ran 'em out—lucky they weren't lynched. When they got back to where Bill and my other ranch hand were hidden, both were gone. There was a letter, hung on a branch over their campfire. I've got the letter. Bill said he was sorry, that he didn't kill the whore, but that they meant to hang him as if he did, and he had to run. He lit out for the border—along with the $25,000 . . . said he had to have something to live on. He said he'd probably go to Europe and he'd write me from there. I got a letter from Jeff McMullen, too. It says he's terribly sorry about what happened, but he says Bill did kill the girl, no question. I'm skeptical."

Doc looked up from his plate. "So, you want us to . . . ?"

"I want you to find out if my boy did in fact kill that girl," said Jacob Bridenbaugh grimly. "If he did, he has to go to trial and maybe to the gallows like any other man, though he's only nineteen. I want you to find him and bring him back. And I want the gold."

"It's a tall order, Mr. Bridenbaugh," said Doc.

Jacob Bridenbaugh nodded thoughtfully. "And," he

said, "if you bring me my son, cleared of murder, and
the gold, I'll turn over half the gold to you two as your
reward. How's that for making a tall order a little
shorter?"

Doc smiled and shook his head. "It's of course very
generous, Mr. Bridenbaugh, but we can't work on that
kind of arrangement."

"Why not?"

"The Pinkerton Agency doesn't operate that way. We
don't work on contingent fees, and we don't accept re-
wards. You'll be billed for our per diem plus expenses.
We don't accept any more or less."

Jacob Bridenbaugh extended his hand across the
table, first to Doc, then to Raider. "Honest men working for an honest business, by God," he said warmly.
"It's rare, and I couldn't ask for more."

CHAPTER THREE

Five miles outside the town of El Aguila, Raider and Doc separated. From now on they were a pair of strangers in town who had happened to arrive at the same time only by coincidence. If they acknowledged each other at all, it would only be as two men who happened to live in the same hotel. It was an effective way to operate. They had often done it before.

Raider had a horse, a big black stallion with wild eyes. He had told Jacob Bridenbaugh his horse had been stolen in Scottsville—though he didn't tell him how—and Jacob had offered horse and saddle. Raider had to sit him tight every minute. The stallion would twist and skitter, just to test him; and Raider understood very well that the first time the stallion caught him loose in the saddle, maybe asleep or half asleep, he would throw him on his head. The Mexican hand who had saddled him for Raider at the Bridenbaugh ranch had muttered *"bastardo!"* when the stallion lunged and nearly crushed him against the fence, and that was what Raider called him from then on—Bastardo.

He rode into El Aguila half an hour ahead of Doc's Studebaker. The town was bigger than he had expected: it had half a dozen saloons, two banks, three churches, stores, a telegraph office, two livery stables, two lawyers' offices, a dentist, an undertaker, a land office, and of course the whorehouse they would have to look into early in the investigation. If it was a bigger town than

24

he had expected, it was no more grubby than he had anticipated. The buildings, whether frame or adobe, were red with dust and sagging in disrepair. Scrawny trees lined the street; under one of the trees, half a dozen Indians lay in the dust, sleeping off a drunk. A cowboy lay on one of the boardwalks outside a saloon. As Raider rode by one of the saloons, a whore called to him from a window, made him a couple of signs that would have brought a blush to one of the drunken Indians, and hauled one of her tits out of her dress. He rode on.

Coming on a man in a respectable-looking four-wheeler—a lacquered rig hitched to a sleek brown mare —Raider stopped.

"Howdy," he said, touching his Stetson.

The man looked up. He nodded. "Howdy," he said. He was well dressed, in a suit, with boots, a gun belt, a dusty white Stetson.

"Stranger in town," said Raider. "Can you tell me where a man finds a good room to stay in?"

"There's no hotel," the man said. "A woman called Blake runs a boardinghouse on the south side of town. You'll see her sign. The Eagle there"—he pointed toward a saloon—"has got a dozen rooms upstairs. Tell the man you want the third floor."

"Obliged," said Raider. He touched his hat again and swung Bastardo toward the Eagle Saloon.

By the time he had rented a room for the week and carried his roll and Winchester up, Doc had arrived in El Aguila. Raider went downstairs to the saloon and was having a whiskey at the bar when Doc came in to rent a room; Doc had seen Bastardo at the hitching rail outside the Eagle. Raider watched the saloon keeper rent Doc a room. The man made it plain enough he did not like the slick easterner, did not like his derby, his suit, his talk. He charged Doc a dollar more per night for his room than he had charged Raider.

Raider went outside. He swung up on Bastardo and rode him to the livery stable down the street, the one the saloon keeper had recommended. On the way, he rode past the McMullen Bank, a small gray frame building under what probably was the town's only real shade tree. There was a bench in front of the bank where three men sat in the shade, smoking. One old man, with a full white beard, wore a badge but no gun —an odd sheriff, to Raider's way of thinking. The old fellow wore a black suit, smeared with dust, a white shirt open at the collar, and no necktie. An unlit cigar hung from a corner of his mouth. If this was the man who had concluded that William Bridenbaugh shot the whore, maybe there was hope that he hadn't.

He asked the man at the stable what the sheriff's name was.

"Jimmy Tate," said the middle-aged man who took Bastardo's saddle as Raider loosened the cinches. "He's been sheriff of Bravo County since there's been a Bravo County. You got business with him?"

"Just saw him on the street," said Raider. "Wondered if he was Jimmy Tate. I'd heard his name before."

"He was a good man in his day," said the stable keeper.

Raider nodded. "I heard that."

"Mind if I ask what brings you to El Aguila?"

"Bastardo," said Raider, slapping the rump of the horse.

Doc, traveling half an hour behind Raider, left the Eagle Saloon as Raider was on his way back from the livery stable. They passed on the street. Raider pretended not to see the dandified eastern doctor driving his mule-drawn Studebaker wagon with the garish medical placards on the side. Doc showed no sign that he recognized the tall, gun-carrying man who walked along the boardwalk before the McMullen Bank. But he did notice that Raider was not subtle in peering into the bank. The lawman sitting on the bench could well take him for a possible bank robber.

The stable keeper shoved a feed bag on Judith's muzzle before he unharnessed her from the wagon. He took an immediate liking to her and promised Doc he would take good care of her.

When Doc left the stable he crossed the street and walked along the side opposite where Raider had walked, opposite the bank, and in front of two saloons, the Snake and Joe Murphy's. There was a boardwalk in front of the Snake and some boards laid in the dust in front of Murphy's, but none after that; as he walked along in front of a dry-goods store and a harness and saddlery shop, he walked in the dust and dried dung. The saloons were doing brisk business at midday. A barber shaved a customer on the sidewalk in front of his shop, in the shade of a dusty, water-starved tree.

"Hey, you!"

Doc turned. A man had come out of Joe Murphy's and was striding after him. He was a young man, no more than twenty, with an ill-trimmed mustache and several days' growth of dark beard. He bore down on Doc with a scowl—obviously a little unsteady from whiskey.

"Who're you? What's your name?" the young man demanded.

"My name is Dr. Weatherbee," said Doc.

The young man stood with his hands on his hips, nodding with skepticism and scorn. "Ummm . . ." he breathed. "Dude. We got a doctor here. Don't need another'n."

"Ah," said Doc. "That's good. I'm glad to hear you've got a doctor in town. I'll have to meet him."

"You better just pack up and move on."

Doc appraised the young man. He was not as tall as Doc himself, but he was heavier, a good twenty pounds heavier. He wore a Colt revolver on his hip. His boots were expensive calfskin, the kind Raider wore, but they were scarred and stained. Doc saw no point in arguing with him. "You're probably right," he said. "Maybe I'll just do that."

"I'll give you an hour," said the young man sullenly.

Doc drew a deep breath. *"You'll* give me an hour? Who are you?"

The young man reached for his Colt. Doc had not anticipated that, exactly, but he had instinctively tensed for something, and he was poised and fast. His fist shot forward and crushed the young man's nose flat against his face. As the young man reeled back, groping for his gun but momentarily disoriented, Doc's right cross struck like a club against his ear. The fellow went down, face first in the dust.

Doc knelt over him. He slipped the Colt out of the young man's holster, broke it open, and poured the cartridges into the street. He flung the gun across the street. It skidded ten yards in the dust and disappeared under the boardwalk in front of the Eagle. He stood. He looked around. A dozen people had seen what had happened. Some turned their faces away; some men just stared curiously, unmoved. Doc glanced around once more for a hostile move from somewhere, then walked on up the street.

He found the doctor's office and went in and paid a call. The doctor was his own age and no more a medical graduate than he was. Dr. Hinkley, as he called himself, said he probed bullets and set bones; he could preside at a birthing but preferred to let the midwives do that. "Heart, cancer . . ." He shrugged. "What you got in your wagon is as good for them as anything I can do. Sell all you can. Makes no difference to me."

"I understand you had a shooting here a couple weeks ago," said Doc. Sitting at Dr. Hinkley's window, he could see the street. He had watched the young man stagger across the street, looking for his Colt, yelling and lurching, his nose bleeding. "Heard about it on the road."

Dr. Hinkley shrugged again. "Couple weeks ago? We've had half a dozen shootings in two weeks. El Aguila is not New York, Dr. Weatherbee."

"This one was unusual. Someone shot a woman."

Dr. Hinkley nodded. "Oh, yeah. Susie Bradford.

Yeah. A drunked-up kid from up at Adena shot one of the little gals in the local whorehouse. Did you know her or something?"

"Name's familiar," said Doc. "I do know a family named Bradford, up around Waco, and they did have a daughter run away from home. Could be . . ." Doc rubbed his chin as if speculating. "Did you examine the body?"

"No. She was dead, and they took her directly to the undertaker. If her family wants to claim the corpse, it can be done. She ain't buried yet."

"How come?" Doc asked, surprised.

Dr. Hinkley smiled. "The undertaker here in town is named Ben Dunlop. Ben likes to get paid for his work. And he's what you'd call an entrepreneur, I guess. He embalmed Susie and laid her out, thinking Sister Edwards, the madam over at the whorehouse, would pay for it. Sister wouldn't pay, so Ben still has the body; and he's gettin' his money, two bits at a time. Hand over two bits and you can have a look at Susie Bradford. He's got her laid out under glass, and I guess a thousand people have paid their two bits and took a gander. There was a lot of curiosity about her killin', you know. It's what you might call a scandal."

Doc took a deep breath and set his shoulders before he pushed open the door and walked into the Benjamin Dunlop Undertaking Parlor.

"Yes?" said the quiet, unctuous voice of the undertaker.

"Uh . . . you Mr. Dunlop?" Doc asked.

Dunlop nodded. He was a man with flaming red hair and a square, freckled face—with the hardest, most uncharitable set to his mouth that Doc had ever seen. He was dressed in black, of course.

"What can I do for you?" he asked.

"Well, I . . . I understand you've got the corpse of that whore that was shot here in town. I, uh, hear you show her. I just arrived in town. I . . ."

"Twenty-five cents," said Dunlop.

Doc dug a quarter out of his pocket. Dunlop gestured for him to follow and led Doc through a door to the rear of the room and down a short corridor. Coming to an open door to the left, he pointed, and Doc walked into a small, windowless room where the corpse lay on display in the yellow light of a single coal-oil lamp.

Two women with two children stood staring. Doc was appalled. The women's mouths were open, and they stared with eyes transfixed, while their children, a boy and a girl, neither more than twelve, stood with their hands covering their mouths and tried to suppress their giggles. The corpse of Susie Bradford lay in a pine box. She had been a girl of perhaps nineteen, a brunette. She didn't look like she was asleep; she looked dead. She was not dressed but covered with a white sheet. Dr. Hinkley had said she was laid out under glass. She wasn't. The coffin was open. A hand-lettered card lay on her stomach. It said DON'T TOUCH.

The undertaker stepped into the room. His hard look at the two women suggested they had stayed as long as their money entitled them to stay. Doc wondered if he had charged two bits apiece for the children. The women smiled wanly at the undertaker and left, dragging the children with them.

Dunlop stepped to the coffin and whipped the sheet off the corpse. She was naked. "I don't let women and children see this," he said to Doc. "That there's the bullet hole."

There was indeed an ugly brown hole just above the breasts and square in the middle of her chest. Doc felt dizzy. He got control of himself by clenching his fists and drawing a deep breath. "Uh . . . is the bullet still in her?" he asked.

Dunlop nodded. "I never tried to get it out. It didn't go on through and out her back; I can tell you that much."

"Who shot her?"

Dunlop sighed as if he were tired of the question.

"Fellow named Bridenbaugh. Haven't hung him yet. He got away into Mexico. May never see him again. She was a whore. He took a fancy to her, but he got drunk and wild and shot her."

Doc was chewing his lower lip. "How long can you keep her?" he asked.

"Heard of a fellow up in Illinois that's kept one twenty years," Dunlop said. "Got ahold of a murderer that was hung, embalmed him good and set him up in a glass case, and he's been showin' him for twenty years." Dunlop shrugged. "I won't keep her much longer. Curiosity about her's runnin' down. I'll put her in the ground one of these days."

Someone knocked at Raider's door.

"Who is it?"

"Doc. Open up."

Doc had made no concession to the heat. He still wore his shirt, his vest, his coat—and of course his silly-looking domed hat, the derby. He came in, glanced with mild contempt at Raider lying naked on the bed, and sat down in the one chair the room afforded. "We've got a job to do tonight," he said.

"You made yourself some trouble this afternoon, Doc," said Raider.

"The bastard was drawing on me," said Doc.

"Yeah, they said that. Even so, they didn't like it. He's one of theirs, son of one of the town's citizens."

"Who you been listening to?"

Raider sat on the bed. "Men at the bar downstairs. They talked about how the new dude in town beat up on Billy Bob Galvin. His daddy owns a ranch outside town."

"I can't help that," said Doc. "I've got more important things to worry about."

"Then I suggest you break out that peashooter of yours and start to carry it," said Raider.

Doc nodded in agreement. "We *do* have a job of work to do tonight," he said.

"It'll have to wait for cooler weather," said Raider.

"It can wait until the wee hours of the morning," said Doc.

" 'Wee hours of the morning,' " Raider repeated sarcastically.

"You hear what the local undertaker has done with the body of the girl William Bridenbaugh is supposed to have killed?"

"I heard. Enough to turn a man's stomach."

"Yes. And what we have to do will turn it even more."

"Huh?"

"We are going to break into Dunlop's funeral parlor tonight and dig the bullet out of the corpse of Susie Bradford."

Raider stared angrily at Doc for a moment, then grabbed his shirt over his hips, as if he were embarrassed to be naked in the face of so obscene an idea. "Doc," he growled. "In a lifetime of listenin' to stupid ideas, I thought I'd heard every damn-fool notion there was; but for sheer goddam stupidity that overtakes anything I ever heard before."

Doc smiled faintly. "There's a very good reason," he said. "I have to do it, whether you help me or not."

"Why?" Raider snapped.

Doc took a cheroot from his coat pocket and scratched a match on the floor beside his chair. "Did you notice the gun Sam carried? I mean Jacob Bridenbaugh's foreman, the Negro. Did you notice?"

Raider frowned. "Smith & Wesson," he said. "Model 2, I think."

Doc puffed on his cheroot. "Caliber?"

"Uh . . . a .32, wasn't it. All Model 2 Smith & Wessons are .32 caliber."

"Right," said Doc. "I saw two more of them on the Bridenbaugh ranch. I asked Sam about it. He told me Jacob Bridenbaugh bought two dozen of them. Just about every man on the ranch carries a Smith & Wesson Model 2."

"Including William Bridenbaugh, I suppose," said Raider.

Doc nodded. "And he was carrying his the day he is supposed to have shot Susie Bradford. So, if we dig the slug out of the corpse and it's not a .32 . . ."

"But hell, Doc, we *can't!*"

"Why not?"

"Somebody'd lynch us if they found out. Allan Pinkerton'd never stand behind you on that."

Doc shook his head. "To the contrary. Where do you think I got the idea? If you dig a slug out of a body and that slug could not possibly have come from the gun that was supposed to have killed the person, you have incontrovertible physical evidence that that gun did not kill that person—and the person who was carrying that gun did not do it either."

"The court that's going to try William Bridenbaugh won't take your 'incontrovertible physical evidence,' " Raider argued sullenly.

"Unfortunately, that's probably true. The Pinkerton Agency is ahead of the law."

"Then why should we go and do a filthy job like that?"

"Because we need to know," said Doc flatly. "If the slug in that corpse is not a .32, I'm going to wire Wagner that he can tell Jacob Bridenbaugh his son did not commit murder."

"And we have to find some other way to prove it."

"It's easier to prove what you know than what you don't. I have to do it, with you or without you."

Opening the rear door to the funeral parlor was no problem for Doc. From his kit under the floorboards of the Studebaker he had taken several items besides a bullet probe, and from his coat pocket he now extracted a spring-steel lock pick. In a minute he turned and whispered to Raider that they could go in.

It was pitch dark inside. They could see nothing,

hear nothing. Doc had been inside the building during the day and remembered generally the layout of the center hallway and the rooms to each side, but Raider was wholly disoriented. With his left hand on the wall, he inched along, following Doc, who was invisible ahead of him even though he was no more than two feet away. He shivered. The night was still hot, but he dreaded happening on a corpse laid out in the funeral parlor.

"Here," Doc whispered quietly.

Raider had no idea what that meant, but he stopped. He heard what sounded like Doc turning a doorknob.

"Damn! Locked."

He heard the rasp of the pick again. In a moment he heard the faint squeak of hinges. He groped for the door, found it, and walked into Doc's back where he stood in the doorway.

"Close the door," Doc said.

Raider closed it. Doc struck a match. In the orange glow Raider saw a small, windowless room, and on a pair of trestles in the center stood the open pine coffin. His eyes fixed on the pale, silent corpse, and he shuddered just as the light went out.

"I brought a carbide lamp," said Doc. "Here." In the darkness he shoved a big piece of cloth—a sheet—at Raider. "Stuff this under the door. I don't want any light showing in the hall."

Raider obeyed. He heard the hiss and smelled the metallic odor of acetylene as Doc opened the valve on the little tank and water began to drip on the chips of carbide in the gas generator. Doc struck a match, the lamp popped to life, and the room was filled with brilliant white light.

Raider stared at the naked corpse. The sheet that had covered it was the one he had stuffed under the door. The body was bruised. Maybe the girl had been beaten before she was murdered. He felt unsteady on his feet, and he backed against the door.

"All you have to do is hold the lamp," said Doc. He

handed over the little carbide lamp. "And stand steady. I'm the one who has to touch her."

Not exactly, he didn't, Raider noticed. Doc pulled back his coat and shirtsleeves, then he pulled on a pair of rubber gloves. He glanced at Raider, shook his head and sighed, then took from his pocket a surgical instrument, a sort of long, flexible needle on a wooden handle. He inserted the needle into the bullet hole in the chest of the corpse. She had been dead for two weeks and more, but immediately the wound began to ooze and stink. Doc's face looked pained, and he shook his head emphatically. But he pushed the probe deeper into the wound, until suddenly it stopped.

"There it is," he said. He wobbled the probe and jabbed it two or three times against the obstruction in the bullet hole. The probe was six inches into the body. "Could be a bone chip," he said to Raider. "Whatever it is, I've got to pull it out."

"Be quick about it," Raider muttered. His stomach was churning, threatening to expel the whiskey he had drunk and the beef and beans he had eaten a few hours ago.

Doc pulled the probe out of the hole. He put it aside and took the bullet extractor from his coat pocket. It was like a pair of scissors, but longer and thinner, with toothed jaws at the end. He was sweating as he pressed the extractor into the bullet hole. He worked in the deep hole with the extractor, opening and closing the jaws, pulling up, losing whatever he was pulling out, getting another grip, working it out. His pale face glistened with sweat. Raider saw him weave as if he would faint and saw him steady himself and concentrate on his work.

He pulled out the bullet. He held it up in the light from the carbide lamp. "There you are," he said. "A .44 slug if ever I saw one. William Bridenbaugh did not shoot this girl with a Model 2 Smith & Wesson; and since that's what he carried, I judge he didn't shoot her at all."

CHAPTER FOUR

"Not many gen'men come round mornin's," said Molly. "Not many come have had a bath. Not many come sober. Fact is, not many come that actual are gen'men."

Doc liked her. She was a plump, short blonde, with big white breasts and a shaved crotch, and she had been the only girl in the house willing to get up in the morning to serve a customer. Beulah Edwards, the hard-eyed madam the town called Sister Edwards, had said he'd have to be satisfied with Molly if he wanted to get laid this time of day. He had said he liked to come to a house in the morning; people weren't in such a big hurry then; and he had paid five dollars and said he might spend an hour or so with Molly. Sister Edwards said that that would buy his hour, but if he wanted to stay longer he'd have to pay two more. He had handed over two more immediately, saying he didn't want to be hurried. That was his cover for spending enough time with the little whore to engage her in conversation about the murder of Susie Bradford.

"A travelin' doctor," Molly mused. She picked up the items of his clothes, one by one, marveling at the silk of his shirt. "All I can't understand is why a gen'man the likes of you would come to a two-bit town the likes of El Aguila."

"How did *you* wind up here, Molly?" Doc asked.

She sat down on the edge of the bed. Both of them were naked, and he had already taken his quick satisfaction of her. She took his limp penis in her hand and began to massage it into another erection. "I come from Looziana," she said. "Always said I'd make some money workin' in a whorehouse and then I'd go home and nobody'd know how I made it. That's how come I picked out a little town like this—that and that I heard Sister Edwards run a fair operation, which she does."

"You going to go home, then?"

She shook her head. "You can never go back, after you do this. It puts a mark on you. Anyway, I'm a drinkin' woman, an' it pleasures me to have three or four or five different cocks a night. I like cock, Doctor. I really like yours." She bent down and licked the glistening fluid off the tip. "I'd like a drink. You put up a dollah for a bottle?"

"I'll put up two dollars if you got something better than rotgut."

"Hee!" She ran to the door and yelled down the hall. "Nigga! Nigga! Bring me a two-dollah bottle. A *real* two-dollah bottle."

Doc took the two dollars from his pants and laid them on the table by the bed.

"Now, Doctor," said Molly. "You just lie still and relax like, and Molly'll show you how she pleasures a tired gen'man."

Pushing him gently, she turned him on his back, and she lifted herself astride him. Pressing his penis into her wet hole with both hands, she let herself slowly down until all of him was in her. She smiled lazily and began a rhythmic, slow undulation of her hips. The movement was minimal, but the sensation was electric. Immediately he swelled inside her, and he could feel himself tensing for another explosion.

"Hmmm-mmm," she admonished. "Don't come. Take it easy, Doctor. We want this one to last and last." She stopped her undulations, but somehow she closed the muscles inside her and began a series of gentle squeezes. "Just relax. This kind stuff it takes a gen'man to 'preciate, and I 'xpected you was the gen'man that would know how."

"I can learn a few new tricks, I guess," he whispered hoarsely.

"No cowboy ever can 'preciate this. He's got to ride a woman like he was trying to bust a hoss. Guess it proves somethin' to him. I reckon there's nothin' much that has to be proved to you, huh, Doctor?"

He did relax. As she had promised, the pleasure lasted. He relaxed, and the pleasure in his loins sustained itself.

A Negro woman came in with the bottle of whiskey. She took his two dollars, opened the bottle, poured two glasses, and handed one to each of them. Doc blushed, but if she noticed, she ignored it. She took the time to pick up a couple of towels from Molly's dresser before she went out.

"I went to the undertaker and saw the body of that girl who used to work here." Doc said to Molly.

"I don' wan' talk 'bout that," said Molly. Her broad, flushed face turned solemn.

"Can't somebody get up enough money to pay that bastard off and get the girl buried?" he asked.

Molly shrugged "Susie don' know nothin' 'bout it and don' care," she said.

"How'd it happen?"

She shrugged. "Stuff like that happens. This ain' no Sunday school, y' know."

"You see it happen?"

"Nobody seen it happen. It happened in her room, when she was alone with the guy."

"You hear the shot?"

Molly shook her head. "This place gits so you cain't hear thunder. Yellin' drunks, somebuddy playin' the pye-anner. And people shoot off guns sometimes, out the windows—sometimes even through the ceiling." She shook her head. "I was downstairs, and this Bridenbaugh boy comes runnin' down the stairs yellin' Susie was dead. He run right out the door. Couple cowboys stopped him out on the porch, 'cause we wuz all yellin' stop, murderer. He was drunk. They took his pistol away from him. It had two empty shells in it. Then these two niggers came up on the porch and pulled their guns and took him away from the cowboys. They worked for him, as I hear tell. They rode off, hell-bent. Later them niggers came back and tried to tell the sheriff their boy hadn't done it. Sheriff tole 'em to go git him and bring him back, then he'd listen to why he didn't do it. That's the last anybody seen of any of 'em. The boy run over into Mexico, and the niggers run back to the man that owns 'em—or used to own 'em, back when you could own 'em."

"Why'd he kill her, do you suppose?" Doc asked.

Molly sighed. She had stopped squeezing his penis, and she reached for her glass and took a big swallow of whiskey. "You ask a lot of questions, Doctor," she said. "You a friend of them Bridenbaughs, come to find out what happened?"

Doc shook his head. "I heard about the shooting of Susie Bradford all the way to Scottsville. I've heard several versions of it. I saw the body. I'm just curious."

"You talk to Sister Edwards 'bout it?" Molly asked, raising one eyebrow.

"I asked her what happened."

Molly shook her head. "Should'n done that, Doctor," she said. "This here's a private town, very private. It won' take to your askin' questions."

"Who runs the town?"

She swallowed more whiskey. "Bankers, saloon keepers . . . some of the ranchers."

"Jeffrey McMullen?"

"Sure. And that son of his, Tom McMullen."

"His son runs the town?"

"Runs over it is more the way to say it. Him and a bunch of his friends, other young fellows, sons of them that really runs things. They shove their way into anything, beat up anybody they want, wave their guns around. Nasty bunch."

"Punks," said Doc.

Molly nodded. "Yeah, punks. They come here and don't pay, is one thing they do. And I know what you're gonna ask me, so the answer is, yeah, Tom McMullen took a particular fancy to Susie Bradford. He climbed on and off her bed all the time, and he never give her a nickel. Now, Doctor, I'm goin' to ask you a question. You want to go on playin' detective, or whatever it is you're playin', or do you want to screw?"

She began again the undulations of her hips, and Doc laughed and thrust himself upward, deeper inside her. "*Molly . . .*" he grunted.

"Just relax, Doctor," she said. "Stick your attention on this. It's much more 'portant."

So an operative could telegraph Wagner in Chicago without the local operator knowing he was sending a wire to the office of the Pinkerton National Detective Agency, it was arranged that a telegram could be sent to any of a number of Chicago business offices and if it were addressed to a Mr. Wagner, it would be forwarded immediately to him. Since the suspicion of the local telegrapher would be aroused if he had to transmit a message that was obviously in code, a number of prearranged signals were used. Doc's telegram to Illinois Pharmaceuticals & Chemicals, Inc., Chicago, read:

PLEASED TO REPORT PATIENT DID NOT SUFFER AS WE THOUGHT STOP DIED OF ENTIRELY INDEPENDENT CAUSE STOP WILL CONTINUE TO PRESCRIBE AS WE DISCUSSED STOP DOCTOR WEATHERBEE STOP

Outside the telegraph office Doc paused to light a cheroot. He was tired. He had slept only two or three hours. Molly had been enough to drain the strength from an elephant. It was nearly noon, and he thought he would go back to the Eagle now, eat something, and take a nap in the heat of the day. He turned to walk toward the saloon.

"You! Your name Weatherbee?"

Doc stopped. A burly man wearing a silver star on his shirt hurried across the street toward him.

"Yes, I'm Dr. Weatherbee," he said as the man came up to him.

The corners of the man's mouth turned down scornfully, and he planted his hands on his hips and nodded. "I bet you are," he said. "And a fine figure of a man you are, too. I hear you're pretty quick with your fists. Want to try them on me?"

"I don't see any reason to do that," said Doc. The man was pot-bellied, but under the flab Doc could see a foundation of big bones and heavy muscle. "What's *your* name, friend, and what's the badge?"

"I'm no friend of yours, dude," the man said. "My name's Horace Chandler, and I'm a deputy to Sheriff Jimmy Tate. I hear tell you busted the nose of a young man on the street here yestiddy."

"He reached for his gun," said Doc.

"Let's me reach for mine and see what you do," said Horace Chandler, and he pulled a Colt Peacemaker from his holster. He pointed the gun at Doc's belly. "Want to take a crack at me, dude?"

Doc shook his head. He had the Diamondback under his coat, but if he reached for it he was a dead man, for sure.

Horace Chandler snapped the pistol upward. The tip of the barrel hit Doc under the chin. It snapped his head back. The sight broke his skin, and when he touched it with his hand, his hand came away with a smear of blood.

"Don't seem to have much fight in you," said Chandler.

Doc could have struck. When the pistol was up, he could have clubbed Chandler hard on the nose with a quick fist, followed by a kick that would have immobilized him sure. But he was a deputy sheriff, and knocking him down would have ended any possibility of Doc continuing to work as a Pinkerton operative in El Aguila. He wiped his chin and restrained himself.

"I'm a man," said Chandler. "You busted a boy's nose, but you don't seem to got the heart to bust a man's."

Chandler's face was flushed and sweaty. His beady eyes were dull and without expression. A lock of greasy yellow hair hung from under his ragged, dirty hat. He could kill; Doc could see that. Doc licked his lips. Chandler's guard was down now. Doc could pull the Diamondback if he had to.

"Hear you like to ask questions," said Chandler. "Why don't you ask 'em of *me?*"

"What kind of questions?" Doc asked cautiously.

Chandler grinned. " 'Bout the dead whore," he said. "Hear you got a lot of questions 'bout her."

Doc shook his head. "Just curious. Heard a lot about her. Just wondered how it all happened."

Chandler lifted his chin high. "How it all happened is the law's business," he said. "And in this town Jimmy Tate and me is the law. You got questions, you ask me and don't ask no others. You understand?" Chandler returned the Peacemaker to his holster. "I said, *you understand,* dude?"

Doc nodded. "I guess I understand. You have a way of making yourself plain."

Chandler's big fist came up faster than Doc could duck. It hit him alongside the jaw, knocked him off balance, and Doc slid down against the wall of the telegraph office. "Wanta git up now and bust my nose like you busted the boy's yestiddy?" Chandler asked.

Doc rubbed his bruised jaw. "I believe I'll sit right here and rest awhile," he said. His right hand was on the Diamondback, and if Chandler had made one more threatening move, Doc would have drawn and fired.

"Figgered you would," said Chandler. He glanced around at the men on the street who had watched all that had happened. "Some way I jus' figgered you would, dude." He grinned at the watching men. "Might be a good idee if you packed up your medicine-show wagon and moved on, too."

"Maybe I will," said Doc. "People here don't seem to take to me too well."

Raider had found Doc sitting on his bed, stark naked in the heat of an El Aguila afternoon, writing in his case diary.

"Don't finish writin' it till I finish the story," said Raider. " 'Fat shit deputy gets jaw busted.' "

"*I* could've busted his goddam jaw," said Doc. "Then I could have loaded up and left town."

Raider sighed noisily and angrily. "Pinkerton don't pay enough for what we have to put up with," he said. He sat down facing Doc from the chair. "Cuttin' up corpses. Takin' beatings on the street. Shit!"

"You've always wanted to quit," said Doc.

"Yeah, and leave you here to get stomped into the dust," said Raider.

"You look at that bullet?" Doc asked.

Raider nodded. "Yeah, while you were gettin' it off at Sister Edwards's. Nothin' odd about it. It could have come from any .44." He pulled it from his pocket and tossed it on the bed beside Doc. "Not a thing different about it from any bullet that come out of any .44."

Doc picked it up. "Maybe," he said. "Look at the gouges in it. Those were made in the barrel of the gun that fired it." He tossed it back to Raider. "You suppose a Remington marks a bullet differently from a Colt, or both of them differently from a Smith & Wesson?"

Raider stared at the bullet. "Could be, I s'pose. Barrels are made different." He shrugged. "So what?"

"The Pinkerton Agency is studying guns and bullets," said Doc. "Maybe someday we can take a bullet like that and tell what kind of gun fired it—maybe even *what* gun fired it."

Raider shrugged. "Maybe," he said. "Right now we don't know what gun this bullet came from, and we have no way to find out. Even if you could read those gouges like Chinese hieroglyphics, what you gonna do, pick up every gun in Texas and shoot it into a cow and pull out bullets till you get one marked like this?"

Doc chuckled. "Anyway, it's not a .32—which is what Bridenbaugh carried. And I'll make you a bet Tom McMullen carries a .44."

Raider shook his head. "You're 'way ahead of your game, Doc," he said. "I looked into the bank this morning. Jeffrey McMullen looks like the respectable, solid banker you'd like to put your own money with. About the same age as Jacob Bridenbaugh. Nice-lookin' old man. They think well of him around here. The cattlemen put their money in his bank."

"Hear anything about his son?"

Raider shook his head. "Nothin'."

"You hear anything about anybody breaking into the funeral parlor last night?"

"No. You cleaned off that corpse. Nobody's goin' to know the bullet's gone out of her. If anybody did, there'd be hell to pay in this town this morning."

"More than I paid on the street," said Doc. "This town's tense about the shooting of Susie Bradford."

"Not exactly," said Raider. "They're jumpy about somethin' else."

"What?"

"Some of them've got an idea that Jacob Bridenbaugh's the richest man in Texas and that he might decide to come down here from Adena with a hundred ranch hands and shoot the hell out of the town that accused his son of murder. I heard more than one drunk at the bar telling how they'll act when what they call 'the Bridenbaugh war' starts."

Doc stood and dipped a cloth in the water in the bowl on his stand. He pressed the wet cloth to his chin and wiped away a drop of blood. "You feel like getting yourself relieved up at Sister Edwards's," he said, "be sure to ask for Molly. Give her enough money to have her awhile and let her do it her way. It's enough to make you forget somebody pistol-whipped you and knocked you on your ass."

Raider grinned. *"You* let 'em do it their way, Doc. With me they gotta do it *my* way."

CHAPTER FIVE

Raider chose to find his pleasure elsewhere. He had been watching a girl work the bar at the Eagle. She was not the best-looking whore he had ever seen—not by a long shot—but she intrigued him. She was small, young, pretty. But she was timid, which was strange for a whore. She appraised men carefully before she approached them, and when she approached, she approached cautiously, as if she were afraid of rejection. When she climbed the stairs with a man, she looked down over the barroom as she went, as if she were afraid someone was watching.

He heard someone call her Kathleen. Her hair was auburn, long and straight. Her eyes were blue. If he did not think she was the prettiest whore he had ever seen, maybe it was because she had so furtive and timid an appearance about her and because she did not have the big bust he liked on a woman. On the other hand, her hair was pretty, and her skin was smooth. Being a whore did not seem to have coarsened her, the way it did most girls. When, on his second night at the Eagle, she approached him, he bought her a whiskey, and then he agreed to take her up to his room for two dollars.

Upstairs in his room, she asked him to turn down the lamp before she took off her clothes, and when she was naked she slipped under his sheet as quickly as she could, giving him only a glimpse of her thin body. He jerked the sheet off her, to have a look, and it was evident it caused her pain to be seen. She spread herself dutifully, and he had her. He could not complain that she did not do what he had paid her for. He came hard in her. He came fast.

When she sat up and reached for her petticoat, Raider seized her hand. "Wait a minute," he said. "That was quick. We don't have to run back downstairs. You don't pick up new customers that fast, anyhow."

"I . . ." she said. It was plain she was afraid of something. "Someone's waiting for me."

"Really? Who?"

The girl looked into his face and blinked as if she were blinking back a tear. "Never mind," she whispered.

"What the hell is this?"

She drew breath. "I'll stay as long as you want," she said. "Your two dollars' worth, anyway."

He tossed the sheet off them both and lay back to look at her. She sat on the edge of the bed, looking down at him. Her tits *were* small, but they were nice— delicate was the word: sort of pointed and hanging down. Her belly was flat. She tossed her head to toss her long hair out of her face, and she stared down at him solemnly.

"I can see a girl not liking what you do for a living," he said. "But if you like it as little as you seem to, why do you do it?"

"I've always done it," she said. "Since I was a little girl. It's not a bad living."

"It's not so good, either," he said. "You came upstairs three times last night."

"I used to come up more."

"'Used to,'" he said. "What's changed?"

She looked away from him. "You're from out of town. A man who lives here won't touch me," she said sadly.

"Why? *You got a disease?*"

"No. You don't need to worry about that."

"Then?"

Kathleen sighed. "Just trouble, that's all."

Raider reached to the lamp and screwed up the wick, brightening the light. He sat up. "What kind of trouble? Have I got into trouble for bringing you up here? You somebody's daughter?"

She shook her head. "You're new to El Aguila," she said.

"I've been here long enough to take a strong dislike to it."

She looked into his face. "Like any town, it's got a bunch of men that own it. You know how that is. McMullen, the banker. Galvin, who has a big spread north of town and runs a thousand head of cattle on it. Murphy, who has Murphy's Saloon across the street. Taber, who owns the Eagle. Hawthorn, the other banker. There's a couple more ranchers, Taylor and Putnam. Some others . . . It wouldn't be a bad town just for them. Every town belongs to somebody, and a girl like me has to live with that and maybe sometimes give away something others would have to pay for. I don't mind that. I'm a realist. But here it's different."

"The punks," said Raider.

"Bullies," she said. "McMullen's son. Galvin's. Taylor's. Both Murphy boys. Sometimes others. They swagger around town. They carry guns. They take what they want from everybody. Well . . . not everybody. They take from people like me, who have no way to stop them. I don't think they'd bother you. You look like a man who could stop them."

"One of them get his nose busted yesterday?" Raider asked.

She nodded. "Billy Bob Galvin. The out-of-town dude hasn't heard the last of that."

"And what do they do to you, Kathleen?"

She raised her chin. "They sort of declared me their property. One or two takes me every night. And they pay. But I can't live on one or two a night. Any man who knows about them won't take me. They don't want the trouble."

"Isn't there anything but cowards in El Aguila?" Raider snorted.

"Yes," she said. "A few men. There are two or three who come in for me, just to show the punks who's what. But the run of men who'd come to me, don't. The least there'd be is a scene downstairs. The worst, they'd get killed."

"These punks really ever kill a man?"

"Yes. Joe Hawthorn shot a drummer about six months ago."

"Over what?"

"I don't know. It happened at Murphy's. Argument. Drunk."

"The law?"

She smiled sarcastically. "Old Jimmy? Or Horace, the deputy? Which one of them's going to uphold the law?"

Raider handed the girl her petticoat. "The more I see of this town," he said, "the less I like it."

When they went downstairs there were twenty men in the saloon. Doc was sitting at a table against the far wall, with a whiskey and a plate of beef and potatoes. The talk in the room subsided as Raider came down the stairs with Kathleen, and Raider saw Doc put his hand under his coat, on the Diamondback. The girl nudged his arm, then she fell behind, and he walked down the last of the steps alone.

He saw the punks at the bar. He recognized the Galvin boy by the bandage over his nose. It was nervy of Doc to sit there and eat with that one in the saloon, and Raider wondered if there had been another confrontation. He didn't know any of the others, but they were an obvious knot at the bar, drinking together a little apart from the other men there. Raider shoved his Stetson a little farther back on his head as he stepped up to the end of the bar and pointed to a bottle of whiskey.

"Kathleen," he said, loud enough for everyone to hear. "Have a drink with me."

The girl shook her head. "No thanks," she said very quietly.

"Why not?"

"Well, I . . ."

Raider looked at the knot of punks. They were staring at him. He could see past them—could see Doc nervously fingering the .38 Diamondback under his coat. The bartender passed him the bottle of whiskey as if it were hot and burned his fingers. Another whore stepped up to Kathleen, took her by the shoulder, and drew her back a few paces. The room was silent now. No one was talking.

"Somebody afraid of something?" Raider asked as he poured himself a generous measure of whiskey. "Personally, I don't see anything to be nervous about." He tossed off a swallow of whiskey.

Doc was slowly shaking his head, trying to signal him without being noticed. He had allowed the deputy to abuse him on the street rather than make a confrontation, and he wanted Raider to do the same. That was Doc's way. He could write it all down in his report later.

It wasn't Raider's way. He looked at Kathleen. "Have a drink, little girl," he said. "It'll put the color back in your cheeks."

The biggest of the punks stepped forward from the knot. "The lady said she didn't want a drink from you, mister," he said loudly. He was a tall, broad-shouldered young man carrying a revolver in a holster he wore outside his coat. The belt pinched in the coat. His sweaty shirt was open. His hat was pushed to the back of his head. He wore a thin mustache.

"What's your name?" Raider asked.

"Tom McMullen," said the young man loudly. "You heard the name?"

Raider shook his head. "No, and I don't think I want to. I don't remember asking you to butt into my conversation with Kathleen."

"Kathleen sort of belongs to us," said McMullen

aggressively, tilting his head and smiling sarcastically. "You've been messin' with what belongs to other men."

" 'Other men,' " Raider repeated. He looked around the room. "Where are they?"

Doc had stood and was shaking his head, his mouth open. His hand remained inside his coat.

"You son of a bitch," growled McMullen.

"Son," said Raider. "You tryin' to get yourself hurt?"

McMullen glanced over his shoulder at his smirking companions. Then he lunged toward Raider, swinging a fist from below, toward Raider's chin. Raider stepped easily aside, then stepped one pace forward, driving his right fist hard into McMullen's ribs. He heard the breath huff out of the big young man and saw his mouth and eyes open wide in shock and fear. Raider's left cross caught McMullen on the side of his jaw. Raider heard and felt the bone crack. McMullen was finished, but Raider was angry and swung again. He knocked McMullen sprawling over a nearby table. McMullen clutched at the table, spilling two old men's drinks, then dropped heavily, first on his knees and then full-length forward, on his face.

Doc screamed, *"Look out!"*

Raider saw the revolver coming out of the holster of the one with the broken nose—Galvin. In the smooth motion he had practiced ten thousand times, Raider drew his Remington and fired. The big bullet hit Galvin square in the chest, flopping him backward. As he fell, dying, he pulled his trigger convulsively and shot himself in the shin and foot.

Raider returned the Remington to his holster. He put his foot on the bar rail and lifted his glass of whiskey. "Somebody better get the sheriff," he said.

Someone had already run for the sheriff, and it was hardly a minute before Sheriff Jimmy Tate was dragged into the saloon by a man who had him by the arm. *"God-a'mighty!"* said the old man, his white beard wobbling. He stared for a moment at the body of the Galvin boy, then he looked at McMullen, who now sat

on the floor, dazed, clutching his broken jaw, blood
oozing from between his fingers. "Who kilt Billy Bob?"

"He drew on me," said Raider.

The old man peered at Raider, surprised that anyone would admit the shooting. "Who you?" he asked.

"The name's Raider. I'm a cattle buyer."

The sheriff glanced around. "He speakin' the truth?"
he asked.

No one answered. Eyes fell to the tables. One man
shrugged.

Raider had Doc's eye. He shook his head. Doc need
not speak up. Not yet, anyway.

"You hurt the boy there, too?" Sheriff Jimmy Tate
asked Raider. He nodded toward McMullen. "Hit him
in the face?"

Raider nodded. "He swung on me."

"That the truth?" the sheriff asked.

Again, no one answered.

The old man shook his head sadly. The corners of
his mouth turned down into his white beard. "Sons of
two of the finest men in this county," he said. "You
in big trouble, mister."

"I don't think so," said Raider. "You've got twenty
witnesses here who saw that one swing on me and the
other one draw on me. If it comes to it, there'll be two
or three with the stomach to speak up."

The old man continued shaking his head. "I don'
know, I don' know," he muttered. "Two fine young
men . . ."

"Have a drink on me, Sheriff," said Raider. He
reached for the bottle and a clean glass.

"What th' hell?"

Raider turned, alert. The big voice in the doorway
had come from the deputy, Horace Chandler, who now
swaggered into the saloon. He stopped in the middle of
the room and surveyed the scene. "What th' hell?" he
said again, stunned. "Billy Bob . . . Tommy. What th'
hell?" He spied Doc, still at his table. "You been at it
agin, dude?"

Doc shook his head.

"It was the cowboy there," said one of the young men still standing at the bar.

Chandler focused on Raider, appraised him with beady little eyes. "Jimmy?" he asked.

The sheriff spoke. "This man here admits he done it, Horace," said the old man. "He claims Billy Bob drawed on him."

"That the truth?" asked Chandler.

"Hell no," said the young man at the bar.

Chandler pushed his battered and dirty hat back on his head. "Didn't figger 'twas," he said. He looked again at Raider. "Well, mister, I'll trouble you for that revolver. Hand it over."

"Don't think I will, fat man," said Raider.

"*Huh?*"

"You heard me," said Raider. He lifted his glass and casually sipped whiskey.

"I'm the law in this town—Jimmy 'n' me," said Chandler, scowling.

"There *is* no law in this town," said Raider.

Chandler glanced around the room, and a smile spread over his face. "You figger you kin shoot all of us in here?" he asked.

"Won't have to," said Raider. "Anybody makes a hostile move, I'll gut-shoot you. Any shot fired in a general easterly direction would hit that gut of yours."

Chandler reached for his pistol, but Raider had the Remington in hand and pointed at the man's belly before Chandler had lifted his pistol halfway out of its holster.

Chandler's face collapsed. He looked around for someone to help him; but now the group at the bar had begun to edge back. Raider had never lost sight of Doc, who had kept his hand on his Diamondback all the while.

Raider spoke to the sheriff. "Send someone to the stable for my horse," he said.

"It's always a mistake to defy the law, son," said the old man. "You ought to reconsider."

"It's only lynch law that I'm defying here," said Raider. "Send someone for my horse."

The sheriff pointed at a man standing by the door. "Dick," he said. "Please."

"Deputy," said Raider. "Drop your gun belt." Chandler unhooked the belt, and the holstered pistol fell heavily to the floor. "Some of the rest of you, the same," Raider said to the young men still edging toward the far end of the bar. They did as he told them. "Deputy," he said then, "have a drink." He nodded to the whiskey bottle. "In fact, have two or three drinks."

In the ten minutes it took the man to return with Bastardo, Raider compelled Chandler to drink more than half a bottle of whiskey. The sweat ran down Chandler's face, and he began to blink at Raider. He slobbered over the mouth of the bottle.

"Yer hoss is outside, mister," said the man called Dick.

Raider gestured with his revolver. "Come along with me, Deputy," he said. "You tell your friends to stay right here and have a drink on you. If any man steps outside the door before you come back, you won't be comin' back."

Chandler nodded at the young men at the bar and at the sheriff. "Do what he says, fellas," he slurred. "He's a crazy man."

Doc rode west out of El Aguila just before dawn, on a spavined horse he had rented from a drunken cowboy he had found lying in the dust beside it. He wore denims and a slouch hat, and the Diamondback was stuck in his belt. Some would recognize him if they saw him, but he did not mean to have the whole town know the itinerant doctor had ridden out of town in the direction the killer of Billy Bob Galvin had taken.

He expected Raider would be watching for him somewhere on the road, and he was not surprised when

Raider stood and waved his hat from behind a rock. Doc turned the horse off the road and guided it toward Raider.

"You got it!" said Raider.

"Got what?"

"My Winchester," Raider said, pointing to the rifle lying across Doc's battered saddle.

"And your money and one or two other things," said Doc. "While they organized their posse—or lynch mob—I went up and picked the lock to your room. I got the bullet we dug out of Susie Bradford, too."

"I couldn't help it, Doc," said Raider. "You saw it. What could I have done?"

"Nothing," said Doc. "Anyway, what's done is done. And what's done is, you're done in El Aguila. You can't go back there."

"Their posse went thundering by in the dark, 'bout midnight I guess it was," said Raider. "They straggled back in twos and threes the rest of the night."

Doc smiled. "Chandler couldn't get on a horse."

"Could the sheriff?"

"They don't worry me. What does worry me is Galvin, the rancher, Billy Bob's father. You can't stay around here. When he starts looking . . ."

"How 'bout you?" Raider asked.

"If you hadn't shot Billy Bob, I might've had to. They were working up their courage at the bar, to come get me for breaking Billy Bob's nose. But that's all forgotten now."

"I've been thinking here tonight," said Raider. He had been examining his Winchester closely, and now he rubbed a thumbprint off it with the sleeve of his shirt. "The only thing for me to do is ride over into Mexico and see if I can find William Bridenbaugh."

"I agree," said Doc. "I thought about it all night, too. We have to remember, finding our client's son is part of our job. The old man has a wire from Wagner by now, telling him his son didn't kill Susie Bradford.

That's going to make him more anxious than ever to get his boy back."

"That's that, then," said Raider. "You take care of yourself, Doc. Allan Pinkerton'd be mighty upset if he lost you."

Doc grinned. "You too, Raider. Be damned careful in Mexico. Don't forget what they did to Maximilian."

Raider grinned and shook his head. "I don't know anybody with a name like Maximilian," he laughed. "I bet he and I are very different fellas."

CHAPTER SIX

Since he left Arkansas after the war, Raider had been in Mexico three or four times, staying eight weeks one time and six weeks another, and he had spent a lot of time in the border counties of Texas. He knew a little Spanish. Even so, he did not like Mexico or Mexicans. There was little law in Mexico—in the American sense of it, anyway—and the Mexicans probably had good enough reasons for hating Americans. Anyway, he never felt safe in Mexico. Not for a minute.

He did not cross the Rio Grande at the nearest river point from El Aguila. If the rancher, Galvin, really was looking for him, he might have men watching the river. He crossed twenty miles north of El Aguila, splashing across just after sunset, when he judged it would be difficult to see him from either side. He rode on until it was dark. He stopped and built a campfire, then rode on a mile or so. He tied Bastardo to a tree and moved a hundred yards away from him, to sleep sitting up, with his Remington in his hand. Just after dawn he approached the campfire he had built the night before. He found no tracks around it. It had burned itself out without disturbance.

The land was poor, yet it had a stark beauty he could not ignore. Mountains rose in the west and in the south. This land was dry and rough, just like the land on the other side of what he should now call *Río Bravo del Norte*—the Brave River of the North—what the Mexes called the Rio Grande. It was land left the way the

Indians had it: wild, poor in one way, but rich in another; the Mexes hadn't messed it up much. They didn't make a living off it, either. It was good to look at. But what a man would live on, Raider couldn't imagine.

He rode south. He judged that William Bridenbaugh had ridden south. Though Texas posses did cross the river, they didn't ride far south. They couldn't carry Texas law or lynch law too far into Mexico or the Mexes would start taking shots at them.

A lone horseman, on the other hand . . . either they would welcome him—and their hospitality could be generous—or they would shoot him. It depended on who you met first. It depended, maybe, on how you looked. It was a mistake to look too rich. It was good to look like a man who could take care of himself. He rode with his Winchester laid across the saddle in front of him and wished Bastardo didn't look quite so good a horse.

On the afternoon of his first day south of the river, he chanced on a village. It consisted of a church—the only brick building in the village—and a few adobe huts. There was no street as such; the huts clustered around the church. There was no square. No fountain. No trees. A few scrawny chickens scattered ahead of Bastardo as he rode into the midst of the huts. A naked girl, maybe ten years old, stared at him for a moment before she ran. A face appeared in a doorway for an instant before retreating. He rode slowly up to the church. He stopped. There was no rail or post to tie his horse to. He dismounted, dropped the reins, and entered the tiny church.

It was cool inside, and dark, in the manner of all Catholic churches in Mexico and southern Texas. No candles burned. Carrying his Winchester and his saddlebags, he ventured cautiously into the quiet interior.

"Señor?"

The priest appeared silently out of the shadows.

"Buenas tardes, Padre," Raider said.

The priest was a muscular, middle-aged man, with a

square jaw and a heavy beard that showed dark through his weathered skin even though he had apparently scraped it hard with a razor this very morning. He wore a dusty black cassock and a gold pectoral cross.

"What is the name of this village?" Raider asked in Spanish.

"San Ignacio del Arroyo," said the priest. "I am afraid it is more commonly known as Parrajaco."

Raider smiled. The name meant "ugly bird."

"You are *Norteamericano,*" said the priest.

"Yes," said Raider. "I am . . ." He could not think of the Spanish word for "detective." "Did you ever hear of the Pinkertons?"

The priest shook his head.

"I have come looking for a man accused of killing a woman in Texas. I am, uh . . . *policía.*"

"Texas Ranger?" the priest asked.

"No. Pinkerton. A national agency."

"Washington," said the priest.

"Chicago," said Raider.

The priest seemed to take the word "Chicago" as Raider's mispronunciation of some Spanish word, maybe a request for a cigar. He smiled and asked if Raider were hungry.

He sat down an hour later at the priest's table and shared a meal of hard corn bread, beans with a little tough meat, and some sour red wine. The priest was grateful and seemed to think his hospitality repaid when Raider offered enough coffee from the little left in his kit to make them a small pot of bitter black brew. After dark he and Raider sat on two wooden chairs just outside the door of the church. A torch was lighted. Villagers squatted in the dust around them, smoking, drinking wine, and watched their naked children run and play.

"This *Norteamericano* you are looking for," said the priest. "How would one of my flock know him if they saw him?"

"There were probably two men," said Raider. "Young. One of them was carrying a lot of gold."

"Do you speak of William Bridenbaugh, then?" the priest asked ingenuously.

Raider did not succeed in concealing his surprise. "As a matter of fact, I do," he said. "Do you know him?"

The priest shook his head. "I have heard of him."

"Who spoke of him?"

The priest shrugged. "Everyone speaks of him. They say he carries much gold. It was very unwise of him to let this be known. A thousand men must be looking for him, for that gold."

"Do they say he killed a woman?"

The priest shook his head.

"As a matter of fact, he didn't," said Raider. "He was accused, but we have now proved he did not kill the woman. The gold is his father's. The father wants his son back, and his gold."

"The thousand men care nothing for the man. They want the gold."

"I suspect so," said Raider. "Do you know anything more about the man?"

The priest again shook his head. "Only that he must be a fool, to come to this country carrying so much gold and telling everyone he has it. I doubt he remains alive, señor."

Raider slept in the church and rode out of the village at dawn. He stopped at a hut where he found a farmer already scratching the earth with a hoe, and he bought corn for Bastardo. The farmer was pleased and seemed amazed that anyone would give money for corn. A track led south from the village. It was not a road. It led, Raider judged, to a town, probably a market town, since he overtook three barefoot families trudging with oversized bundles on their backs. The red sun turned white, and the sweat poured down him long before what would be the heat of the day was reached.

The horse grew touchy and began to skitter and shy. At a small stream, Raider tested the water and let Bastardo drink. The horse would have run away from him there, if he had let him loose.

He overtook a farmer driving a burro laden with bundles of firewood. The old man told him the town of Cedro Grande was just ahead, in which it was market day. The old man shook his head at the mention of William Bridenbaugh—or of a *Norteamericano* carrying gold. He had never heard of him.

Cedro Grande was bigger than Parrajaco, and more prosperous, but it was a poor place just the same. A market was in progress in the small square before the church, as the farmer had said. Men and women squatted in the red dust with their wares spread out on blankets before them—foodstuffs mostly: grain, dried peppers, live chickens, onions. He saw a few sellers of household utensils: bowls, pots, knives; and a young man with a fierce black mustache and angry black eyes offered a pistol, a shotgun, and a battered Bowie knife. A fat priest stood in the door of the church, smiling, waving. A fat man beside him wore sweat-dampened and stained white clothes, sandals, a huge sombrero, and a Colt Peacemaker in a belt around his belly. Raider guessed he was *el jefe*—the headman of the town. Whoever he was, he had taken notice of the *Norteamericano* on the big stallion, and when Raider looked at him, their eyes met.

Raider dismounted and tied Bastardo to one wheel of a collapsed cart. He pushed his way through the small crowd and walked up to the apparent headman. *"Buenos días, señor,"* he said. *"Hoy hace calor, eh?"*

"Demasiado," the man grunted. He agreed it was hot; it was too hot.

Raider nodded greeting to the priest, then he spoke again to the fat man with the Colt. *"Está usted el jefe aquí?"* he asked.

The man smiled, showing broken teeth. He acknowledged he was, one way or another, the headman here.

"Could I buy you some wine, and can you and I sit down and talk somewhere?" Raider asked.

The man shrugged and stepped down from the church door. He pointed toward an adobe building across the square—the local cantina apparently. Raider asked him what he should do about his horse. The man snapped his fingers at a young man not far away in the crowd and told him to guard the horse of the *Norteamericano*. He led Raider into the cantina, where two men sat on a bench near one wall, already drunk in mid-morning. They passed through and out into a small courtyard behind, where two tables waited in the shade of a small tree. The man lowered his bulk heavily onto one of the chairs. Raider sat down across the table.

"My name is Francisco Marquez," said the fat man.

"Mine is Raider. I'm a Pinkerton. You ever hear of the Pinkertons?"

The man shook his head.

Overnight Raider had decided the Spanish word he couldn't think of for the priest was probably *detectivo*. He tried it. *"Detectivo . . . policía Norteamericano."*

"Ah . . ." said Francisco Marquez.

A middle-aged woman, fat and barefoot, came to the table, bearing a clay pot of red wine, two clay cups, and two plates piled with Mexican food—the beans they ate smashed, their tough flat bread, peppers. Francisco Marquez doffed his sombrero to her and dropped it to the ground beside his chair.

"I am looking for the American, Bridenbaugh," said Raider.

"Ah . . ." said Francisco Marquez again.

"The gold is his father's," said Raider. "It is possible his father will give that gold and send some more besides, as a reward, to the man who returns his son."

Francisco Marquez had filled his mouth with bread and beans, but he spoke anyway. "They will hang him, the Texans. They say he killed a woman."

"They lie about him," said Raider. "The woman was killed with a big pistol, a .44 like your Colt and my

Remington. William Bridenbaugh carries a little pistol, a .32. The bullet in the woman's body was a .44."

"How do you know this, señor?"

"Another detective, a partner of mine, dug the bullet out of the body."

"*Madre de Dios!*" whispered Francisco Marquez. He crossed himself.

Raider tasted the wine and the food. They were good, better than the impoverished priest at Parrajaco could offer.

"I have heard of this American and his gold," said Francisco Marquez. "There are two men, Bridenbaugh and another one. They are fools—but dangerous fools."

"How so?"

"They told everyone they were carrying gold. Within a day after they crossed the border, the story was everywhere. Men from this village insisted on riding out, looking for them. It was fortunate they did not find them. Bridenbaugh and the other one are quick to kill. They killed at least two men who tried to approach them."

"Tried to rob them," said Raider.

Francisco Marquez shrugged. "Perhaps."

"Have you heard where they went?"

"There has been no word of them for the past two weeks. They meant to reach Monterrey perhaps. Before, everyone talked of them. Now . . . silence."

"What is the last place you heard mentioned?"

"Santa Rita. It is on the Rio Sabinas."

Raider sighed and nodded. His thought was of two days' ride in the hot sun.

"You have money, señor?" asked Francisco Marquez.

"A little."

"If you can pay, I can send men out to inquire for you. You stay here. I can offer a clean bed, food, wine, and I think we can find a woman who will please you. I can send, say, three men in different directions, to ask your questions for you."

"I am grateful to you, señor," said Raider, "but while I wait here for your men to go and return, my two Americans keep moving."

"*If* they are moving. If they are alive."

"Yes."

"Another suggestion, señor," said Francisco Marquez. "You don't know this country. You can become lost. You can blunder into bad places. I suggest you remain here today and tonight. In the morning, my son will go with you. He can ride and shoot. If you do not find this Bridenbaugh, you can pay him a little for his trouble. If you do, you can share with him the reward the Bridenbaugh father will pay. It is an opportunity for him, a benefit for you."

"It sounds fair," said Raider.

They rode out of Cedro Grande at dawn. The son, whose name was Perfecto, was the black-eyed, mustachioed young man Raider had seen selling weapons in the marketplace the day before. His father had provided a sound gray horse and a battered saddle for his son. The young man was maybe twenty years old, an angry, sullen boy whose eyes were hard with some unspoken resentment he harbored. He wore loose white cotton clothes, with a sombrero but no shoes. He carried a Colt like his father's—maybe it *was* his father's—in a holster he wore on his left side with the pistol butt forward for a cross draw.

They rode in silence, Perfecto choosing one rough track over another, sometimes leaving the tracks and leading across the open country, among the rocks. The country was hilly, but mountains lay ahead. They stopped at a hovel and bought bread at noon. By early afternoon the sun was too hot for travel, and they dismounted on the bank of a stream, almost dry, and rested in the shade of overhanging rocks.

Mexican food had begun to disturb his bowls, as Mexican food always did, and Raider took from his saddlebag a box of dyspepsia powders Doc had pro-

vided him, mixed one with water from the stream, and
took it. He sat down in the shade again. His belly
wheezed and rumbled, but he dozed.

Raider wakened with a wrenching pain in his gut. He
trotted downstream twenty yards, dropped his pants,
and relieved his churning bowels noisily into the sand
and water. He was some minutes at it, sweating and
nauseous, and he was cleaning himself when he heard
the sounds of Bastardo and Perfecto's gray, snorting
and pawing. Alerted, he slipped away from the streambed and retreated into the rocks.

In a moment he heard Perfecto grunt from pain.
Then he heard voices.

Working his way quietly, he returned to where he had
left Perfecto—but behind rocks and in the cover of
some thorny brush. He inched up to where he could
see.

Perfecto was standing, slumped, rubbing his mouth,
from which a trickle of blood ran and smeared his
fingers. Confronting him were three Indians—naked but
for breechclouts, their grim faces framed with strings
of greasy black hair, two of them armed with rifles, the
third with Perfecto's Peacemaker Colt, which he was
examining with satisfaction.

"Dónde está el gringo?" one of them grunted at
Perfecto.

"No sé," muttered Perfecto.

The Indian struck him with the butt of his rifle, and
Perfecto fell.

Raider's Remington was in his hand, but he could
not be certain of hitting all three of the Indians before
one of them got a shot into Perfecto. He watched and
waited.

"Los caballos," the leader barked at the Indian with
Perfecto's pistol.

Carrying the pistol in his hand, for want of a belt
or holster to put it in, the naked Indian walked away,
toward the scrub trees a few yards away, where Bastardo and the gray were tethered. Raider slipped away

and followed, keeping quiet and keeping rocks and brush between him and the Indian. The Indian reached the horses. Immediately he spied the Winchester in its scabbard on Raider's saddle. He dropped the pistol and with a grunt of delight rushed forward and pulled the rifle from the scabbard. Raider, sneaking closer, could smell the Indian's filthy body. He hefted a rock and lunged forward. The Indian's head was bent forward as he intently examined the Winchester, and he neither saw nor heard Raider until it was too late.

Raider recovered his Winchester from the sand. He walked back directly, the way the Indian had come.

The other two Indians had stripped Perfecto. One wore his sombrero. The other wore his shirt. They were laughing over his pants, one of them holding them up, the other grabbing at them as if to snatch them. Perfecto was on his knees, doubled over. They had hit him in the stomach, apparently.

As soon as he saw them, Raider raised the Winchester and shot the Indian leader in the chest. He turned the rifle on the other and shot him through the neck.

He knelt beside Perfecto and asked how badly he was hurt. Perfecto shook his head and clutched his belly. He was ashen. For a moment Raider was afraid they had stabbed him, and he seized his hands and pulled them away from his belly to see. He saw the angry imprint of a rifle butt. Perfecto gagged, but he said he would be all right in a few minutes.

"You saved my life, señor," he said without looking up. "They were going to kill me."

"They were going to kill us both," said Raider, "and if you had told them where to look for me, they might have done it. You're a brave man, Perfecto."

The young Mexican looked up. It was as if Raider had struck him, he was so surprised and puzzled. "You . . . believe that, señor?" he asked quietly.

Raider nodded. "I believe it. Now we had better move on. The shots may have told others we are here."

CHAPTER SEVEN

The banker Jeffrey McMullen puffed appreciatively on the Old Virginia cheroot Doc had given him. "It's not that we don't trust our Dr. Hinkley, you understand," he said. "In a small town in south Texas, we're lucky to have any kind of doctor. But a specialist like you . . . well, I'd be grateful for your attention to my son. I'm only sorry there's nothing you can do for Tod's son."

Rancher Tod Galvin, father of Billy Bob Galvin, the boy Raider shot and killed the night before, sat heavily in McMullen's office. He was a big man. He wore a tall Stetson and was smoking a big cigar. "Only one can do anything for Billy Bob now is me," he said. "And what I'm gonna do is get that drifter, if it takes me a hundred years."

"Yes," said McMullen sadly. "Billy Bob was trying to protect Tom. He gave up his life trying to save his friend. It was a noble thing. You witnessed it, Dr. Weatherbee. Was it not a noble thing?"

"Well," said Doc hesitantly, "it's difficult for me to find much nobility in any situation where two men draw guns and fire at one another."

"That man Raider is a shootist," said Galvin. "Billy Bob drawed on a shootist, so it wasn't a fair fight by any stretch. I know he drawed on you, too, Doctor, and I know you busted his nose. That was fair. He had that comin'."

"I regret that, Mr. Galvin," said Doc.

"Billy Bob was playful, Doctor," said Galvin. "He

wouldn' never've hurt you. You couldn't know that, of
course, and when he drawed you hit him. He didn't hold
no hard feelin's 'bout that. He'd a shook your hand
and had a laugh over it, if he hadn't died. He was just
a playful bear of a boy."

The banker sat before his rolltop desk, his nutria fur
railroad hat on his head, his crossed legs showing a
pair of calfskin boots. He was a small, wispy, late-
middle-aged man, clean shaven, with watery blue eyes.
"You're interested in the Bridenbaugh case, I hear," he
said.

Doc shrugged. "Traveling around Texas, I heard
about it. Then I saw the body. I believe I may have
met Mr. Bridenbaugh once, some months ago. I recall
I prescribed some pulsatilla for him. He's a ranch
owner, isn't he? Up around Adena?"

McMullen nodded. "Yes, and an old friend of mine.
The matter of his son is another tragedy."

"Seemed like a nice family . . ." Doc mused reminis-
cently. "Is there any doubt he killed that girl?"

"None whatever," said McMullen firmly. "If ever
there was, the fact that he ran disposed of that."

"Took some gold with him, they say," said Doc.

"Twenty-five thousand dollars in gold, his father's
money, paid to him from this bank only hours before,"
said McMullen.

"*Twenty-five* . . ." Doc exclaimed, letting his mouth
drop open as if he were astounded. "You can pay out
amounts like that *in gold* from this bank, Mr. McMullen?"

"Occasionally," said McMullen calmly. "We held it
for Jacob Bridenbaugh, on payment from a railroad
company."

"Where the San Antonio, Houston & New Orleans
Railroad Company got $25,000 in gold is what I'd like
to know," said Tod Galvin. "Anybody deals with that
crowd takes a beatin'."

"I've heard of that company," said Doc. "Isn't it
sound?"

"Sound as a dollar," said the banker, nodding.

"Sound as a whore's fart," said Galvin.

The door opened again, and Tom McMullen came in. Dr. Hinkley had set his jaw last night, and this morning his swollen face, fixed in a contraption of straps and wires, was blue and red. He flexed his lips nervously, in some pain. He was missing two front teeth. He glowered at Doc, then frowned at his father and sat down.

"Hurts, huh?" asked Doc.

"Ughh."

"Well," said Doc. "Laudanum is not exactly a homeopathic medicine, but it's sovereign for severe pain." He took a bottle from his kit—laudanum, tincture of opium. "Be careful," he said. "Don't take more than what it says on the bottle. It's powerful."

Tom McMullen fixed a venomous stare on Doc. He muttered through his teeth. "You's th' one that yelled 'look out' las' night."

"Huh?" said his father.

Tom pointed a finger at Doc. "When Billy Bob went t' pull his gun, *he*"—pointing accusingly at Doc "yelled 'look out.' He give that Raider warnin'."

"Guns were being drawn," said Doc. "I did yell 'look out.' Anyone might have got hit."

Tod Galvin looked at Doc with an expression of resigned grief. "You done what any man would have done, Doctor, and I don't hold it ag'in you," he said. "Maybe, though, the shootist wouldn't have got his shot off ahead of Billy Bob's if you hadn't yelled."

"Damn right," grunted Tom McMullen.

Doc stopped at the telegraph office and sent off another wire to Illinois Pharmaceuticals & Chemicals:

DOCTOR GOLD'S SPECIFIC MAY NOT HAVE ARRIVED BY RAILROAD STOP NEED REPORT STOP GOLD'S VITAL TO PATIENT'S CASE STOP COULD RAILROAD HAVE LOST IT STOP DOCTOR WEATHERBEE STOP

Wagner would have to decipher as best he could. If Tod Galvin thought the San Antonio, Houston & New Orleans Railroad Company was unsound and Jeffrey McMullen insisted it was, their statements might throw an interesting new light on the case.

He returned to the Eagle and ate a light lunch in the saloon. The Murphy boys were there. They glared at him, but no one spoke or came near him until the clerk from the telegraph office came in. He brought a telegram to Doc that read:

COMPANY SUPPLYING DOCTOR GOLD'S SPECIFIC APPEARS INSOLVENT STOP UNABLE TO PROVIDE MEDICINE IN QUANTITY YOU ASKED STOP BEST OF LUCK WITH PATIENT STOP ILLINOIS PHARMACEU-TICALS STOP

In the afternoon he hitched up Judith and pulled the apothecary wagon to the center of the town. For two hours he dispensed homeopathic specifics to townspeople who wandered by. Horace Chandler stood lounging against the front of a store for a few minutes, watching him curiously. Apparently he was satisfied that Dr. Weatherbee did, indeed, sell medicines as he advertised himself to do—which was part of Doc's purpose in setting up shop.

At five o'clock he was in his room. With him were two women: a Mrs. Penelope Crittenden and her daughter, Charlotte, a girl of eighteen. The mother had approached Doc at the wagon and had consulted him urgently about her daughter's problem. Doc had told her he could treat the condition but that the treatment could obviously not be administered on the street. The two had followed him to his room above the saloon when he returned from reinstalling Judith in the stable, and they were there now: the mother sitting stiffly upright on the room's one chair, the daughter, stripped to the waist, sitting with her head hung down, blushing, on the bed.

"The deficiency—if, indeed, that is what we should call it—can indeed often be remedied, Mrs. Crittenden," Doc said. "Actually, of course, Charlotte is not without symmetry. . . ."

"But can medicine improve her 'symmetry,' Dr. Weatherbee?" the mother inquired anxiously.

Doc cocked his head and pretended to study the girl's small naked breasts. "The treatment is guaranteed to add two or three inches," he said.

"Ah," said the mother, pleased. "You see, Charlotte?"

The girl covered her breasts with her folded arms. "What is the treatment, Dr. Weatherbee?" she asked timidly.

"Fleur de Lis Bust Expander is massaged into the bosom daily until the supply is consumed," said Doc. "After that, Seroco Bust Cream or Food should be regularly rubbed on the bosom. Even you, Mrs. Crittenden, could benefit from daily application of the cream or food, to keep the skin smooth and firm—even though you are already generously symmetrical."

"No . . . ? No . . . ?" the girl stuttered.

"No implement? No, indeed, Miss Crittenden. Most doctors do in fact recommend a cup and pump device that draws the blood to the surface and the flesh into the desired contour. I prefer that my patients rely on frequent massage with the two specifics I recommend."

"Massage . . . ?" the girl whispered.

Doc nodded. "The technique is simple. I can apply the first treatment if you wish."

"Yes, please, Doctor," said the mother. "Show her how to use it. May I . . . may I ask the price of this specific?"

"A bottle of the expander and a jar of the cream or food, together, cost two dollars. I suggest you buy at least two jars of the cream. I receive one dollar as my fee for teaching you the method of application."

When the knock on the door interrupted, twenty minutes later, he was massaging the mother's big soft breasts, and the daughter, still sitting on the bed, was studiously rubbing more expander into hers, following the technique Doc had demonstrated. Whatever enlargement of the breasts he might have achieved for the two, certainly he had accomplished a marvelous increase in the size and firmness of his penis, and it was only with care that he was able to walk to the door without letting them see how he had grown.

"Yes?" he said in a firm voice. He half suspected Mr. Crittenden, husband and father, might be in the hall.

"Dr. Weatherbee?" a female voice inquired through the door.

"Yes. Who is it?"

"Kathleen Reilly. I need to talk to you."

"Return in half an hour, Miss Reilly," he said.

When she returned he was alone, lying on the bed. He let her in. "I'm glad you've come," he told her. "After my experience of the last hour, I am definitely in need of your services."

"You shall have them, then," said Kathleen Reilly. "But first I have to talk to you."

"There's a bottle of whiskey there," he said, pointing to the bottle beside the wash basin. "Pour one for me while you're pouring one for you."

"You are a friend of Mr. Raider," she said. "You are not strangers to each other." She did not look up from pouring whiskey into two glasses. "I was watching him and you last night. You had your hand on your pistol. You were going to help him if need be. You and he exchanged signals. I could see."

"You have a vivid imagination."

"No. I saw."

"Assuming you are right, then what?"

"I need help," she said.

"What kind of help?"

"You know what happened to Susie Bradford," she said. It was a statement, not a question. She tossed her head to toss her auburn hair out of her steady blue eyes, where a draft from the window had blown it. She handed him his glass of whiskey and took a sip from her own. "Susie Bradford was killed because she let another man have her, without Tom McMullen's permission."

"A man named Bridenbaugh killed Susie Bradford, as I hear it."

Kathleen smiled bitterly. "Tom McMullen killed her. Or if he didn't, Billy Bob Galvin did. Or one of the Murphy boys. And one of them is just as likely to kill me, after last night."

"Are you telling me they kill a girl like you just because you . . ."

She shook her head. "Not till they get drunked up and decide to prove how tough they are. All Susie Bradford did was get too friendly with the Bridenbaugh boy. I was friendly with the man who killed Billy Bob Galvin and broke Tom McMullen's jaw—not to mention that he humiliated Horace Chandler." She lowered her head and blinked back tears. "I'm afraid," she whispered.

"What do you think I can do for you?" Doc asked.

"I don't know. I know one thing, though: that you and Raider are friends. I know something more. Raider is not the . . . what he said, a cattle buyer; and he's not a shootist, the way they're saying around town today. I wonder if he doesn't work for the father of William Bridenbaugh. I wonder if you don't, too."

"How much do you really know about the killing of Susie Bradford?" Doc asked firmly.

She shook her head. "I wasn't a witness. But I know the town punks. I know what they've done to me. I know they killed her, just as sure as if I had been there and seen it."

"How much stuff do you have in your room, that's yours I mean?"

"Not much. Clothes . . ."

"Money?"

"Yes."

"And a bag to pack it in?"

"Yes."

"Go down and pack. I'll knock on your door in about ten minutes, when there's no one to see you come out. Three knocks, then one."

Kathleen nodded. "Thank you, Dr. Weatherbee, or whatever your name is," she whispered. "Thank you so goddam much. I'll make it up to you."

The next morning about ten a limping Irish veteran of the Union Army hobbled up to the bar in the Eagle. His red hair burst from under his blue hat with crossed cavalry sabers, and his cheeks and nose were red. He wore thick eyeglasses with small gold frames, and he carried a cane of gnarled blackthorn. In his belt, in front, on his belly, he wore an old percussion-cap revolver.

"Whiskey," he demanded of the bartender.

The bartender poured him a shot of the raw, cheap whiskey he habitually dispensed, and the Irishman tossed it down and ordered another.

"Where's the whorehouse in this town?" he asked the bartender.

The bartender told him, and the man tossed a coin on the bar for his whiskey, turned, and strode out.

Half an hour later the Irishman was back. "Sister Edwards doesn't have the girl I'm lookin' for," he said. The bartender shrugged. "I'm lookin' for a particular girl. Sister Edwards says she works here. Her name is Kathleen Reilly."

The bartender looked up, startled, into the blue eyes of the Irishman, swimming behind the thick lenses of his spectacles. The hard Irish face barely concealed an anger that threatened to burst forth in rage. "We don't need no trouble," the bartender said. His hand was on a pistol under the bar.

"Me neither," said the Irishman in his brogue.

"She a friend of yours?" the bartender asked cautiously.

"Me daughter," said the Irishman grimly.

"Your name is Reilly, then."

"The same."

The bartender sighed heavily. "Well, Mr. Reilly, she did work here. She had a room upstairs. Yesterday she packed up and left. Took her things and left. I didn't see her go, but she's gone."

The Irishman nodded. "Strange," he mused. "This is the third time. The girl has a sense of it."

"A sense of what?"

"That I'm ketchin' up with her. This is the third time she's left a town a day or two or three ahead of me. Me grandmother had a power like that, too. It was born in Kathleen. She knows things other people don't know, just like me grandmother did. It's eerie. Damn! Pour me a shot o' your best."

The Irishman was in town only an hour. He rode out of town, muttering, cursing under his breath, drawing stares on the street.

About noon a woman rode into El Aguila, drawing stares by riding astride her horse, her skirt riding high on her booted legs. She was a severe-looking woman, with jet black hair and fierce black brows. Her ample bosom bounced as she dismounted and strode into the Eagle. She wore a belt and holster and carried a pistol. She strode up to the bar.

"I'm looking for Dr. Weatherbee," she announced.

The bartender glanced at the men who were smirking from the two ends of the bar. "He has a room here, ma'am, but I think he's out."

"I'll have the key to his room, then."

"Well . . . I'm not sure I can accommodate you, ma'am."

"I'm his wife."

When Doc walked in half an hour later, loud laughter followed him as he climbed the stairs toward his room.

Kathleen was sitting on his bed, her hair and brows still as black as he had dyed them in the grove ten miles out of town, where they had set up camp overnight and where at dawn Doc had applied what he had brought from the Studebaker wagon.

"Well, Patrick Reilly," said Kathleen, "I trust yours went off as well as mine."

Doc smiled and nodded. "It's a Pinkerton specialty," he said.

"Don't forget to sponge the marks off the horse before you take him back to the livery stable," she said.

Doc nodded. "Don't venture out," he said. "Don't press our luck."

Kathleen smiled. She cupped her hands under the padding in her blouse and lifted it up. "Yes, husband," she said.

"I'll bring you a bottle of Bust Expander and a jar of Bust Cream or Food from the wagon," he laughed. "Maybe we can dispense with the artificial augmentation in a few weeks."

"It is a fine thing, Mrs. Weatherbee, when a traveling man's wife can join him from time to time." Lifting a glass of whiskey, Jeffrey McMullen saluted Kathleen; and his wife, Martha McMullen, beamed and nodded. "We are so pleased you could join us."

Kathleen accepted his salute and tossed off her whiskey exactly as he did. Her eyes met Doc's over her glass, laughing with mirth that she was containing only with effort.

"It is a shame that your trunk was lost," trilled Mrs. McMullen in an artificially melodious voice. "On the other hand, what good fortune to be able to buy a new wardrobe all at once."

"I've bought only a little," said Kathleen. "Just this— and a few other things."

It would have been awkward to decline the McMullens' invitation a second time. Anyway, Doc wanted to study the man more closely. Tom McMullen, with his jaw broken, would hardly sit down at dinner with them. He would see Kathleen in the house probably, though, and Doc did not want him to see her wearing anything he might have seen her wear before. The Dr. Warner's Health Corset she was wearing—though Doc had laughed as she snapped and laced herself into it—afforded her a generous symmetry of the bust without the danger of slipping stuffing. Her blue linen blazer suit and straw hat looked matronly and severe. Her black-dyed hair was tied up under her hat. Even if Tom McMullen sat down with them, it was unlikely he would guess that his father and mother had for their dinner guest the little whore who only the day before yesterday had offered herself at the bar of the Eagle.

"I am frugal with the doctor's money," said Kathleen primly. "We are both so pleased to become friends with a banker with a fine reputation for honest and prudent dealing. I wonder, Mr. McMullen, if you can offer us any advice about investments?"

"Indeed I can," said McMullen, visibly flattered.

He was interrupted by the housemaid, who entered carrying a tray and began to put their dinner on the table. McMullen himself stood and lighted the coal-oil lamp over the table. The maid placed the silver castor, bearing cut-glass salt and pepper shakers and bottles of vinegar, oil, and mustard, in the center of the table. She placed tumblers with silverware standing in them on the table. She put a loaf of bread and a knife before Mrs. McMullen.

While the maid was in the kitchen again, McMullen tucked his thumbs into his vest and said, "Indeed I can, Mrs. Weatherbee."

"I wonder about the railroad," said Doc. "You spoke well of it the other day, even if Mr. Galvin didn't. Are its shares on the market?"

McMullen's jaw trembled. "Yes . . . yes," he said.

"Would you recommend I buy?" Doc asked.

"Uh . . . certainly," said McMullen. "I couldn't recommend a sounder investment."

"Do you hold any shares you might be willing to sell?" Doc asked.

McMullen's brows rose, and his eyes seemed to bulge. "Uh . . . yes. Yes, indeed."

"Are you thinking of Wagner?" Kathleen asked Doc innocently.

Doc nodded. "Yes, my elder brother, Wagner Weatherbee. He inherited some land and money through his wife's family. He might be interested."

"To what extent, Doctor?" asked McMullen.

"Oh, say . . . five or six thousand dollars. Would that buy him some shares?"

"I should say so!" said McMullen with a broad grin.

"You understand," said Doc soberly, "it would be all my brother has. He is not a wealthy man, and this would represent what his family expects of him when he's gone. It is, you might say, the support for his widow and children—that is, should he die."

"I quite understand, Doctor," said McMullen. "I could recommend no investment sounder than shares of the San Antonio, Houston & New Orleans Railroad Company, and if your brother is interested, I might be persuaded to part with shares worth the amount you mention. I just might be persuaded."

CHAPTER EIGHT

Weakened by his churning, spewing bowels, Raider could ride only half a day on the day they reached the Rio Sabinas. Perfecto was stiff and rode in constant pain from the beating he had taken from the Indians. Both of them were glad enough to make camp on the river, twenty-five miles or so from Santa Rita. They hobbled the horses. By now Raider was willing to trust Perfecto and allowed him to stand watch, with all their weapons, while he, Raider, stripped and plunged into the river to wash the dust and sweat and stench from his body. He went in with all his clothes on, and he wrung them out and spread them on a flat rock on the river's edge to dry. Perfecto, with his Colt in hand, concealed himself at a distance, ready to fire from cover on anyone who surprised the defenseless Raider in the water.

Later, Perfecto went in the water, and Raider stood guard. After, they sat and let the sun dry them.

"You say you are of the *policía*," said Perfecto. "My father believes you have come to seek the gold, like everyone else."

Raider glanced at Perfecto. The young man had mostly kept his silence during the two days they had ridden together, saying only what was necessary, avoiding conversation. It had been apparent, nevertheless, that he pondered heavily, weighing ideas, speculating, uncertain but trying to understand. "I seek the gold," Raider said. "But not for myself. For the man who owns it."

They built a fire and cooked a meal, allowing the smoke to rise only because a hot, gusty wind quickly dispersed it. They had bread and beans and coffee—the last of the coffee Raider had carried with him in his saddlebags.

"I need meat," Raider said as he scrubbed the bean pot with sand. "These beans go through my guts too fast."

He pulled on his clothes, even though they were still damp. Carrying the Winchester, he climbed away from their camp, to the higher ground above the river to the south. It was as he had thought. There was game. He could have shot a deer if he had wanted to track it far enough. But his gut was churning, and he was still weak, and he contented himself with two large jack-rabbits, brought down with two shots.

Out of curiosity to see a little more of the area where they had camped, maybe out of an unconscious instinct for self-preservation, he waded across the river and headed back for their camp on the north side. He was not quite sure how far he was from Perfecto and their campsite when he heard horses. Quickly he climbed to the top of a low bluff overlooking the river. Hiding in the cover of brush and rocks, he peered down toward their campsite, wondering if Perfecto had heard, wondering if Perfecto would be more alert to these horsemen than he had been to the Indians who had attacked him. He had to orient himself. He looked for landmarks. He saw a dead tree that looked familiar. Then he saw the horsemen.

There were four of them, Mexes in white clothes and sombreros, armed with pistols and rifles. They splashed into the river and crossed it, north to south. On the south bank they stopped and looked around. Raider watched. They stood on the edge of the river, their horses' hooves in the water. They stood in their stirrups, looking all around. Then Perfecto emerged from the brush and raised his hand to them.

They talked with Perfecto. The talk was short. They splashed back across the river, and he stood with his hand raised in salute to them as they left. Raider watched them ride up to the higher ground north of the river, and when they were out of sight he still heard their horses for a while as they rode away.

He said nothing to Perfecto when he returned to the camp. He waited for Perfecto to tell him about the horsemen, but Perfecto said nothing. The young Mexican helped him dress the rabbits, and he built up the fire so they could roast them. They ate in silence.

It would be pointless not to sleep. If Perfecto wanted to kill him, he could have shot him with the Winchester while he was naked in the water. He could have shot him last night while he slept. If he wanted to steal Bastardo and the Winchester and the little money he was carrying, he had had every chance. His father—if in fact Perfecto *was* the son of Francisco Marquez—had pressed him on Raider for another reason, without doubt: to take the gold William Bridenbaugh was carrying, assuming the *Norteamericano* was more likely to find Bridenbaugh and the gold than any of the Mexes were.

Raider could kill him easily enough—and leave him for his four friends to find. Or he could do exactly what Perfecto himself was doing to him—keep him alive until he had been all the help he could.

In Santa Rita he bought supplies—corn, bread, peppers, onions. He could find no coffee for sale, no bacon. He bought a bag of beans. In a *botica* he bought a fistful of an herb the proprietor and Perfecto assured him would stop his running gut. He brewed the stuff as tea, as Perfecto insisted, and drank it with little confidence. It worked. His gut stopped churning overnight. Before he left he bought more.

Or maybe it was the whiskey that stopped him. He

found whiskey in the cantina—raw, white, of doubtful origin, and fiery. Perfecto would not touch it. He drank the equally fiery Mexican liquor they called tequila, distilled from the juice of some kind of cactus and flavored—so they said—with the carcass of a big blue beetle in each bottle.

The town was bigger than the two others he had seen on this trip to Mexico. Here again it was market day, but the market was bigger and livelier than the one he had seen in Cedro Grande. Horses were on sale, and cows and goats and pigs—and, as Raider discovered, girls. Between the wall of the church and the wall of a row of adobe houses, just off the main marketplace, a pair of ugly, heavily armed men were trading in girls, the daughters of the poor farmers who brought them to be sold. It was a furtive business, not only against the law but obviously offensive to most of the town; yet it was a commerce that was tolerated, apparently because the traders would carry on their business somewhere else if the town stopped them here.

The town knew about William Bridenbaugh. Raider bought a pot of wine for the local *jefe,* and the man said yes, he had seen the two *Norteamericanos,* two weeks ago.

"The word that they were carrying gold came only after they left," the man said regretfully—the implication being clear that they would not have left carrying it if he had known about it.

"Where were they going?" Raider asked.

"Ah," the man said. He pulled hard on a big, ragged cigar. "Monterrey, I think. They wanted to reach Mexico City. They would find the railhead at Monterrey and could ride the train from there."

It would have been an easier ride to follow the river another fifty miles, then turn south again; but Perfecto said they might gain time if they rode directly south from Santa Rita to Dolores, then on to Villaldama. He asked Raider what he would do if he found no trace of Bridenbaugh at Monterrey.

"If I find they went on to Mexico City, then I go to Mexico City," said Raider. "I wonder also if they might not have gone toward Tampico. Bridenbaugh wrote his father he might cross the Atlantic."

"Will you follow across the water, señor?"

Raider shook his head. "I won't. Some Pinkerton will, if we find out that's where they went. I'll send word to Chicago."

"If they reached Monterrey and boarded the train for Mexico City, we will never recover the gold, señor."

"Why not?"

"*El Presidente*," said Perfecto. "Díaz. He will get it. His men. You will never pry it from their grasp."

The streams were dry south of Santa Rita. The road toward Dolores was a rutted track, hard to identify in places, but they had to follow it because the desert to both sides was at places impassable for horses. They carried water; Perfecto had advised Raider it would be necessary. It was only a day's ride, twenty-five miles, to Dolores, Perfecto promised. Then it would be fifty to the next town, Bustamante.

Raider glanced back often. If Perfecto's four friends were following, they were keeping their distance. He concentrated so much on who might be following them that the men who approached from the south were almost on them before he saw them.

"*Soldados*," grunted Perfecto.

They were coming at full gallop, five of them, and Perfecto guessed they were soldiers because of the uniform worn by the first one: a blue jacket with brass buttons, breeches, boots, a military cap, a pistol, and a sword. They reined up when they reached Raider and Perfecto, and the four men behind the officer leveled their rifles on them.

"You speak English, I suppose," said the officer in accented English.

Raider nodded.

"I am Lieutenant Jésus Adolfo García y McDowell," said the officer. He was young, not much older than Perfecto, a slight man with a pointed, waxed mustache. "Who are you?"

"My name is Raider. I'm an operative of the Pinkerton National Detective Agency."

"Ah. Come to Mexico for what purpose?"

Raider glanced past the lieutenant at his four soldiers, four men dressed like Perfecto, except that they wore boots and crossed cartridge belts. "I am trailing an American who stole his father's money."

"Bridenbaugh," said the lieutenant.

"Bridenbaugh," agreed Raider.

"A murderer," said the lieutenant.

"Not a murderer," said Raider. "It's been proved he didn't kill the girl."

"Then you want the money."

"His father wants the money. It's his. He also wants his son back."

The lieutenant nodded. "Hand over your pistol and your rifle, Mr. Raider," he said.

"Why?"

"Because you are under arrest."

"Why?"

The lieutenant shrugged. "Because I choose to arrest you. I doubt you are a Pinkerton. I suspect you are just an American shootist, come to hunt Bridenbaugh like so many others."

"I can identify myself as a Pinkerton," said Raider.

"You will have the opportunity to do that."

"When? Where?"

"In Saltillo. It is the provincial capital. You will receive justice there."

With four rifles leveled at his chest, Raider had no choice but to surrender. They tied his hands behind his back and looped a noose around his neck with which to lead him. They treated Perfecto the same way, only more roughly. They turned south again. Perfecto muttered to Raider that it was more than a hundred miles to Saltillo and it would take four days to get there.

They reached Dolores at sunset. The town had no jail; Raider and Perfecto were locked into heavy irons and housed in a stable. In the morning they were fed and allowed to relieve themselves. The chains were taken off. They mounted their horses again and were tied as they had been on the road the day before.

The lieutenant rode beside Raider, holding Raider's halter loosely in his hand. "I am sorry you could not enjoy the pleasures of the town last night, Mr. Raider," he said lightly.

"I am sure Dolores offers cosmopolitan pleasures," said Raider.

"Indeed it does," said the lieutenant. "The truth is, a man can find 'cosmopolitan pleasures,' as you call them, anywhere he may be."

"If he knows what to ask for," said Raider.

"For example," said the lieutenant. "I had an interesting bath last night."

"Really?"

"You've seen a cat wash her kittens, Mr. Raider? Well, I was washed by the kittens, four kittens, four little girls who gave me a bath with their tongues, like four dutiful little mother cats. Every inch of me, Mr. Raider. Every last inch."

"Slave girls?" Raider asked. "Bought in the market?"

The lieutenant frowned. "One of my duties, Mr. Raider," he said grimly, "is to stamp out the trade in little girls. I have ended the careers of eleven traders. With the rope. In fact, I was on my way to Santa Rita, where, according to report, there has been trading in little girls lately, when by chance I encountered you."

"I saw them buying and selling little girls in Santa Rita," said Raider.

"I will be there for the next market day. Or the one after that."

Raider flexed his shoulders. His wrists were already rubbed raw from having been bound all day yesterday and chained all night. His sweat itched in his two-day growth of beard. His arms were stiff.

"I have learned where your Mr. Bridenbaugh has gone," said the lieutenant.

"Not to Saltillo, I imagine," said Raider.

"No, not to Saltillo. To the mountains. To the Sierra Madre."

Raider glanced at him, to see if the lieutenant were making a sarcastic joke. "Why there?" he asked. "Why would he go there?"

"He did not go there voluntarily," said the lieutenant. "He was taken there, as a captive."

Raider sighed. "Someone got him."

The lieutenant nodded. "Don Miguel de Melchor."

"*Don* Miguel?" Raider asked.

"Yes. A hidalgo."

"A hidalgo? In the republic of Díaz?"

"Don't be scornful, Mr. Raider. His days are numbered, but for the present Don Miguel is a hidalgo. He lives like a feudal baron. He is a wealthy man. He commands more men than my colonel."

"What, then, does he want with Bridenbaugh's gold?"

The lieutenant laughed. "What man would scorn $25,000 in gold?" He laughed again. "A thousand peasant bandits dreamed of taking that gold, and it turns out that the man who captures it is already wealthy. The rich get richer, as they say, hmm?"

They rode through the village of Lampazos de Naranjo, where barefoot women and naked children scattered and hid from the troop of soldiers. Some dared to stare curiously at the two bound prisoners. The lieutenant stopped to take water from the fountain before the church, and he ordered his men to hold gourds to the mouths of the prisoners and let them drink. As much was spilled on Raider as he was allowed to drink. The lieutenant cursed the soldier and made him offer the water gourd a second time.

They rode on into the heat of the day. Raider marveled at the lieutenant, stiffly erect in his saddle, wearing his blue wool military jacket buttoned to the chin. Raider's stomach had begun to churn again. He wondered if the lieutenant would allow him two or three stops an hour. His shoulders ached. He wondered if he could endure three more days riding like this. He swayed in his saddle. The sun was dizzying.

When the lieutenant pitched violently forward over his horse's neck and fell headlong to the ground, Raider was stunned and confused. He had not heard the shot. He heard the others. The four soldiers fell one by one, picked off by riflemen firing from cover and out of sight. Not one of the soldiers got off a shot. None of them saw the men who killed them, and Raider didn't see them either. Six or eight shots were fired, no more, and the road was again silent except for the whinnying and stamping of frightened horses.

For one dangerous moment Raider thought Bastardo was going to bolt. But he didn't. Raider sat, looking all around, expecting the riflemen to emerge from their cover. None appeared. Perfecto, stunned and afraid, sat gaping. Raider drew a breath, threw a leg over Bastardo's neck, and dropped to the ground. He squatted beside a dead soldier and, straining behind him, managed to take the man's knife from his belt and cut his bonds. Then he cut Perfecto loose.

In half an hour he had recovered his Remington and his Winchester and his saddlebags, had drunk more water and was chewing on some of the herbs that seemed to settle his guts, and was mounted to ride on. Perfecto had taken the lieutenant's Colt and his belt and holster. They had scouted the surrounding area but had found no sign of the riflemen who had ambushed the little troop of soldiers. Raider had decided it would be dangerous to remain on the road—it went on south anyway, which was no longer where he wanted to go—and he led Perfecto off to the west, toward the Sierra Madre.

Perfecto had not overheard the conversation between Raider and the lieutenant—which had been in English, anyway—and was puzzled by their turn to the west. He had been leading the way until they were captured by the lieutenant, and now he kept suggesting turns to the left, to resume their southward course, and Raider kept shaking his head and urging Bastardo upward, into the higher hills west of the track they had followed before. Stopping wherever there was a view behind, Perfecto peered back.

"Can you not tell me where we are going, señor?" he asked at last.

"I'll make you a deal," said Raider. "You tell me who your friends are, and I'll tell you where we're going."

They had stopped at the flat crest of a low hill, where they could see all the way back to the village of Lampazos de Naranjo, through which they had passed three hours ago. On the road, now more than two miles behind and below, they could see four white-clad horsemen. Raider assumed they were the men Perfecto had spoken to on the bank of the Rio Sabinas and the men who had shot down the lieutenant and his soldiers. They had freed Raider and Perfecto and expected them to ride on south. Now they knew they hadn't. They were looking for a track, and they wouldn't find it, not in this country, not unless they were as good as Cheyenne or Apache, and they weren't.

"It is my father," said Perfecto. He was shamed. "He has followed us from Cedro Grande."

"To move in and take the gold if we caught up with Bridenbaugh," said Raider.

"Yes, señor."

"And what were you to do?"

Perfecto shook his head. "What I would not have done," he said firmly.

"Betray me?"

"*I would not, señor!*"

"Why not?"

"You saved my life from those Indians. You called me a brave man. I would never betray you. I am my father's son, but my father is the father of ten sons and five daughters, all of which he uses like property, like horses or cattle. I have no respect for him."

"I will tell you where I am going," said Raider. "The lieutenant told me William Bridenbaugh was captured by Don Miguel de Melchor. I am going to find him. You can return now and tell your father where I am going, or you can ride with me, as you choose."

"I ride with you, señor. My father will not follow us into the country of the hidalgo. He fears him."

"He won't follow us anyway," said Raider. "He's lost the trail."

Perfecto peered back. He nodded. "We are free of him."

CHAPTER NINE

Traveling became more and more difficult. To travel west it was necessary to climb the mountain ridges to their crests, struggle downward to the dry streambeds between, and climb again. At Perfecto's suggestion, Raider bought a suit of Mexican clothes—white cotton pants and shirt and a sombrero. Why, Perfecto asked, should everyone who saw them, even at a distance, understand that a *Norteamericano* was riding into the lands of the hidalgo? He bought fish line and hooks. Perfecto said they could catch fish in mountain streams and pools and not alert the Don's men by firing at game.

From a mountain ridge they climbed they could see the snow on the tops of peaks a hundred miles to the west. The mountains spread out before them, a formidable barrier. Don Miguel's land was in the lower mountains, Perfecto said. The people in the mountain country raised sheep and cattle and hunted endlessly for gold and silver, of which they found little. The dryness condemned the land to perpetual poverty. That was why every man was potentially a bandit. A poor man will steal, he said.

They made camp in the afternoon of their second day in the mountains, choosing a pine grove near a mountain stream and pool for a place to rest and try to recover. Perfecto tried his luck with the fish line and caught a pair of large trout. They built a fire and cooked. Raider bathed in the cold mountain water.

"The Don will not give you the gold, you know," Perfecto said as the dark gathered around them and they stretched out to sleep. "He will not give up the Bridenbaugh boy either if he thinks he can obtain a ransom for him. He is not an evil man, but he keeps what he thinks is his. Do you plan to try to *take* them from him, señor?"

"If I have to."

"You and I alone?"

"I alone. When you have guided me where I must go, you can return."

"No, señor."

"It's not your fight, Perfecto."

"It is not yours, either, señor. Still you propose to risk your life."

"I have my reasons," said Raider. "Anyway, I'm paid for what I do."

"Enough to fight the fifty men who will be in arms around the hacienda of Don Miguel de Melchor?"

"No."

"Then you and I go for the same reasons, señor."

"And what's that?" Raider asked.

"When I was a small boy, I wanted to be a priest, so I would be respected in Cedro Grande. The priest told me that was not a good enough reason for taking up the vocation, and I had no other reason, so I could not become a priest. Later, I thought I would become a hard man, a fighter and shooter, so people would fear me. That's a kind of respect. But I was beaten, knocked down in the dust and kicked, so I knew I was not a fighter. When you saw me I squatted in the dust, selling whatever my father had to sell in the market that day. I ran and fetched, at my father's bidding or at the bidding of others. I sat in the dust and waited for my orders. If I go back, that's what I will do again. You have won respect, I judge. But you will lose some of it if you go back to Texas and have not at least tried to save Bridenbaugh and the gold. Even if you lie and say you tried and could not save him, you will know yourself you did not, and you lose respect for yourself. That's important. I will go with you, señor."

Three days later they stood on the side of a mountain and looked across the valley at the hacienda of Don Miguel de Melchor.

It was a house of stone and timbers, no adobe, built on the slope of a mountain, overlooking the valley and a village on the edge of a dry streambed. It had the aspect of a feudal castle, with only narrow windows in its stone walls, a tower at one end, roofing of dusty red tile. The outbuildings were of like construction, and they clustered around the rear of the house, lending more to the appearance of a walled baronial castle. The road to the hacienda wound up the mountainside— narrow, not walled but passing between rocks like gates at three points—and was the only approach by horse. The mountainside above the hacienda was wooded with low pine. Below, only scrub pine and thorny brush grew among the rocks.

There were two ways to approach. Raider could ride up to the house, identify himself as a Pinkerton, and ask Don Miguel de Melchor to release William Bridenbaugh if not his gold; the alternative was to try to recover man and gold by stealth and force. As they sat on their horses and stared across the valley at the hacienda two or three miles away, Raider had not made up his mind. Neither alternative was attractive.

The village was typical. From this distance they could see the adobe church. Surprisingly, they could hear its bell, the tone rising from the valley as distinct as if they had been at the edge of the village. A knot of white-clad horsemen rode out of the village and up the road toward the hacienda.

Nothing distinguished Don Miguel's men from any other horsemen on the roads, except that they all were armed with Winchester rifles, exactly like Raider's. He and Perfecto had seen a few of them as they rode into the Don's domain. Keeping away from the valleys and roads and out of the villages, they had encountered none of the Don's men at close range. They had seen that there were many of them and that they watched the approaches to this village and the hacienda. The Don did not live in a fort, but no force of soldiers or any troop of bandits could reach the hacienda without his having ample warning.

"I want to cross to the other side of the valley, climb the mountain behind the hacienda, and see it from that side," said Raider.

"That will be difficult," said Perfecto, "with the horses. And we will go at night, *sí?*"

Raider nodded. "By moonlight."

"I could go into the village instead," said Perfecto. "I might learn much."

"They will want to know who you are, where you came from, where you are going, and why," said Raider. "I called you a brave man. I'm not sure you're a brave liar."

They kept to the woods, high above the valley, and rode south, watching for the place where they could cross the valley and climb the mountain on the other side. Two miles south of the hacienda Raider found the spot he wanted. They settled down there, still in the woods, to eat and rest and wait for night.

They crossed over just before midnight. It was easy. The Don's domain was watched but not tightly guarded. On a high slope they chose a place where the pines were thick and tangled with vines and brush to tether the horses and make themselves a camp. They slept the rest of the night in two-hour watches.

In the morning Raider ordered Perfecto to guard the camp and the horses. For himself, he would reconnoiter the hacienda, approaching it along the wooded ridge above.

"*Vaya con Dios, señor,*" said Perfecto.

He had two miles to travel, north along the mountain. The terrain was rough: steep at places and rocky, with scrabbly, stunted pines clinging to the rocks. As the sun rose overhead, it turned hot. He was glad for his good American boots. After an hour's walking and scrambling, he began to move more cautiously. He was not far from the hacienda.

He found a place directly above, where he could lie on his belly on a rock and peer between two pines at the compound, the house and outbuildings of the hacienda.

It was a busy place. Two farm carts on the road in the valley were delivering something—food apparently, and Raider wondered if the Don paid for it or if the farmers had to offer it to him as gifts. A dozen women and children were carrying bundles up the winding road from the carts to the entrance to the hacienda. At the rear of the house, near a small building that was apparently a chicken coop, a girl was scattering grain for a flock of chickens. A man near her was splitting firewood. The other outbuildings were a barn, another barn that looked like a stable, two tiny houses, and —of interest to Raider—a long, two-story stone building that looked to be the quarters for some of the men who carried guns for the Don. It was what a Texan might have called a bunkhouse. As he watched, two men with Winchesters emerged, mounted horses at the stable, and rode down the twisting road to the valley.

Bridenbaugh could be held anywhere on the hacienda, and a man could lurk around the edges for days and never gain a clue as to where the prisoner was. Having slipped as close as he dared—so close he could hear the talk of the people working with the cows and pigs and chickens kept in the compound—Raider lay on his stomach for what had to be three hours without seeing any sign. They did not at noon carry food to one of the outbuildings, which would have suggested a prisoner in one of them. Neither the main house nor any of the other buildings had a grated window. None of the men who moved in and out of the hacienda with rifles seemed to be a guard over any particular building.

Early in the afternoon he saw Don Miguel de Melchor. An elderly man with deep wrinkles in his tanned skin, with white hair and a white spade beard, emerged from the house and mounted a big gray stallion held for him by a bowing attendant. The old man was dressed in black except for a ruffled white shirt. The people working around all bowed to him as he rode around the house, down the road to the valley, and then toward the village. He was confident of the loyalty of the people in his domain. He rode alone. He was not armed.

Patience was not one of Raider's virtues. He thought of Doc. Doc would lie here on the ground, uncomplaining, for a week, if that was what it took to find out where Bridenbaugh was being held. Doc would do nothing rash. Patient, methodical . . . he was infuriating. It wasn't in Raider's nature. He fought with himself. He told himself the only way to scout this place was to lie here until he knew at least the comings and goings, the routine of the hacienda, even if he did not discover Bridenbaugh's whereabouts.

There was a routine. The Don's horsemen went out in the morning—some of them not very early, as if they had drunk too much the night before. Some carried saddlebags and blanket rolls on their horses and probably would not return tonight. Some carried ropes on their saddles. The hacienda was a ranch house. He saw cattle grazing on the poor, scant grass in the valley.

He was disgusted when he slipped back up the mountainside and began to make his way toward the camp. The day had not been wasted, but in his impatience it seemed it had been.

Perfecto hovered over a small pit he had dug in the ground. In the pit he had charcoal burning, hunks of it glowing. "Such a fire makes no smoke," he said. He had a pot of beans cooking, and he had rolled out corn dough and made flat Mexican bread. He handed Raider a clay jar of red wine.

"Where'd you get it?" Raider demanded. "All this?"

"In the village," said Perfecto.

"You went into the village?" Raider asked angrily.

Perfecto nodded. "The name of this village is San Ysidro. The man we seek is in fact here. I never entirely believed the lieutenant."

"Where do they keep him?" Raider asked. "I've spent a day staring at that goddam hacienda, and I'm as ignorant as I was when I left here this morning."

"He is there," said Perfecto.

"Has the Don sent a ransom demand?"

Perfecto shook his head. "I don't think so. I could not ask too many questions."

Raider glanced around. "How did you buy all this?" he asked. He saw a sack of corn, more wine, a bag of beans, another bag with onions and peppers. "I didn't know you had any money."

"I traded the old pistol my father gave me," said Perfecto. "The one I took from the dead lieutenant is better."

"The Don rode into the village from the hacienda this afternoon. He rode alone."

"In San Ysidro, some love him, some hate him, some fear him—but no man would dare speak a hard word to him, much less touch him."

Raider drank some of the red wine. "If we don't know where in the hacienda they are keeping Bridenbaugh, how are we going to get him out?" he asked. It was a rhetorical question. He did not expect an answer. "We can't assault the place and take it. We have to know where our man is, or we can't snatch him out of there."

"There is no way to find out, señor," said Perfecto. "No one in the village would know that much. We can't see what we need to know, and no one can tell us."

Perfecto dipped a piece of his flat bread in the pot of beans. He lifted out a dollop of beans on the bread and handed it to Raider. He had mixed onions and peppers with the beans; the mixture was hot and tasty. Raider chewed the hard bread and savored the beans.

"What would make them bring him out?" Raider asked.

"Señor?"

Raider looked up at the red sky. "What would cause them to bring Bridenbaugh out? Money? The idea they were going to get money? If they thought they were receiving a big ransom from his father?"

"The people in San Ysidro spoke with no animosity of the *Norteamericano*," he said. "They don't hear that the Don wants to kill him. He wants a profit."

After a brief silence, Raider said thoughtfully, "Well, I don't have the money for Don Miguel's 'profit,' but I have an idea about something that he might trade for William Bridenbaugh."

Perfecto, sitting on his haunches over his fire and eating, looked up sideways into Raider's face. "Is this idea fixed in your mind?" he asked. "Is it ready to be told?"

Raider grinned. "I don't know," he said. He stood and drew a long breath. "It's dangerous. The alternative is to give up and go home. I don't have any other idea."

Perfecto ate, waiting.

"Suppose . . ." Raider began. He hesitated. "Suppose we took Don Miguel prisoner. Suppose we meet him on the road tomorrow, if he rides alone to the village, and capture him. I'm sure he would trade his own life for Bridenbaugh and the gold."

Perfecto looked up. "You would kill him if . . . ?"

Raider shook his head. "No. In the end, no. But . . ."

"It is very dangerous."

"Yes. Half a dozen strings hang loose from the idea, too. But maybe . . . Maybe it's the best way. Maybe it's the only way."

CHAPTER TEN

Two horsemen on the valley road—particularly if one rode as handsome a horse as Bastardo—would alarm the hacienda and the village. So Raider and Perfecto left their horses at their pinewoods camp, two miles from the hacienda, and walked the mountain ridge to reach the point between the hacienda and the village where they might be able to take the Don from his horse on the road.

They looked for some cover—rocks or brush not too far from the road—where they could lie in wait. The valley varied. It was wide at points, narrow at others; cattle grazed in dusty fields along some parts of the road, and mountain slopes approached the streambed at others. There were no houses between the hacienda and the village; the Don owned all the land. It was almost barren land. The cattle were few; it would not sustain herds, and no cowboys worked the few cattle. The road was little traveled. They found a place that looked suitable.

When the Don rode from the hacienda to the village, when the sun was high, he was not alone. Only one man rode with him, but Raider decided it was better to wait for his return or even for another day, rather than try to take the Don when he was with one of his men. He had a better look at him, though. Don Miguel was in his sixties, maybe his late sixties. He sat his horse erect and confident, like a man who had spent much of his life in the saddle, who had not lost much of his vigor in his old age. He was not tanned as Raider had supposed; he had a dark complexion, probably from an inter-mixture of Indian blood with the Spanish. His hair and beard were snow white, but it was his eyebrows that marked his face with a brave, even fierce, character—they were thick and black and curly.

"He goes to the church," Perfecto said. "He is a religious man."

"Does his religion say nothing against kidnapping an American, stealing his gold, holding him prisoner?" Raider asked.

Perfecto shrugged. "What man's religion persuades him to give up the pursuit of gain?"

In mid-afternoon the Don returned. This time he was alone. For a time it seemed they would be frustrated again, because three of his horsemen rode toward the village as he rode out. They encountered him at some distance from where Raider and Perfecto waited, how-ever, and saluted him and rode on into the village. He approached. On his big gray he was a majestic figure. He rode placidly, absorbed apparently in his private thoughts. He looked neither to the right nor the left.

Perfecto stepped into the road ahead of Don Miguel. "Señor," he said. "Don Miguel."

The old man reined his horse to a stop. He looked down at Perfecto, calmly, condescension on his face. His eyes dropped for a moment to Perfecto's belt and pistol, and he frowned.

"Don Miguel," said Raider. He stood atop a flat rock by the side of the road, his Winchester leveled on the Don. Today he wore his own clothes: black Stet-son, gray flannel shirt, black pants. "Dismount," he said.

Don Miguel said nothing. He swung down easily from his horse.

"Come," said Raider. "You will come with us."

The Don sighed audibly. With a slight shrug, turning his mouth down, he walked into the brush and climbed toward Raider on the rock. "You work for Jacob Bridenbaugh, I assume," he said.

It was not possible to return the two miles and more to their camp and their horses. Don Miguel was too old, too unused to hard and sustained physical effort, to climb the rough mountain slope and follow the rugged mountain ridge at the same pace as Raider and Perfecto. He did not complain, but his breath came hard, and he sweated. If he died, the whole purpose of coming here and taking him would be lost. Besides, Raider was sympathetic. The old man asked no quarter. He kept up with them as best he could. He did not look afraid.

They stopped often, to rest and drink water. Once when they stopped, Raider climbed a tree for a view of the valley. It was as he expected. The Don's men were out in force, riding up and down the valley. They would suspect at first that his horse had thrown him and run on. When they began to suspect he had been taken, they would enter the woods, climb, and begin to search the mountain. Then maybe the Don would have to be a shield against his own gunmen.

Don Miguel spoke as they sat beneath the cover of a thick copse of pine, resting; Raider was in fact thinking they might spend the night there. "His son says Jacob Bridenbaugh is a strong, brave man," the Don said. "I was not sure he would come to Mexico in search of his son and his gold. Anyway, I thought he would come otherwise—at the head of a band of men."

"Have you heard of the Pinkerton National Detective Agency?" Raider asked.

The Don nodded. "I have, yes."

"I am a Pinkerton operative. Perfecto is my guide, provided me by his father."

"You came alone?" the Don asked incredulously.

"My partner is working to prove William Bridenbaugh did not commit murder back in Texas. I came to Mexico to bring him back."

"With his gold?"

"With his gold."

Don Miguel stroked his spade beard. "I never dreamed one man would come alone. Either you are a very brave and clever man or you are the biggest fool in Christendom."

"I want to ask you a question," said Raider.

"Of course."

"Since you have the Bridenbaugh gold, why didn't you let William go?"

The Don shook his head. "I don't have the gold," he said simply.

"What do you mean?" Raider asked quickly.

"William Bridenbaugh was paid twenty-five thousand *Norteamericano* dollars by the McMullen Bank in El Aguila, Texas," the Don said quietly, precisely. "Within hours he was accused of murder and fled across the border. Immediately it became known that he had the gold, and he rode south as hard as he could, he and his companion, fleeing not only the Texas Rangers but Mexicans of every stripe and character who hunted him. He killed to protect his gold—his father's gold. But when my riders captured him, on the road between Sabinas and Monclova, he was carrying less than $8,000."

"What happened to the rest of it?" Raider asked.

"You asked why I have been holding him. That is why: to make him tell me what he did with the remainder of the gold. Obviously he hid it somewhere. I meant to find out where."

"How?"

The Don shrugged. "Not by treating him very severely," he said easily. "We have threatened more severity than we have practiced. I will tell you, however—a few days ago I found my patience wearing thin. He has been given no food since then and will be given none until he tells what he did with the gold."

*   *   *

Raider stopped where the winding track toward the hacienda left the valley road. He stopped to wipe the sweat from his forehead with the sleeve of his shirt. He rode alone, but the Don's men rode all around him. It was obvious they knew he had captured the Don—or had something to do with it—and they allowed him to ride up the valley and approach the hacienda. They would not have let him ride past or turn back—that was obvious, too. They kept a distance of twenty yards or so, staring at him with sullen black eyes, itching as he well knew to shoot him in the back. They were well disciplined. He was safe.

He turned up the track toward the hacienda. Riflemen among the rocks to either side of the road guarded well this one approach to the compound. It had been a measure of the Don's confidence that no one guarded the woods and the mountain behind.

He dismounted at the top and hitched Bastardo to a post. No one came out to meet him. No one looked out. He stepped to the door and knocked with the iron knocker. It was two or three minutes before the door opened and he was confronted with a grim, middle-aged woman in a white blouse and black skirt.

"I have come to speak to Juan Cardenas," he said. "Don Miguel has sent me."

The woman nodded and stepped back from the door. He entered the house. It was cool inside. The light from the narrow windows fell cool and gray on whitewashed walls. His boots set up an echoing beat on the stone floors as he followed the woman toward the wide double doors at the end of the entrance hall. The woman knocked quietly on the double doors, then opened them. She stood aside, and he walked into a large room, sparely furnished with chairs of dark wood and leather, a heavy table, a bookcase filled with leather-bound books behind glass doors. A man stood by the table. "I am Juan Cardenas," he said gravely. "I am the Don's son-in-law. May I offer you food and drink before we talk?"

Seated at the table, Raider handed Juan Cardenas the gold signet ring the Don had given him for identification. It was not necessary. Juan Cardenas assumed he had kidnapped Don Miguel. Raider accepted wine and some cheese and fruit. The wine was far better than any he had tasted since he drank at Jacob Bridenbaugh's table.

Juan Cardenas was clean-shaven except for a mustache he wore shorter than Raider wore his own. His black hair was combed back over his head and held down with some kind of dressing. He wore clothes much like Raider's. He wore no pistol. He sat across the table from Raider, his square, handsome face sad and apprehensive.

"I have no wish to harm the Don," said Raider. "I promise you without condition that he will not be harmed—with the sole exception that . . ."

"I can imagine what your exception is, Mr. Raider," said Juan Cardenas. "What I want to know is when and where, precisely, will you release Don Miguel, assuming your various conditions are met?"

"He will be released in Texas," said Raider. "As soon as my party is back in the United States, in a town large enough that I can be sure you won't ride over after us. The Pinkerton National Detective Agency will arrange with the Texas Rangers for his safe return."

"What you propose is quite impossible, Mr. Raider," said Juan Cardenas. "What you seem not to understand is that the mountains beyond the area under the Don's protection are swarming with lawless bandits who will be more anxious to capture him than to capture you and William Bridenbaugh. You will be hunted like animals, and the richest prize among you will be the Don."

Raider bit into an apple. It was the first fresh fruit he had eaten since he left Texas. "And if I release him while you can still get to me, you will shoot me down the first chance you have," he said.

"You may be sure of it," said Juan Cardenas. "If the Don is harmed, we will pursue you into Texas or wherever else you go."

"The president's soldiers would like to have the Don, too, I imagine," said Raider.

"Maybe," said Juan Cardenas.

"There are five in my party," Raider lied. "With the two men you will release, we will be seven, plus the Don. I think we can move safely back to the border—particularly if we are as careful as we were coming here —without being stopped. You can follow me, so long as you keep your distance. That will discourage these bandits you talk about."

Juan Cardenas lit a long, thin cigar. He rose and walked to the window and looked out. "I wish I could think of an option. It would give me great pleasure to have one that would allow me to have you seized and hanged, Mr. Raider. In the absence of an alternative, I will grant what you demand."

William Bridenbaugh sat at the table and wolfed down cheese and fruit. He was a tall, long-faced boy with blond hair. The ranch hand who had accompanied him all the way from the Bridenbaugh ranch and had shared his captivity here, and even the Don's decision to starve the two of them, ate hungrily but without William Bridenbaugh's crude grabbing. His name was Foster, Jack Foster, and he was a hard, rangy cowboy, the kind who drifted from one ranch, one bunkhouse, to another, all his life. He was deferential to William and to Raider. He was accustomed to taking orders.

When they left the hacienda, William and Jack rode the horses they had ridden in on, and they carried the weapons they had carried when they came. Raider took notice that both men wore Smith & Wesson Model 2 revolvers, .32 caliber. Only Jack Foster had brought a rifle, and Raider had asked Juan Cardenas for a Winchester for William—or for Perfecto, if he proved more effective with it. Juan Cardenas had provided the rifle without comment. He had personally led out Don Miguel's gray horse, with a blanket roll neatly tied behind the saddle and saddlebags bulging with clothes and provisions for the Don. Bags of corn and other foodstuffs were hung over Foster's horse.

The gold rode with Raider. They had counted out the double eagles inside the house—$7,780. William acknowledged that it was the same amount, exactly, that had been dumped out of his saddlebags the day they were captured. "There was $7,800 originally," he said. "I spent twenty dollars."

When they turned away from the house to ride down the track to the valley road, a dozen women and children watched from the windows. Twenty men watched from the rocks and walls, hate in the eyes of every one.

Raider stopped and looked back at Juan Cardenas. "If we get out of Mexico alive, so will Don Miguel," he said. "I promise you that."

"If he does not, you will not, Mr. Raider," said Juan Cardenas. "*I* promise *you* that."

"Where's the rest of the gold?" Raider asked William when they were away from the hacienda and riding along the valley road.

"Them saddlebags had locks on 'em," said William. "Banker McMullen said he'd send my daddy the key by another man. I broke 'em open in Mexico. The $7,800 is all the gold there was. Where I was a fool was, I didn't know what $25,000 in gold ought to weigh. McMullen didn't even bother to put the lead in the bags. I carried off $7,800, thinkin' it was $25,000. My daddy had made such a point about what a good friend McMullen was, I never asked to count what he'd handed me before we left—thinkin' he'd be insulted."

"It'll be his word against yours on that, won't it?"

"Yeah, and if they could make it out I murdered a whore . . ."

"Who did kill her?" Raider asked.

"I don't know, and that's the truth, too. When I got to her room she was already dead."

Raider and William rode ahead. Jack Foster followed, leading the Don's gray stallion. Half a mile back, Juan Cardenas and ten white-clad horsemen followed.

They turned off the road and began the difficult ride up the mountainside, through the rocks and pine and brush, to the camp where Perfecto waited with Don Miguel. The horses struggled, resisting, lunging forward only when prodded and spurred. They had to lean down close to their horses' necks at times to make their way under overhanging branches. Their slow progress was hard, noisy work. When they had covered a distance of three or four hundred yards up the slope, Raider stopped.

"You two work your way up to the top of this ridge and wait for me there," he said.

"Wait a minute, we . . ." William protested.

"*Go,*" Raider barked. He slapped the rump of William's horse and turned away from him.

William and Jack struggled on upward and soon were out of sight. Raider sat on Bastardo and waited. He could hear the Mexicans below, following, clattering and grunting upward over the path he had just come up. In five minutes the first of the Don's horsemen came in sight. When they saw Raider, they stopped and sat staring sullenly at him. In another minute or so, Juan Cardenas caught up with them.

"Señor," Raider said to Cardenas. "You follow too close."

Cardenas said nothing. He sat his horse, heaving with exertion, containing his anger.

"Don't make my people angry or nervous," said Raider. "It's not the best way to save the life of Don Miguel."

Juan Cardenas nodded, abruptly and silently.

Raider turned Bastardo and resumed his climb.

At the top of the ridge he came on William and Jack. They had dismounted, but when they saw him they remounted their horses and were standing waiting as he rode up.

"I think we ought to get somethin' straight," said William as Raider forced Bastardo to make the last upward lunge.

Raider stopped. He faced William and let him speak.

"You work for my father," said William. "That means you work for me. If you expect to get paid when this is over, stop trying to give me orders. It was smart of you to kidnap the Don. You got me out of the hacienda. But I'll give the orders from here on out."

Raider said nothing. In an instant the .44 Remington was in his hand, the muzzle pointed at the middle of William's chest.

"Gawd a'mighty!" exclaimed Jack Foster.

Raider replaced the revolver in his holster, as smoothly and almost as fast as he had drawn it.

"I take your point," said William hoarsely. He had flushed. His eyes were wide. "Okay," he breathed. "It's settled."

Raider tossed his head to the right. He reined Bastardo around and started north along the ridge.

CHAPTER ELEVEN

Kathleen sucked the tip of Doc's foreskin between her lips, and holding it there she fluttered her tongue over it. He moaned, and she let it go. "You are more kinds of crazy man than any other man I've ever met," she said with a smile.

"Well, don't leave me like this, Kathleen," he protested. "You've got me ready to explode."

She lifted her breasts in her hands and flexed her shoulders. "If ever I get out of this mess and go back to making my living my own way, I'm going to raise my price. I could put up a sign—'Kathleen Reilly, student of the famous Dr. Weatherbee, offering tricks plain and fancy—$10.' What do you think?"

"I think the day will never come when a man will pay a woman that much money," said Doc.

"You're ignorant about some things, Doc," she said. "What do you think it cost Napoleon to enjoy the favors of Josephine?"

"Was she a whore, you think?" Doc asked lazily.

"And Nell Gwynn," said Kathleen. "King Charles paid her more than ten dollars, you may be sure."

Doc laughed. "I didn't know you were an expert on the history of whores. Tell me more."

"Well, to start with, there are other words than 'whore,' and I wish you'd use one," said Kathleen primly.

"Like what?"

"Well, we have been called trollops, strumpets, harlots, tarts . . . and . . ."

"Sluts . . . floozies," Doc suggested. "What would you like me to call you? Katie?"

"No, not Katie," she said emphatically. "Call me Kathleen, Doc. Just call me Kathleen." She bent over him and sucked in and licked the tip of his penis. She rolled over then, on her back. "C'mon," she whispered.

Doc rose astride her. "This is going to be quick," he said. "You've got me going."

"Then save some for another time," she said. "And maybe a third time. About the third time is when you're best."

He thrust into her hard and deep, at the same time trying to hold back, as the pressure in him rose to a maddening level. He knew he could not hold back long enough to give her her pleasure, but he wanted his own to be as intense as possible. It was. It was hard to believe something inside a man didn't break from the strain when he came that hard. He settled down on her, sweating, drained, and grateful.

Kathleen ran her fingers through his hair. "Do you have any brothers?" she murmured.

"Raider's as close to a brother as I have," Doc said quietly.

"He'll be back," she whispered.

"It's a dangerous thing, what he went to do," said Doc.

"It's a dangerous thing you're doing," said Kathleen. "Raider is a strong man. He can take care of himself. The question is whether you can take care of yourself." She reached up and gently touched a bruise on his forehead.

Jeffrey McMullen was anxious to sell Doc's "brother" $5,000 worth of railroad stock. Doc had sent a telegram to his "brother," care of Illinois Pharmaceuticals:

MR. MCMULLEN PRESIDENT MCMULLEN BANK
WILLING SELL FIVE THOUSAND DOLLARS WORTH
STOCK IN SAN ANTONIO HOUSTON NEW ORLEANS
RAILROAD STOP ASSURES ME SHARES WORTH EVERY
CENT STOP DESCRIBES RAILROAD AS SOUND INVEST-
MENT STOP YOU SHOULD CONSIDER STOP WIRE
YOUR DECISION STOP DOC STOP

The response had come two days later:

MCMULLEN PROPOSITION VERY INTERESTING STOP
WILL CONSIDER AND ADVISE STOP GET ALL ADDI-
TIONAL INFORMATION YOU CAN STOP WAGNER
WEATHERBEE STOP

"Your brother Wagner is a careful investor," said
Jeffrey McMullen. "I admire that in a man. I do admire prudence in matters of money."

They sat at a table in the Eagle, where Doc was
eating a breakfast of steak and eggs. The banker had
coffee.

Doc had begun to wonder in the past couple of days
if McMullen's attention to him and Kathleen was really
a part of his effort to sell railroad stock, or if the
banker wanted a closer look at Kathleen—if he suspected something. Kathleen had been playing sick and
coming down only when necessary. "I have her on a
regimen of ipecac," he said, "and you can imagine the
result. She really is not able to venture forth much."

"Dear lady," said the banker sympathetically.

Every day Doc sold homeopathic specifics from the
Studebaker wagon; it was necessary if he was to maintain his disguise. He made enough money to pay his
hotel bill, to pay the livery stable, and to eat and drink.
He bought Kathleen a derringer to carry in her purse.
He carried the Diamondback himself. He disliked carrying a gun, but he had rarely spent time in a town where
he felt so menaced. The bruise on his forehead that
Kathleen had caressed had been dealt him by one of

the Murphy boys, who had slapped him across the mouth, then struck him with a fist to the head. He was the butt of their ill-humored jokes. Tom McMullen was at it again. Even he, who had slept three days under the influence of the laudanum Doc had prescribed for him, menaced Doc on the street with his Colt .44. He and the Murphys stood at the edge of the crowd around his wagon and yelled that he was a quack, a sawbones, a pill pusher. They threw clods and dried horse dung at the wagon. It was a good thing Raider was in Mexico. He had killed one of them; he would have killed the rest.

Doc led Judith along the street toward the livery stable. Near the end of the street the deputy, Horace Chandler, fell into step beside him.

"You don't take no man's advice, do you?" he said to Doc.

"What advice is that?" Doc asked without looking at Chandler.

"You been tole to clean out," said Chandler.

Doc glanced at him. "More than once," he said.

"I ain't 'bout to keep tellin' you," said Chandler. "This is it, medicine man. You just keep walkin', right now. Don't unhitch that mule. You jus' pick up that woman you call your wife at the Eagle, and be sure you pay yer bill, and move on."

Doc led Judith through the doors of the stable. The stableman was out. It was not unusual. He had unhitched Judith and fed her himself several evenings. He began to unbuckle her belly band.

"What'd I say?" Chandler growled.

Doc went on unbuckling. "You've been drinking, Chandler," he said.

Chandler grabbed Doc by his coat and spun him around. "You're an ugly man, Doctor," he said. Doc could smell the whiskey on his breath, and the hatred in his narrow eyes was deep and cold. "You got a ugly mule, too." He doubled a fist and staggered Doc with a

blow to the side of his neck. Then he drew his fist back
and struck Judith on her ear.

Judith screamed and tried to pull away.

Doc pulled himself erect again with a hand on the
wagon. "Chandler . . ." he grunted. He shook his head.
His right fist shot out and caught Chandler on the chin.
Chandler stumbled back against a box stall. Doc's left
cross hit him on the side of his jaw, and another short,
hard jab of the right broke his lips against his teeth.
Chandler slumped to the ground. "There's a limit,
goddam you," Doc growled at him. "There's a limit."

Chandler crawled away, toward the back of the
stable, shaking his head. Doc turned to Judith and
patted her reassuringly on the flank. She was not hurt,
only stunned. She twitched nervously at his first touch,
then eased as he patted and spoke to her.

A pistol shot exploded behind him. He threw himself
against Judith, almost knocking her over, and fumbled
for the Diamondback, knowing it was too late, that the
next shot would hit him and there was nothing he could
do to stop it. He turned, at least to see who . . . It was
the rancher, Tod Galvin: a big, bulky figure, wearing
a tall Stetson, silhouetted against the light from the open
stable door. He was shoving his Colt Peacemaker back
into its holster. He looked past Doc.

"Chandler, you drunken bunkhouse bum," he yelled.
"Kick it! Kick it farther!"

Doc turned to look. Chandler's pistol lay beside him
on the ground. He was covered with dust and dirt, and
a deep gouge in the ground marked the place where
Galvin's bullet had hit and exploded dirt over him.
Chandler reached out with his leg and nudged his revolver farther from him. He stared at Galvin, shocked
and uncomprehending.

"Get up," Galvin said to him.

Chandler rose, first on his knees, then lurched to his
feet. Galvin walked by Doc, swung heavily on Chandler,
and knocked him down again. Chandler this time lay
unconscious.

The big rancher picked up Chandler's Colt. He handed it to Doc. "I suggest you keep this, Doctor," he said. "You may need it. You know how to use one?"

Doc nodded.

"I saw you on the street, followed you; I want to talk to you. Good thing I followed you. He meant to kill you."

Doc glanced at Chandler, who lay silent in the dirt and horse dung. He sighed. "He'll probably try again."

"No. Not his type. He'll be afraid of you now."

"Well, I thank you, Mr. Galvin," said Doc. "I do indeed thank you."

"I'd consider myself repaid if you and your lady would ride out to my ranch with me this evening," said Galvin. "You can be my guests for dinner and the night, and I'll bring you back to town in the morning. What I want to talk to you about will require some time."

It would have been awkward to refuse. Kathleen was uneasy, but Doc insisted she go with him, not stay in their room alone. Galvin drove an open buggy, and the three of them were squeezed tightly together on the seat. He had tossed a few items he had purchased in town into the back. His gray horse needed no driving once it saw they were headed home. It stepped out smartly, and the town was soon behind them and red in the light of the low sun.

"I am surprised at how long you are staying in El Aguila, Doctor," said Galvin conversationally.

"Business is good," said Doc.

"Ten days is a long time for a traveling man to stay in a town like this," Galvin persisted.

"I stay as long as I make sales," said Doc.

"Besides," said Kathleen, "it is not often I can be with him."

"I'm surprised you didn't meet him at a rail town," said Galvin.

"It was an easy journey," she said.

For half a mile Galvin drove in silence, probably

collecting his thoughts, forming a judgment. "It is suspected you are not really his wife," he said then to Kathleen. "Forgive me if that's an impertinence."

"You are forgiven, but it certainly is," she said.

Galvin nodded. "It is suspected his name is not Dr. Weatherbee," he said. "It is suspected he is not a doctor."

Doc's hand moved slowly toward the Diamondback under his coat.

Galvin noticed. "Relax, Doctor," he said. "It's all right with me, one way or the other. I'm curious to know who you two really are, but I can't see how it makes any difference to me who you are. I have a feeling you are the law, some way or other—bank examiners, railroad detectives, something."

Kathleen laughed. "The idea is ridiculous," she said.

Galvin shrugged. "Like I say, it makes no difference to me. But there are those who do care. I mean to warn you about them."

"Why?" Doc asked bluntly. "Why should you give us a warning?"

Galvin smiled and changed the subject. "Tell me, Doctor," he said. "What do you think of this buggy? I notice your wagon is a Studebaker. This buggy is a Columbus, made in Columbus, Ohio, where they make the finest rigs in the world. Had you noticed?"

His ranch house was not nearly as fine as the Bridenbaugh house, but it was a low, comfortable house, roomy, homelike, warm. His wife, as he explained, had been dead for ten years. The house was kept for him by a daughter, Jennie, a girl of eighteen, and he had two sons, sixteen and fourteen, who had survived Billy Bob. He served whiskey in the living room before dinner and again on the dinner table, and they ate beef and potatoes and eggs, served in mountainous quantities.

After dinner the boys left the room, and Jennie busied herself supervising the removal of the dishes. Galvin lighted a cigar over the coal-oil lamp in the center of the table. Doc lighted a cheroot. Kathleen ignored his frown and poured herself another whiskey.

"You spoke of a brother, Wagner Weatherbee," said Galvin. "You told McMullen he might be interested in some stock in the San Antonio, Houston & New Orleans Railroad. You sent off a telegram. You got one back. You've asked a lot of questions about the railroad. McMullen's beginning to put two and two together, Doctor—or whatever your name is."

"And what does two and two add up to, Mr. Galvin?"

"That you're here to look at the bank," said Galvin.

"Would Mr. McMullen object to having bank examiners look into his bank?" Doc asked.

"Right now he would," said Galvin. "I don't know how bad it is, but I know the bank's in trouble. If the slightest word of it got out, the bank would go bust. I'm worried, I can tell you."

"Are you an investor in the McMullen Bank, Mr. Galvin?" Kathleen asked.

"An investor, and a depositor," said Galvin. "If the bank goes bust, I'm gonna lose a lot of money."

"What's wrong with the bank?" Doc asked.

"I don't know. I'm not sure," said Galvin. "All I know is, I had a chance to buy a spread of cattle land north of here about two months ago, and when I went in and told Jeff I'd be making a big withdrawal soon, he begged me not to. He said he could cover it—though, to tell you the truth, I doubt he could've—but he asked me to wait a little, till he could handle it a little easier. I figure he put a lot of money in the railroad, and the railroad hasn't panned out."

"He's supposed to have paid over $25,000 in gold to that Bridenbaugh boy," said Kathleen. "Did that hurt the bank?"

Galvin shook his head. "That was only escrow money. The railroad sent in the $25,000 for the bank to hold until Bridenbaugh delivered a deed to some land the railroad bought. The boy brought the deed, and Jeffrey turned over the railroad's gold. That was never the bank's money."

"You said you doubted the railroad could come up with that kind of money," said Doc.

"That's somethin' else that makes me think Jeff's in trouble," said Galvin. "His tellin' you that stock would be a good investment. He knows better. He's hard-pressed for cash, is what's the trouble."

Doc smiled faintly. "And you think I'm a bank examiner," he said. "Supposing I am, what do you want me to do?"

"Supposin' you are," said Galvin, "ain't it your job to keep banks sound, to keep the financial system sound? Is it your job to bust a bank?"

Doc shook his head.

" 'Course not. What I'm askin' is, you let Jeff McMullen have a little time, and he'll make that bank sound again. You let it be known in this town you're an examiner—just by askin' the wrong questions of the wrong people—and you can bust the bank."

"How will he make it sound, Mr. Galvin?" Doc asked. "By selling worthless stock?"

"He'd not do that, if he wasn't scared," said Galvin. "He's scared. He needs money."

"Where's it going to come from?" Doc asked.

"He thinks the railroad company'll pay out. It bought the Bridenbaugh land, y' know; that was an investment and ought to pay out. What Jeff needs is time."

Doc smiled at Kathleen. "Well, I won't break the bank, Mr. Galvin. That's not what I'm here for."

Kathleen stood nude except for a pair of black stockings, rubbing her body vigorously, trying to rub the red marks of the corset off her skin. The room was lighted by a single candle, and Doc lay on the bed, waiting for her.

"A dollar will get you five," said Kathleen, "there was no gold in the saddlebags McMullen turned over to William Bridenbaugh. It was lead or rocks. They killed the Bradford girl, tried to make it look like William killed her, and let him get away from them. They laid for him somewhere, either between here and the border or over in Mexico, and killed him. Now nobody will ever know there was no gold in the saddlebags he carried, and the banker is $25,000 to the better. Maybe his bank is goin' under, and he needs the money bad enough to make him do a thing like that."

Doc shook his head. "I don't think it's that simple."

"Where's the hole in it?"

"Well, in the first place, how could McMullen have known William Bridenbaugh would take it in his head to stop at the cathouse on the way out of town? Sam said that was on impulse. Besides, it was Sam and his son who drew their guns and broke William loose from the cowboys that had him. They're the ones who made it possible for him to escape. No. Doesn't work, Kathleen."

"I bet it's something like that," she said.

Doc nodded. "The railroad company is insolvent. The bank isn't sound. I . . . I think you're right about one thing, Kathleen."

"Good for me. And what's that?"

"There wasn't $25,000 in gold in those saddlebags."

"And that explains a lot."

"It doesn't explain anything unless we can prove it. William is in Mexico, if he's still alive. He still stands accused of the murder of Susie Bradford, and though I have the evidence that proves he didn't, it's evidence I don't think a judge or jury would look at. He ran off. He was drunk in this town, and he spent a lot of his time at the whorehouse. If he swears there was no gold in those bags, and the banker swears there was, who's a jury going to believe?"

"Maybe William, if in the meantime the bank has gone under and the town knows the banker had been stealin' from it."

Doc laughed. "Kathleen," he said. "You and Raider

would work well together. You think alike. But I'm afraid Mr. Pinkerton would never make an operative of you."

"Any more than I could make a whore of you, Doctor," she said as she hurried toward their bed.

CHAPTER TWELVE

Don Miguel had as much interest in their reaching the border safely as did any of them, and Raider decided he could trust him. The old man knew the country. He had fought with Santa Anna against Taylor at Buena Vista, and in years since he had campaigned all over northern Mexico. He considered President Díaz, not himself, to be the outlaw. He believed, quite simply, that well-born, cultured men like himself were entitled to rule; and he had spent his later life insisting on that principle, even to the point of declaring his own personal war against the government in Mexico City.

"It is 175 kilometers to the border at Nuevo Laredo," said the Don. "The same roughly, at Hidalgo. But there is dangerous country between here and there. If we move north, toward Piedras Negras or even toward Ciudad Acuña, the way will be difficult but maybe safer. It is more than 300 kilometers, however."

"Your health . . ." said Raider. "Can you endure the ride?"

The Don lifted his chin. "I can ride where you can ride, Señor Raider," he said.

Raider smiled at him. "I believe you can."

"Sounds like you two have decided we're going the long way," said William.

"I've had worse advice," said Raider.

Perfecto was deferential in the presence of Don Miguel, yet he guarded him closely and clearly would restrain him roughly if the Don tried to escape. Usually they rode with Raider and William in the lead, Perfecto and the Don following, and Jack Foster—whom Raider trusted as an obedient man and handy with a gun—guarding their rear.

As they rode north the land was drier, the mountains more barren, and from high points they could look back. Often they saw Juan Cardenas and his troop following. Cardenas stayed back a mile or more, but he was always there. From the sun's reflection, Raider could tell Cardenas was watching their progress through a long telescope.

For two days Raider led them along mountain ridges, avoiding roads and the meager streams in the valleys, circling well away from villages, even from ranches. Since they saw no one, it was unlikely that anyone but Juan Cardenas saw them.

When they camped for the night, everyone took turns guarding the Don. He expected them to share the food that had been sent for him; there was no question of that. He shared, too, the flask of old brandy his son-in-law had sent.

The second morning, Raider awoke in the first light of dawn. It was Jack Foster's watch. Raider had tried to waken during each watch, to see if the others slept. William had dozed, and Raider had given him a hard kick in the ass. Jack was awake, hunched against a rock, with his blanket wrapped around him, smoking the butt of a cigar he had dismounted to retrieve after the Don threw it away. The Don was up and had moved a few yards away from all the others. He knelt in prayer, clutching a gold cross to his breast.

"Figure he's prayin' for the Devil to take us?" Jack asked Raider very quietly.

"Wouldn't you?" Raider asked.

When the Don had finished his prayers, he sat on a rock and carefully trimmed his beard with a straight razor and a tiny pair of scissors. Raider had shaved before he went to the hacienda and confronted Juan Cardenas, but not since; and now, a bit shamed by Don

Miguel, he scraped off his dark whiskers with cold water and no soap. The old man ate fastidiously, with fork and knife from his kit, which he washed carefully and returned to their leather case after each meal.

At first there was water: mountain pools, little springs, stagnant pools in the beds of almost-dry streams. By the afternoon of the second day, there was water left in their canteens but none for the horses, and it was plain they would no longer be able to avoid every village, every house, every real stream. Raider scouted for a source of water. He would have avoided a house if he could have spotted a stream they could have visited after dark, but by nightfall he had seen nothing but the occasional poor adobe hut, each one guarding some small source of water lived on by the inhabitants and their few chickens. It would be necessary to approach one.

It was better to go in daylight. If they approached a house at night, someone might shoot. Raider spotted a house, and after they made camp for the night, he sat among the rocks above it and watched as long as daylight lasted. He saw a woman come out once. He saw no men. He decided to go in in the morning.

As it had been the night before, Jack had the last watch. He was awake when Raider woke and moved to sit beside him. "I'm going to take Perfecto to the house with me," he said quietly to Jack. "He'll do the talking. I've got a suit of Mex clothes. Maybe we can pass as a pair of poor Mexes needing water. I'll ride your horse. Bastardo looks too good for a poor man to be riding. We won't be gone over two, three hours. I depend on you to be sure things are the way I left 'em, when I get back."

Jack nodded. He glanced at William, sleeping. "He ain't such a bad feller, Raider," he said. "Don't hold too hard ag'in him."

Raider took off his boots and rubbed his feet and legs with dust. Dressed in his white Mexican clothes, with a sombrero on his head, he mounted Jack's horse.

He carried the Winchester across his saddle and shoved his Remington down inside his loose shirt. Before the sun had risen out of the gray mist over the mountains to the east, he and Perfecto rode among the rocks and down the slope of the mountain, raising a cloud of dust.

"I don't mean to sneak up on this house," Raider said to Perfecto. "Better to ride right in."

A streambed ran at the base of the mountain. It was a gully, actually, where rainwater ran when there was rain. The land on its banks was dry. Nothing grew but desert plants: cacti, thorn. They saw sidewinder tracks, and once they spotted a Gila monster.

There had to be a well at the house. From the distance they could see half a dozen cattle, and a patch of green. The little adobe house shimmered in the sunlight.

"I've never known a man like Don Miguel," said Perfecto, breaking the silence of half an hour.

"Neither have I."

"Be warned, señor," said Perfecto. "He says his prayers. Well he might; he has many souls on his conscience."

"You don't trust him."

"No, señor. He will offer the two men we left behind much gold for his escape. We should return very carefully. They may call in the Don's friends while we are gone. They may try to shoot us and then call them in."

Raider nodded. The thought had occurred to him.

"They will regret it if they do," Perfecto went on. "The Don will watch them suffer an unpleasant death."

When they were a hundred yards from the house, Perfecto rode a horse's length ahead of Raider. *"Hola!"* he yelled. *"Hola!"*

They rode closer. The mud house was a wretched hovel. As they had expected, there was a well to one side, with a bucket hanging on a rope that was attached to a boom. It was obviously a shallow well. Near it was a trough where the cattle drank. The half dozen head they had seen were what the ranch had. A vegetable garden grew behind. Lying on the ground by the well was a yoke with two buckets. Someone carried water to the garden and irrigated it by hand, almost an acre of it. A shed behind the house was for the cattle, probably, maybe for a horse if they had one. The windows of the house—there were only two of them—had no glass, only wooden shutters that were open now.

"Hola!"

The barrels of a shotgun appeared in a window, and Raider heard the click of the hammers being pulled back. A woman's voice asked who they were, what they wanted. Perfecto said they needed water. All they wanted was to fill their canteens. They could pay for water.

The barrels were withdrawn from the window, and in a moment the woman appeared in the door, holding the shotgun warily, the muzzle pointed at Perfecto. She was maybe twenty years old, maybe thirty; it was impossible to tell. Her hair was light brown and dirty. Her eyes were blue. Her skin was sun-browned. She wore a ragged, faded dress that barely hung together, and the skirt stopped just below her knees. She squinted into the morning sun.

"Please," said Perfecto. "We are only poor men who need water."

The woman stepped out of the doorway. She eyed Perfecto skeptically, keeping the shotgun pointed at him; but her eyes shifted, and the gun could have been moved toward Raider in an instant. She took only a moment to stare at Perfecto. She stared harder at Raider.

"Who the hell are you, gringo?" she asked in English. She shifted the shotgun toward him. "You better get your boots back on. You get down off that horse barefoot like that and you'll have no feet to walk on in ten minutes. It takes practice to go barefoot like a greaser or an Indian, and you ain't had it."

Raider smiled. "Texas?" he asked.

"Arizona," she said.

He glanced around. "Long way from home, aren't you?"

"Hell of a long way."

"Can you sell us water?"

"Maybe. Who the hell are you?"

Raider pointed at Perfecto, who now watched uneasily as Raider and the woman conversed in English. "His name is Perfecto. He works for me as a guide, helper. My name is Raider. I'm a Pinkerton. You know what a Pinkerton is?"

"I ain't been in Mexico that long. Christ! That means you're the one who kidnapped Don Miguel de Melchor!"

"Tit for tat," said Raider. "He kidnapped William Bridenbaugh and Jack Foster, so now we've kidnapped him."

"You're takin' him to Texas," she said.

"That's right."

"Maybe you are and maybe you ain't," she said, pointing past him, down the valley through which he and Perfecto had just approached the house.

He looked over his shoulder. A large cloud of dust stood over the valley a mile or so away, spreading in the wind.

"Cardenas," said Raider to Perfecto.

Perfecto stared at the dust cloud. His eyes widened with fear. "We must go," he said.

Raider nodded.

"You make dust like they make dust," said the woman. "You go ridin' hell-bent out of here, they'll spot you."

"I don't see how we got much choice," said Raider. "Cardenas catches up with us and sees us separated from the Don, we'll be in trouble."

"You got a choice," she said.

"Which is?"

"Unsaddle them horses, hitch them in the shed, and hide inside."

"And trust you," said Raider.

"And trust me," she said. "I don't owe Don Miguel no favors."

"If it doesn't work, if they find us, what'll they do to you?"

"I'll show you," she said. In an instant she had dropped her dress to her waist and turned her back to them. Her back was crisscrossed with old welts. She had been whipped.

"You're taking a hell of a chance, then," said Raider.

She pulled the dress up. "You can repay me."

"How?"

"Tell you later. You ain't got more'n a minute to get unsaddled and . . ."

They did as she said. When Juan Cardenas rode up to the house, followed by more than twenty horsemen, Raider and Perfecto were in the house. The woman stood in front. Her shotgun was behind the door. Raider could not see outside, but he could hear.

Cardenas wanted water. For half an hour, Raider could hear the creak of the boom as the bucket was lowered repeatedly to the bottom of the well. Cardenas had apparently dismounted and was standing talking to the woman—Raider could not make out much of the conversation. He fingered his trigger nervously. He and Perfecto had little or no chance if the woman betrayed them.

Suddenly the voices got louder.

"Buena suerte, amo," the woman called out.

Cardenas laughed. *"Adios, esclava,"* he returned, as he and the horseman clattered off.

She had called him "master," and he had called her "slave." There had been a jocular tone in the voice of Cardenas but no such tone in hers.

The woman came into the house. "My name is Ellen Kirtland," she said. "If you're the Pinkerton you say you are, you're the first honest American that's come by here in five years, and that's how long I been here. I was caught by Apaches and carried down into the Sierra Madres—not these Sierra Madres, the other ones, farther west. The greaser that owns this place bought me. There ain't no slavery in Mexico, by law, but you gotta get away to prove it."

"Who whipped you?" Raider asked.

She jerked her head over her shoulder, in the direction of the departing riders. "Cardenas," she said. "One of his boys. I tried to get away from here. I run off. My greaser, the one that owns me—him and his brother belong to Don Miguel. They're his men. They take his orders. When I run off, some of the Don's men caught me. They took me to the hacienda and give me a beatin'. When my greaser come to pick me up, he was grateful."

Raider grimaced. "Jesus . . ."

"Now you owe me somethin', and you can guess what it is," she said.

"I'd take you with us if I owed you or not," said Raider.

She took everything they could use—all the food from the house, water bottles, knives, the shotgun, an old percussion-cap revolver and ammunition, a can of coal oil, a coil of rope—and in the cactus not far from the house she roped a burro. It carried everything she had taken, lashed on its back, and she rode behind Raider on Foster's horse. Just before they left, as Raider was filling the last bottle with water from the well, she disappeared for a moment inside the house, and when she came out the smoke followed her. She had set the house on fire.

There were no trails in the mountains around there, Ellen said. They could be glad of that; it made it harder for anyone to try to follow them.

"That all the clothes you've had since you've been here?" Raider asked. Ellen wore a ragged dress that rode all the way up around her hips as she straddled the horse.

She nodded. "I worked stark naked in the garden to save it. But I never got used to it. My father is a Baptist minister, a missionary to the Apache savages that took me and sold me. I'll be obliged if I don't have to go naked."

"I got some Mex clothes you can have," Raider offered.

Ellen nodded thankfully. They rode in silence, climbing the mountainside. They could see Cardenas and his horsemen riding back and forth in the valley, looking for the trail of the Americans and the Don. It was plain they would return to the adobe house and find Ellen gone and the adobe house burned out. They would guess who had come, with whom she had gone.

"Makes no difference," Raider said. "Once we took the Don, they hated us as much as they could. Taking a woman Cardenas thinks is part of the estate won't matter any which way."

Leaving Perfecto with Ellen and both horses and the burro, Raider slipped among the rocks to have a look at the camp before he entered. He found the Don sitting with his back to a rock, his legs stretched out before him, in his white shirt; he had removed his coat in the heat. He was talking to William and Jack, who sat facing him, listening. "He was no ignoble man," the Don was saying as Raider reached a point where he could listen but still remain hidden. "They put him before a firing squad, and he faced it bravely. Maximilian. His name is slandered in the United States, I understand. It is slandered here, criminally. But he was a brave and noble man, and Mexico suffered a misfortune when he was overthrown."

Raider nodded and helped the Don to his feet. He led the old man to where Ellen stood dressed in Raider's white cotton pants and shirt. Raider then led her and the Don a little way from the camp, and when the three of them were alone he had Ellen raise the shirt in back and show the Don her scars.

The old man shook his head. The corners of his mouth turned down into the corners of his spade beard.

"I did not authorize this," he said. "I did not condone it. I did not know of it."

"If you were in the hacienda, señor, you heard my screams," she said in Spanish. "It is a fearful thing, to be whipped."

"I know," said Don Miguel. "I myself bear scars like yours." He glanced at Raider. "If you do not believe me, I can show you. Have you ever heard of General Isturbide, the Emperor Agustín? He imposed a severe discipline, more than fifty years ago. I could never countenance the lashing of anyone. I have too vivid a memory."

Ellen looked at Raider. "I believe Don Miguel," she said. "It was Juan Cardenas who did it."

Raider shook his head. "Let's not stand here jawing about who did it," he said. "In the morning we've got to move north—and faster than we did yesterday and today."

CHAPTER THIRTEEN

The next day they climbed higher into the Sierra Madre Oriental. The heat moderated at the higher altitude. As night came on, it was cold. Raider agreed they might build a fire for cooking hot food—though not in the campsite where they would sleep, but half a mile from it.

They had lost sight of Juan Cardenas and his men. Moving upward, they had left the valley where horsemen raised conspicuous clouds of dust and entered an area where tough, thin grass covered the slopes and a few trees clung to the rocky soil. Raider stopped from time to time to peer back, searching; but he saw nothing of the score of men that had followed them until today. Juan Cardenas, though, with his long brass telescope, probably could see them.

They stopped early. The Don seemed tired. They had come across a thin mountain stream with a pool. Raider refused to let them camp near it; it was certain to attract anyone moving in the area who knew this mountain; but he made camp a mile or so from it, and when Perfecto had a fire blazing and had begun to cook food, he took Ellen on the back of Bastardo, and they rode back to the pool where the horses had drunk their fill and where they had replenished their canteens. He carried a bar of the Don's soap.

"It's cold, I know—goddam cold," he said to Ellen. "But if you'd like a bath . . ."

"I'd bathe in ice water for a bath with that soap," she

said. "It's the first I've seen since I left Arizona. The Don must've imported it. Nobody here knows what it is."

She was not modest. She stripped off her clothes and plunged into the water without hesitation. He sat on a rock near the pool and watched her. She washed her hair, her face, her body, with eager vigor and obvious pleasure. She was not as old as he had at first guessed. She was not more than twenty-two or -three. Her tits were nice. They were suntanned. He had never seen suntanned tits before—or, for that matter, a suntanned belly and butt. She had said she worked naked in her garden to save her one dress from disintegrating, and now he had to believe it. The scars across her back were thin and white. He took off his boots and socks and stuck his feet in the water. It *was* cold. It was a measure of how much she wanted a bath to see her endure it.

"Toss me my clothes," she said. "I'm not going to put this clean body in them filthy clothes."

He had brought a blanket for her to huddle in while she dried, so he tossed the white cotton clothes in the water. She washed them with the soap and wrung them and spread them on a flat rock in the sun.

She emerged from the water shivering, covered with goose flesh, and wrapped herself in the blanket. She sat down, drawing her knees up against her tits. "Wouldn't hurt *you*, you know," she said. "You don't smell like frankincense and myrrh yourself. Gimme the thutty-thutty."

Raider grinned. He handed her the Winchester, stripped quickly, and jumped in the water. His balls shriveled. "God, woman!" he yelled. "Why didn't you tell me you're an Eskimo?"

He lathered and rinsed quickly, meaning to get out as fast as he could. Ellen laughed. He shook his head and scowled at her, and in a minute he came out and jerked the blanket off her and began to rub himself with it.

"God a'mighty!" she said, eyeing his cock. "You use that for a club to stun mules?"

"Stun you," Raider muttered, rubbing hard, trying to stimulate the circulation of warm blood.

"Son of a bitch! I s'pose I owe you somethin', anyway. And I look at that, I want it. Raider . . ."

He nodded. "I haven't had a woman since . . . I haven't counted the days. But if you don't want to . . ."

"I want to," she said. "Lord forgive me, I want to."

They spread the blanket feverishly, fumbling in their hurry, careless of the possible intrusion of someone coming to the mountain pool. He mounted her and plunged himself into her as quick and hard as he could. He came before he had shoved five strokes into her.

"Oh, no!" she breathed. "Not yet, for God's sake!"

"In a minute, lady," he panted. "Again, in a minute."

He took time then to nibble her nipples, to caress her pussy, to do all he had learned to do over the years of his manhood, to bring her on. She encouraged him with moans and writhing. She thrust her hips upward to meet his exploring fingers. When he entered her again, she wrapped her legs around his hips and held him tight. She humped. She rolled. He thought he would slip out of her, but she clamped him tight inside with her legs. She yelled when she came. He thought the camp would hear her. She broke into a sweat, even in the cool air. He came the second time almost as hard as he had the first.

She clung to him on Bastardo as they rode back toward the camp. She was wrapped in the blanket; her clothes were still wet. "It ain't like that with people very often, is it?" she whispered to him. "It wasn't nothin' like that for my ma and pa, I know. For five years I've had to give it to any greaser that nodded at me, and it's never been like that. Has it ever been like that for you before, Raider?"

"You're good, Ellen," he said. He didn't want to tell

her he had never had better. "You're a real fine woman."

She understood. He could feel her quiet sigh. "Can we do it again as good?" she asked.

"Well, s'pose we try, first chance we get."

Ellen hummed a small tune as she clung to Raider's back on the horse. "Do I smell them beans Perfecto was cookin' when we left, or am I imaginin' things?" she asked. "I can eat some of them. Ummh!"

Raider laughed. The camp was a quarter of a mile's ride yet, as he figured. With the right wind, she could smell Perfecto's beans. The way he used onions and peppers, you could smell his cooking a long way.

"Wait!" she said suddenly. "Stop!"

He reined up and turned to look at her. "What's the matter?" he asked.

She was pointing at the ground, at the tracks of horses in a bit of damp earth near where a rivulet ran down the mountainside. "Look," she whispered. "Which one of our hosses has throwed a shoe?"

"None of them," he said. He saw what she had seen: the track of a horse's hoof with no horseshoe.

She slipped down off Bastardo. "Gimme the revolver or the thutty-thutty," she said. "I'm better with the thutty-thutty."

He dismounted and handed her his Winchester. He tied Bastardo to a tree, and while he was doing that she slipped forward into the brush for a look ahead. She raised her hand. He slipped up beside her. She put a finger over her mouth and pointed.

Their camp wasn't a quarter of a mile away; it was fifty yards away; they had almost stumbled into it. Four Mexicans were in the camp, four shabby men in dirty white clothes. They held William, Jack, and Perfecto at gunpoint. Don Miguel sat on the ground, looking up openmouthed. His beard was stained with blood from his mouth. The biggest of the four Mexicans, a fat man with crossed ammunition belts, held his pistol to William Bridenbaugh's face.

"El oro," the man growled. *"Veinticinco mils de dollares gringos!"*

"Dios . . . " groaned Don Miguel.

"Se callase!" barked the fat man. "Shut up."

Ellen nudged Raider. She pointed at the two men to the right—the fat one who was threatening William and a smaller one beside him—and patted the barrel of the Winchester. She touched his Remington revolver and pointed at the two to the left. Raider nodded.

Ellen lifted the rifle to her shoulder. Her blanket slipped. She muttered something under her breath and shrugged it off. Stark naked, she stepped forward, out of the brush that had concealed her and Raider, for a clear shot. She leveled the Winchester on the fat Mexican, squeezed off a shot, and dropped him. Raider fired on one of his men. That one fell. Ellen worked the lever of the Winchester fast and fired her second shot. Her second man dropped, shot between the shoulders. Raider fired. His second man had spun around, and Raider's bullet hit him in the chest and flopped him on his back.

"Gawd!" yelled Jack Foster.

Raider stood, still outside the camp, his legs apart, glancing warily around, looking for others. Ellen stood with the Winchester held up before her, ready if other bandits should burst from the brush behind the camp. Her eyes were wide and wild, and she ran her tongue over her lips. She heaved with excited breaths.

"There were just the four," said Perfecto.

Raider turned to Ellen. "Y' hear?" he asked.

She nodded. She bent down and picked up her blanket. She handed him the Winchester and wrapped the blanket around her. She walked forward and stood staring down at the fat Mexican she had killed with her first shot.

"Are you hurt?" Raider asked Don Miguel.

"It is nothing," said Don Miguel. He wiped the blood from his mouth and beard with the back of his hand. "They are men who swore allegiance to me, years ago.

They were sent out by my son-in-law to hunt for me. When they found me, they decided they would rather have the gold than whatever reward I might pay. They were too ignorant to be on guard against others of us. God sent you, Mr. Raider. I believe they would have killed us all."

"It's Jésus," said Ellen, prodding the body of the fat one with her foot. "For $25,000 in gold, he would have killed Christ."

"You knew him?" Raider asked.

She looked up into Raider's face and smiled bitterly. "He is the one who bought me from the Apaches. It is his burro that is carrying our supplies. It is his house I set on fire when we left." She nodded at the other man she had killed. "His brother. They shared me. I am the only thing I ever knew either of them to share with anyone."

Don Miguel frowned at Ellen. "I thank God that you and Mr. Raider arrived and killed these men before they killed us," he said solemnly. "You should beg God's forgiveness, however, for the satisfaction you take in their deaths."

Ellen kicked the body of Jésus. "I wish he was alive so I could kill him again," she said.

Raider would not allow them to camp there. He and Ellen had not eaten any of Perfecto's beans, and they wolfed them in a hurry while the others broke camp. Ellen rode Jésus's horse, and she strapped his holster around her waist and carried his pistol. With the light of day fading rapidly, Raider led them higher on the mountain, out of the trees and brush of the middle slope and among the jagged, tilted rocks above. They struggled upward, making false starts into impenetrable masses of rock and having to track back and try another way. By darkness they had moved up only half a mile. They dismounted. Raider set Don Miguel under a sheltering rock, out of the worst of the wind, and Ellen helped make him comfortable with blankets and a saddle. They hobbled the horses. Raider ordered Jack Foster to remain and guard the Don, and he stationed William, Perfecto, and Ellen as sentries in the rocks around.

He heard what he expected. Horsemen clattered around in the wooded area they had left. The shots had attracted them—maybe Juan Cardenas and maybe others. They had probably found the bodies. They might be enraged. Or they might not be. Certainly they would be cautious now.

"Don't fire a shot unless it's absolutely necessary," Raider told William, kneeling beside him. "What's more important, don't fire a shot unless you are absolutely sure who you're shooting at. I'm going out to have a look."

He told the others the same, then he slipped away among the rocks, keeping as quiet as he could. There was a half moon that appeared and disappeared as clouds slid by. In the open intervals he could see the shapes of the rocks around him, could see bits of brush clinging here and there to the sandy soil in pockets among the rocks—could see a man if he came on one. In the intervals when the moon was behind a cloud, he could see almost nothing.

The night animals were out—and that would include snakes. He heard a sidewinder crawling across dry sand and gravel. He heard the frightened cry of a small animal caught by some predator.

Raider worked his way down. It was slow going. In the periods of darkness he stood still and listened. In the dim light he chose his path and moved.

He watched the moving clouds. A big one was coming, one that would hide the moon for two or three minutes, maybe more. He crawled up the face of a tilted rock, to the edge, where he could look down over some little distance. The cloud moved across the moon, and he froze there, lying quietly on the rock.

He could see nothing. He heard nothing. After a moment, though, he began to smell something. It was the stink of a cigar. The smoke off a cigar would stink for fifty yards, he knew. Probably not more. He listened, straining to hear a sound. Nothing. But the stink was sure. He lay tense. The man could not be far away.

The cloud moved off the moon. Raider peered down, searching among the rocks for a movement. The cigar smoke was more distinct. The light faded again.

Then he saw the tiny point of orange light: the fire on the tip of the cigar. He could have taken aim on that little point of light and shot the man's head off.

The light returned. The man was tall and slim, not a barefoot Mexican in white, a Texan maybe, wearing dark clothes, a dark hat. He carried a rifle. He walked carefully, stopping every few steps to stare into the shadows among the rocks. He was coming directly toward the base of the rock where Raider lay. He walked into the little area of flat, sandy soil below the rock and stopped within ten feet of Raider. He put his rifle down, leaned against the vertical surface of the rock, and blew a weary sigh. Now he was almost within arm's reach, and Raider breathed as quietly as he could. Who was he?

The man stood, resting. In a minute, to Raider's surprise, he whistled two low notes. After a moment the same two notes were repeated somewhere down the slope. Raider knew he had at least two men to contend with now, and he quietly drew his Remington from its holster.

The moonlight faded again, and Raider was effectively blind but for the sight of the orange point at the tip of the man's cigar. The smoke rose toward his nostrils, sharp and nauseating. He listened and heard the sound of the second man, stumbling in the dark but not careful. As the light returned, the second man walked up to the first.

"Any sign?" the new man asked quietly.

"Naw," said the first man.

They spoke English, and the new man said, "Whatta a figger?"

"They're up there somewheres," said the one with the cigar. "I ain't heard a sound."

The new man was quiet for a moment; then he said, "Be hard to do much in the dark. I ain't fer takin' no chances. The way they gut-shot them greasers . . . Shit!"

"Wish I knew who that American is that's runnin' the game," said the one with the cigar.

"It ain't the Bridenbaugh kid, that's fer sure."

"No, it's somebody that's come down here lookin' for the gold, same's we are."

"And right now he's got it."

"Uhmm. Fer now."

The light faded, and when it returned the two men were sitting on the ground. The new one was drinking from his canteen.

"Harry," said the new one. "What we gonna do?"

Harry shrugged. "Sit out the night, I figger. Later, we'll jis have to find a spot where we have a good field and pick 'em off with rifles, one by one."

"Shots are gonna bring on more greasers, Harry."

"It'll take more greasers half a hour to git up here. Cardenas and his bunch are at least that far off."

They talked a little more. They carried whiskey, and both of them took a few swallows. Harry told the new man to sleep a couple of hours. He promised to stay awake and keep watch. He'd wake the new man then and let him keep watch awhile.

Raider lost all sense of time. It seemed the two hours were gone even before he heard the second man begin to snore. As he lay on the rock, cramped and afraid to move, he decided he had to kill these two. Their plan to snipe at his party with rifles was too deadly.

He saw Harry toss his cigar butt away. Peering down from above, he saw him sit erect for what seemed forever. Harry took another swallow of whiskey, then one of water. He grew restless. He stepped a few paces away and took a piss. He sat down again, and this time his head dropped to his chest after no more than a minute. He jerked awake, let his head drop again, jerked awake again, and finally slumped and began to snore.

Raider let him snore for a while. Cautiously then he backed off the rock and crawled around to the side of it. With his revolver in his right hand, he edged up until he could peer around the corner of the rock and see the two men. The second one was sprawled in sleep, snoring loudly. Harry was slumped forward, his head down. His sleep was not so sound. He could waken. Raider pulled his hunting knife from his belt. He put it in his right hand and switched the Remington to his left. He edged forward. In a moment he was directly in front of Harry and within striking distance. Harry stirred but did not waken.

He means to kill us, Raider reminded himself. He will, if I give him half a chance. Raider closed his eyes for an instant and locked his resolution. Then, in a quick swing, he drove the point of the knife into Harry's throat.

The man did not move. If he experienced a moment of understanding, it was also a moment of resignation. He stiffened for a few seconds, then relaxed. He did not reach for his pistol. He did not open his eyes to see who had killed him.

The other man had not moved. Raider turned to him. The man was dead asleep. Raider sat for a moment looking at him. It occurred to Raider that there was an option to killing this one. It might be a better option. Quietly he picked up their two rifles. He took Harry's pistol. The other man's revolver lay beside him, in the holster he had slipped off when he turned over to sleep. Raider took that. Raider stood and began his slow trek back up the mountainside. Maybe what the second man would say when he faced Cardenas again—as now he surely would—would be more valuable than having Cardenas learn he and Harry were dead.

*   *   *

At noon they reached the crest of the mountain ridge, where in the cold a harsh wind swept over bald rocks. Raider led his party over the crest and only a short distance down the other side. He left them to rest while he stood on the crest and surveyed the valley and the mountainside they had climbed. He watched for a while, and in time he made out a party of horsemen climbing below. Tiny figures, they were more than an hour's climb behind.

Raider returned to his party and brought the Don to the crest. For a quarter of an hour he and the Don stood on the crest, watching the party of horsemen. "I hope Juan Cardenas is looking at us through his telescope, Don Miguel," Raider said. "Yesterday he did something careless and stupid. He told a pair of American renegades where we were. If he sees that you are alive and well, maybe he will be more careful."

The old man nodded. "I am beginning to regret it was not you who married my daughter, señor," said Don Miguel.

CHAPTER FOURTEEN

Doc sat on the bed, his writing board before him, making an entry in his case journal. Kathleen was combing out her damp hair, to which she had just applied more of the black dye Doc had supplied her from the wagon. She wore only her black stockings, held up by ruffled garters around her knees. Doc worked in his shirtsleeves.

Kathleen ran the comb from the crown of her head to well below her shoulders—the length of her hair. "Even Galvin doesn't want you to win, you know," she said.

"Win?"

"To figure out who really killed Susie Bradford. Even Galvin doesn't want you to prove it was someone besides Billy Bridenbaugh. He's got it figured out the same way you have, and if he's got it figured out, then Jeffrey McMullen's got it figured out, and so have some other people. But it will bust the McMullen Bank and cost this town dear. They'd all rather leave it the way it is: that a boy from out of town killed a whore and ran off to Mexico with his daddy's money. That leaves El Aguila unshook."

He knew now who killed Susie Bradford. It was Tom McMullen. Besides what he had known before, he now knew that McMullen had been at Sister Edwards's house that afternoon. He'd been there, in fact, before William Bridenbaugh, and had left before William arrived. No one had seen Susie Bradford alive after he left. Horace Chandler had investigated the murder and announced in five minutes that William Bradenbaugh was the murderer.

Doc went on writing. He did not respond to Kathleen's analysis of the attitudes in town. He knew them well enough.

"If anyone ever gets his hands on that journal of yours, you're in terrible trouble."

"I rely on you to see that they don't," said Doc. "Right now, you're the only one who knows where I keep it."

She put down her comb and came to the bed. She sat down beside him. "What are you writing?" she asked.

"I'm a little behind," he said.

The entry he was writing read:

Six days after the murder, Horace Chandler, the deputy, purchased a house, outbuildings, and 200 acres of the widow Richardson. He paid $2,000 in cash. The following day, that is September 16, he borrowed $500 from the McMullen Bank, It is understood he used that money to purchase cattle. The Richardson premises are operated for Chandler by the hands who had worked for the widow. The past week, Chandler has spent nearly all his time on his property. He has not been in town except occasionally and for short periods.

The source of his $2,000 remains an open question. He was not observed before September 15 to have resources sufficient to allow him to purchase property.

"We've reached an odd stage, Doc," Kathleen said.

Something plaintive in her voice distracted him from his writing. He put down his pen and looked at her. "What's that, Kathleen?"

"I've been in this room naked with you the past

half hour. You hardly even notice. It does nothing for you."

He smiled gently. "Not so, Kathleen," he said softly.

Watching the stableman brush down Judith while the boy cleaned her stall, Doc counted the money he had taken in selling medicines that afternoon. El Aguila continued to be a good market for homeopathic specifics, so much so, in fact, that he was running low on many of his items. Two or three hours a day was enough to maintain his status as itinerant medicine man, and he was coining a small profit besides. It was well that he was. He paid double for his room, now that Kathleen was living in it as his wife. He bought her meals, too, even though she offered to pay for her own, out of her savings. It was not in him, somehow, to let a woman buy her own food while she was living with him.

"Dr. Weatherbee, I believe."

The man who had spoken stood behind him and to one side. Doc turned. The man was tall, thin, red of face, white-haired, handsome. His white hair suggested an old man, but this man was erect and hard. His blue eyes were sharp and intent. He wore a gray cassimere suit and a Stetson Dakota hat. Doc's experienced eye noticed the slight bulge of a pistol worn in a shoulder holster under his left arm; another man would not have noticed.

Doc nodded.

"My name is Keene," the man said. "Douglas Keene. I am the chief security officer for the San Antonio, Houston & New Orleans Railroad." He extended his hand. "I'd like to talk with you."

Doc shook the man's hand. "At the bar in the Eagle?" he suggested.

"Fine."

Keene ordered a bottle of bourbon and two glasses. He took a sip of the bourbon in his mouth, rolling it around over his tongue, working his lips. "Well," he said then. "Suppose, to begin with, you tell me who you really are. Hmmh?"

Doc looked him in the eye. "What makes you think I'm anybody or anything besides what I say I am?"

"I have a commission from the State of Texas to act as a railroad security officer," said Keene. "I am not Jimmy Tate, and I most certainly am not Horace Chandler. So don't play games with me. I have a pair of bright, brand-new handcuffs in my kit, and if I don't receive straight answers, we are going to put them on you, and you are going to go to San Antone with me, till we figure out just who you are and what your business is. I hear you are fast with your fists, and I suppose you are not reluctant to grab for that revolver you have stuck in your pants. Well, sir, I will take my chances on that. I have some little facility with a pistol myself. I am known for it. Let's see, I asked who you are, didn't I?"

"They call me Doc."

"You are not a homeopathic physician," said Keene. "None of the schools of homeopathic medicine ever heard of you. Oh, and, yes: There is no Wagner Weatherbee at Illinois Pharmaceuticals. What is more, there is no Wagner there either. Who receives the telegrams you send there?"

"What is your interest, Mr. Keene?" Doc asked. "Here you are, a railroad policeman where there is no railroad . . . Or are you really a railroad policeman?"

Keene extracted a small leather case from his coat pocket. He opened it and showed Doc a folded document, a commission from the State of Texas—railroad security and investigations officer. He had a badge, too.

"It seems to me, sir," said Keene, "that you or someone who has hired you are taking an extraordinary interest in the affairs of a railroad and a bank—which is none of your business, I suspect. So again I ask you: Who are you?"

"There are some who seem to think I'm a bank examiner," said Doc.

"But you're not," said Keene. "As I said, I'm not a small-town sheriff, mister. I've checked you out."

"And the railroad sent you here to find out who I am and put a stop to my inquiry, I suppose," said Doc. "I have a question: Why?"

"If you start a run on the McMullen Bank," said Keene, "you'll ruin the bank and hurt the railroad. Maybe you and some friends of yours plan to pick up bank shares or railroad stock, cheap."

"What would I want with stock in an insolvent railroad?" Doc asked.

"So that's it," said Keene, nodding. "If you circulate that story, you'll be able to buy a substantial quantity of our stock for very little. A stock manipulation. Just what I expected."

"A facile conclusion," said Doc.

Keene reached inside his coat and took out a small silver case. He opened it and extracted a cigar. Doc shook his head when he offered one to him. Keene closed the case and returned it to his pocket.

"I've drawn my pistol," said Keene. "It is pointing at you under the table. Regard yourself as under arrest."

"An illegal arrest," said Doc.

"But effective," said Keene coldly. "I believe you have a pistol in your belt, as I said. Hand it over."

Doc took the Diamondback .38 from under his coat and pushed it across the table. Keene took it and shoved it inside his own coat.

"I have a rig at the stable," said Keene. "We'll be riding to San Antone, starting tonight. Depending on how much trouble you try to give me, you can go simply handcuffed or you can go thoroughly trussed. I will leave that to you."

"You are a gentleman, and I will try to be one," said Doc.

"We'll see," said Keene. "Have another drink. Then we'll leave."

Doc drank a swallow of the bourbon. He did not, for

the moment, see any alternative to accompanying this man to the stable. In fact, Keene seemed a careful, capable man. There might be no alternative to accompanying him to San Antonio. It was not in the least clear that telling him he was a Pinkerton operative would change anything. Keene showed a chilling single-mindedness.

"Oh," said Keene when they stood. He held the pistol close to himself, to be as inconspicuous as possible, but anyone who looked closely would see that Doc was being led away at gunpoint. He did not expect anyone in El Aguila to interfere. "I think we'll have a look in your room before we leave. I might find the answers to my questions there." He nodded toward the stairs.

They walked to the third floor. He took Doc's key and opened the door.

"Sorry, little lady," Keene said to Kathleen. She was asleep on the bed, covered with a sheet. "Your friend here is under arrest. Just lie where you are. I'm going to search the room."

Kathleen, waking slowly, gaped and stared at Doc, looking for an explanation. She took note of Keene's Iver Johnson Hammerless Revolver—a .38 with rounded lines that made it easy to draw from under clothing. Doc shrugged at her. She frowned. Her face reddened.

"Jesus, mister," she said to Keene. "Why don't you let me leave. I got nothin' to do with . . . whatever's goin' on."

"Give me ten minutes and you can go back to sleep," said Keene. "I'm a railroad policeman, and I'm taking this man, whatever he is, to San Antone. It's not your problem."

Keene waved the Iver Johnson at her, and Kathleen cowered and shook her head.

"Sit down there," Keene said to Doc, pointing at the chair.

Doc sat, and Keene opened the drawers of the bureau and began to pull out his clothes and toiletries.

Kathleen sat up. She was naked under the sheet, and

Keene glanced and saw her bare breasts before she jerked the sheet up over them. "Be decent enough to toss me my chemise," she said.

"I told you to lie still," said Keene firmly. Nevertheless, he tossed her the white, lace-trimmed chemise from the top of the bureau. As he rooted in the drawers, Kathleen pulled on the chemise and rolled off the bed. "Careful there, little lady," Keene said. He waved the pistol in her direction once again. Kathleen walked to the window, parted the curtains, and looked down at the street. Keene glanced at Doc. "Tell her to sit still," he said.

"She doesn't take orders from me either," Doc said.

Kathleen's purse was on the windowsill. As Keene faced Doc, with his back to her, she reached into the purse and pulled out the derringer Doc had bought her to carry. It was in her palm but hidden as Keene glanced back at her. She stepped a pace closer to Keene. She looked past him, inquiringly, and Doc nodded at her.

"What—"

Doc interrupted him. "Mr. Keene," he said. "The young lady's name is Kathleen, and she has a .41-caliber Remington derringer pointed at your back and within a foot of it. Two barrels. If she fires, the very least you can expect is a shattered spine. If you don't die, you will spend the rest of your life a helpless cripple. Drop your pistol. If you make the slightest quick move, she will pull her triggers."

"I don't believe it," said Keene.

"It's a chance you can take," said Doc. "Your revolver is not pointed at me. If you move your arm to point it at me, she will fire. Try it if you want."

"You're making a terrible mistake, young lady," said Keene. "You said you have nothing to do with this, and now you're pointing a gun at an officer of the law. Hand me the gun, and we'll forget the matter."

"I'm his wife," said Kathleen simply.

Keene's shoulders slackened. He sighed. He let the

Iver Johnson drop from his hand. Without prompting he pulled Doc's Diamondback and dropped it, too.

Doc picked up both revolvers. "I'm not quite sure what to do with you," he said to Keene.

"Take him out in the country, put a couple of bullets in him, and let the crows have him," Kathleen suggested. She sat down on the bed, still holding the derringer pointed at him. "Arrogant son of a bitch."

"I am not," Doc said to Keene, "the kind of man who takes another man out in the country and puts a couple of bullets in him, the way Kathleen suggested. I'm going to let you go, Keene. I don't have much choice. I wish I could think I'm not going to see you again, but I'm afraid it won't be that easy."

"I'll come back with more officers, is what I'll do," said Keene. "I'll protect the honest businessmen of the railroad and bank against the likes of you."

"I'll be here," said Doc. "You had better think about that. Why will I still be here?"

Kathleen sat beside him the next day as he ordered their lunch in the restaurant four doors from the Eagle. They had met Tom McMullen on their way along the street. He had glowered angrily at them. His broken jaw remained wired, and the flesh around it was still swollen, still purple and red.

When their eggs and sausage and corn bread were on the table, both of them became aware of a commotion on the street. They ate anyway. Yelling, fighting, even shooting, were not unusual on the main street of El Aguila. The commotion this time lasted longer than usual. By the time their meal was finished, Doc was intensely curious as to what was going on.

They walked outside. Jeffrey McMullen was at the center of a noisy crowd of men. Horace Chandler was with him. So was his son, Tom. The sheriff, Jimmy Tate, was at the edge of the crowd. Doc approached the old sheriff and asked him what was going on.

The sheriff nodded in the direction of the Eagle. Doc

and Kathleen walked to the saloon with him, away from the noisy, surging little crowd. They sat down at a table—the same one, in fact, at which Keene had arrested Doc the afternoon before.

"I 'preciate that stuff you give me for my eyes, Doctor," said the sheriff. "I do b'lieve it has did me good. They say you ain't no doctor, but there's folks in this town thinks you are, for what you've done for them."

"I do the best I can," said Doc.

"That's a fact," said Kathleen, her eyes merry.

The sheriff nodded. "That out there," he said, tossing his head toward the noise from the street. "You asked me—"

"Yes. What's going on?"

" 'Fore you came here, some weeks back," said the sheriff, "we had a killin'. You've heard all about it, no doubt. Boy name of Bridenbaugh kilt a . . . You'll excuse me, ma'am. Kilt a prostitute. He run over into Mexico."

"I've heard," said Doc.

"Well, now all north Mexico is in a uproar," said the sheriff. "Word's come acrost the border. The story of Bridenbaugh and his father's gold had died down some, but it's all astir ag'in. And worse. It ain't safe for an American to cross the border, no way at all. Every *jefe* in Mexico is riding around with guns. *Federales* is out—the Díaz army. Everybody's lookin' for Bridenbaugh."

"Why?"

"The story is," said Sheriff Jimmy Tate, "that Bridenbaugh has kidnapped an important man, what they call a *don,* what they call a hidalgo. The Mexes has gone crazy over it. There's reason to think they might start raidin' acrost the border ag'in."

"Why does that make such a stir here?" Doc asked.

"They's more," said the old man. "You remember that Raider feller, that kilt Billy Bob Galvin and busted Tommy McMullen's jaw?"

Doc nodded.

"He's in on it some way. The Mexes say he's workin' with Bridenbaugh. What's more, he's told the story that he's a *Pinkerton*. Think of that! He says he's a Pinkerton—and him a murderer and God knows what more!"

Doc was hard put to hide his soaring spirits. Raider was alive! He had found Bridenbaugh. And, likely as not, what they said was true: that he was holding a hidalgo hostage, probably for good reason. And, probably, all Mexico was up in arms and wanting his neck.

"But Jeff McMullen has got more troubles than that," the old man went on. "That's why he's tryin' to organize the town out there."

"Organize . . . ?"

"He says Jake Bridenbaugh, the father, is puttin' together an army of gunmen. The word is that Bridenbaugh don't believe his son kilt nobody here and don't believe the boy run off with his gold, and he's comin' down here with every shootist he can hire, to have it out on the town that done him dirt."

CHAPTER FIFTEEN

All day they had ridden a mountain ridge, following its northward line, winding among the rocks, making slow progress. It was tiring for the Don and tiring for the horses, and not much after mid-afternoon Raider called a halt. They made another of their makeshift camps, where they would spend another night without fire, without hot food, without a source of water. Ellen, the Don, and Perfecto suffered from saddle sores. The horses were visibly weakening.

"I don't think we'll make it if we keep to the ridges," said William. "It's too slow and too tough."

They sat now on a high rock, from which they could see the valleys to both sides of the mountain. It was as it had been for days: They could see dust clouds raised by horsemen, and they understood that most of those horsemen were looking for them. Not for two days had Raider seen anyone he could feel certain was Juan Cardenas. Some of the dust clouds were raised by groups of horsemen, ten or more. Others were smaller.

"They know we're up here," said Raider. "They're just waiting for us to come down."

"They're afraid to come up after us," said Ellen dully. She was exhausted. She was a strong woman, but she was not accustomed to days in the saddle. Her face was drawn. Her eyes were sometimes vacant.

It was true, apparently. They knew, down below, that four Mexicans and the American called Harry had died for their recklessness in coming up the mountains after this group. No one down there knew exactly where they were. To come up not knowing could be fatal. That was the way Raider wanted it understood, and from the looks of it, that was how their pursuers did understand.

"They look for us to go on north or to cut east for the border somewhere," said William. "Suppose we went down the west side of these mountains and hit for west Texas or for New Mexico even?"

"I've never seen that country," said Raider.

"I have," said Ellen. "I rode all the way from Arizona to San Francisco del Oro on an Apache pony, with my hands tied behind my back. It's evil country west of here, eviler than this. These mountains ain't nothin' compared to what's there."

"What you figure we're making, Raider?" William asked. "Ten miles a day?"

Raider shrugged.

"We could be two more weeks getting to the border," said William. "Or more. And it's going to get tougher, the closer we get."

Raider stared at the valleys below. There were ranches in the low country. And villages. They needed supplies. "I think I have to go down tonight," he said. "I'll take Perfecto. I'll take your Mexican clothes, Ellen."

"I want to go," said William.

Raider shook his head. "Perfecto is Mexican. He speaks the language—speaks it right. He's a good boy. He can go where I can't. Perfecto and I will go. We'll try the west side."

They went crashing down the west side of the mountain, carelessly, in a hurry. Raider meant to reach the bottom before the daylight disappeared entirely. Perfecto, openly glad to be riding alone with him again, rode hard, bouncing half off his horse as the beast lunged over rocks and through thorn. Even Bastardo raced down the tricky mountainside, as if he understood that fresh water and forage were at the bottom.

By the time they reached the valley floor and stopped to let the horses drink from the water pooled in the bed of a poor stream, night had fallen. Dim moonlight offered little to the eyes. They rode back and forth across the stream and up its banks on both sides. They found no road at all, not even a track. The land was dry. They saw no cattle, nothing growing. The village seemed so remote that it might be on the moon.

This time he would ride Bastardo in. He would not play the role of a poor man seeking a little water, a little food. This time he would be the angry, dangerous, gun-carrying renegade, not to be trifled with. Likely the village had seen the type before.

It was a village like every other village in Mexico: centered on a church and a well, with a single tree growing in the square. Lanterns and candles burned in doorways and opened windows. It was quiet. The priest sat on a chair before his church door. No *jefe* sat with him. A few tired men and women sat on the ground around the square, drinking wine, smoking, talking, while their naked children played. Raider and Perfecto frightened the children as they rode into the center of the village. The children scattered. The men and women watched apprehensively as the two horsemen rode up to the church and saluted the priest.

"Buenas noches, Padre."

"Bienvenida, señores."

Raider swung down from his horse, but he stood aside and let Perfecto talk.

"We come in the peace of God, Father," said Perfecto in Spanish.

"We extend to you the hospitality of our village in God's peace," said the priest. He was a young man, no more than twenty-five years old. He wore a black cassock, but he was barefoot, as were all his villagers.

"We should like to buy food for our horses and for ourselves," said Perfecto. "We have money. We will pay what is fair."

"Pedro!" The priest called to one of the men squatting at a respectful distance, and the man rose and approached deferentially. "The gentlemen would like to buy food and drink. They say they have money and will pay a fair price."

Pedro nodded wordlessly to Perfecto.

"Grain for the horses," said Perfecto. "Enough for a week or more. Beans, onions, vegetables, meat . . . whatever you can sell. We will pay in gold."

The man nodded solemnly and trotted off. He spoke a word to a woman as he left the square, and she rose and trotted after him.

"What is the name of this village?" Perfecto asked the priest.

"La Esperanza," said the priest.

"Can one buy a pot of wine, which we will share with you while we wait?"

The priest pointed to a woman sitting among the solemn watchers. *"Vino,* Carmen," he said, and the woman rose and trotted away.

Perfecto squatted on the dusty ground. Raider remained standing beside Bastardo. "We are riding north," said Perfecto. "What news, Father?"

The priest shook his head. "No one troubles himself to bring us news," he said.

Raider watched the people around the square. Some silent signal had passed between them and their children. The naked children were gone—suddenly, as if a hand had swept them off the square. It was silent without their cries and laughter. The solemn villagers sat watching—staring in fact—wordlessly. One rose and slipped away, into the darkness between two adobe huts. As Raider watched, another rose and followed. He looked around. The village was too quiet. Too solemn. Too apprehensive. He looked into the face of the priest. It was bland. It was too bland, a study in impassive, rigid absence of expression.

"Perfecto," said Raider.

"Señor?"

"Mount. We go."

Perfecto's face showed he was puzzled, reluctant; but he was obedient; he had seen the señor was right too many times. Without a word to the priest, he swung up into his saddle.

Raider spurred Bastardo and reined him around the church. He had decided not to leave the village the way they had come in. Shots began to split the quiet night. He looked back. Twenty horsemen burst into the square. In the light of the two torches burning before the church, Raider caught sight of their uniforms. Soldiers! The president's soldiers.

"Follow me!" he yelled to Perfecto. He reined Bastardo to the left, and the big stallion crashed through the vines growing in an irrigated garden and pounded across a beaten-down yard, where, from the looks of it, chickens pecked at the ground in the daytime. He had passed between two adobe huts, and twenty yards farther he jerked Bastardo to a stop. He pulled his Winchester from its scabbard, and as the first soldiers dashed into the passageway, he fired, worked the lever action, and fired again. To his surprise he heard the crack of Perfecto's Winchester. He could not see if they had dropped soldiers, but none came through the passage. He spurred Bastardo, and they rode out of the village to the west, across a narrow strip of irrigated land and into the desert. The troop of soldiers followed. He turned to the south, toward the streambed which they had followed in entering the village.

The soldiers came on, firing. Only two or three of their ill-aimed shots came close enough for him to hear the whine of a bullet. Perfecto's horse was slower than Bastardo, but it was frightened now and running in headlong panic. Raider could not tell if the soldiers were falling behind or gaining. He knew all they could do was run, run as fast as they could in the near-darkness and hope a horse did not stumble.

They reached the bed of the stream. Bastardo leaped, nearly throwing Raider, but he kept his saddle, and the big horse lunged up the bank and galloped across the rocky desert toward the mountain slope it seemed instinctively to know was safety. Raider heard Perfecto's horse stumble in the streambed. He slowed Bastardo and turned to look. Perfecto, too, had kept in the saddle, and his horse now dashed toward Raider and Bastardo. The soldiers were spread out now, all on the far side of the streambed, only half of them keeping up and still constituting a threat. Raider called to Perfecto, "Hurry! Come on!" The soldiers were firing.

Perfecto threw up his hands. Raider saw the shock of the bullet that hit him. It threw him forward in the saddle. The horse ran only one more lunging pace before Perfecto fell to the ground. The horse ran on. It caught up with Raider and ran past him.

Raider stopped. The soldiers—five or six of them—plunged into the dry streambed. Others stopped on the far side and took aim with their rifles. Their bullets whined angrily around Raider. He looked at Perfecto. He was spread out on the ground like a discarded rag doll, his arms and legs tangled in no natural position. A bullet whipped past Raider's ear so close he was deafened. He dropped his reins. Bastardo needed no other command. The horse turned for the mountainside and the scrub and brush and rocks, and galloped in wild panic.

Bastardo lunged upward, gaining higher ground. After a minute or two, he shuddered and slowed. He was nearing his limit. Raider let him slow, then he reined him to a stop. He jumped off and climbed on a rock. He picked out a soldier coming up the mountain after him and knocked him out of the saddle with one shot from the Winchester. He moved the muzzle of the rifle to the right and fired again. He hit a horse. He heard its scream. It reared and threw a soldier. He had to reload. In the silence he heard the soldiers slow their chase. More cautious, they began to work their way slowly up through the rocks. He spotted another one, and he was able to reload in time to shoot that one off his horse. He remounted Bastardo and began to climb again. When he stopped a second time, he heard no clatter of horses lunging up after him. He poured water from his canteen into his hands then and wet Bastardo's muzzle.

Raider sat among the rocks, eating sparingly of cold beans and bread. William and Jack were out somewhere, guarding the approaches to their camp. Ellen poured a bit of Don Miguel's brandy into a little silver cup. Everyone had been silent since Raider returned with the news of Perfecto's death. William and Jack had walked off to guard, without being told. The Don had handed Raider the brandy flask. Raider sat on the ground, staring at his boots, tired and discouraged and distressed. As he ate, he remembered that Perfecto had cooked these beans. His throat tightened. It was difficult for him to eat at all.

"Tell me, Don Miguel," he said. "If the soldiers catch you, what will they do with you?"

"It is difficult to say," said the old man.

"Weren't those last night trying to rescue you?"

"I think not. To capture me for their own purposes, now that I am away from the territory where people are loyal to me."

"There are troops on both sides of the mountain, I suppose," said Raider.

"I should expect so."

"It's a standoff," said Raider. "They force us to stay up here until we starve. They can't come up after us, for fear of our rifles, but we can't go down."

They traveled slowly north along the mountain ridge for only half the day. William Bridenbaugh rode ahead, Jack Foster rode behind, and Raider rode beside Don Miguel, with Ellen close to him, watching him carefully as he dozed in the saddle. Toward noon he noticed that they were descending. William came back to say there was a break in the mountains ahead, a pass through which an arroyo ran east to west. To continue north they would have to come down off the mountain, cross the arroyo, and climb the far side.

"They'll be waiting for us if they're halfway smart," said William. "We can't cross in daylight for sure—if we can cross at all."

Raider rode forward a little with William, so they could talk out of the Don's hearing. "There is an advantage here," he said. "If they really concentrate on that arroyo, it leaves them thin to the east and west. If we could cut to the east and run for the border . . . It can't be more than sixty miles from here."

"We're too slow," said William. "If we leave the Don and run for it, we might make it."

"We don't owe him anything," said Raider. "But I'd hate to leave him for those soldiers. And he's the only one of us who knows the country. He knows where we are. We don't."

Don Miguel did know where they were. "I have ridden over all this country in years past," he said. "The Texas border is farther than you think. These mountains do not run directly north and south. We have been traveling west as well as north. If you come down from these mountains and travel east, you cross poor country, with few villages, few ranches. It is bandit country. If you travel west, the mountains are higher, the country more difficult to cross. Going on north . . ." He shrugged. "It would not be so difficult if the presence of troops did not compel us to keep to the high country. If we could follow river valleys . . ."

Raider nodded. "Thank you, Don Miguel."

They slept in the afternoon. They poured water for the burro and horses from their canteens and drank little themselves. They did not wash or shave. Food was short, too. They stretched out on the sandy soil, in the middle of scraggly brush that was thicker at this lower elevation, and Raider slept at last. The others, except the Don, stood watch. The sun was fiercely hot. Ellen brushed away stinging insects as Raider slept.

He awoke before sunset. It was quiet. The lowering sun blazed hot and red in the west. There were no dust clouds in the valleys. Maybe the troops were resting, too. Maybe they had moved on to guard the arroyo in the mountain pass.

Raider rose. He sipped a little water, then replenished his supply of .30-.30 cartridges.

"I'm going hunting, so to speak," he told the others. "Ellen will come with me. Keep your guard. This might be the night they decide to venture up the mountain. If you hear them coming, retreat."

Ellen had a pair of sandals from the supplies they had taken from Jésus and his companions. When she saw that Raider meant to go on foot, she tied them on. In the last light of the day, they struck out, carrying two Winchesters and two revolvers and one canteen with a little water.

"Can I ask where we're going?" she asked when they had walked south along the ridge for a few minutes.

"We're going to find Juan Cardenas," said Raider.

"How do you know he doesn't want the Don dead?" she asked.

"I don't."

"If he does, he'll shoot us down like dogs."

"That's a chance," said Raider.

They could travel almost as fast afoot as they had on horses, covering in an hour the ground they had covered the last hour before noon. It was two miles or more. After that Raider slowed their pace, and they stopped often to listen and to peer into the moonlit night, looking for intruders on their mountaintop.

"I think he's been avoiding the troops in the valleys by following us up here," said Raider to Ellen. "That's why the troops haven't come up, really—they're afraid of Juan Cardenas and twenty to fifty men, not the five or six of us. They must have figured he's driving us forward, and they're keeping us up here, and they can wait for us to have to come down—at the pass and the arroyo."

They hiked southward for the better part of another hour. Ellen fell behind often, but she caught up when Raider stopped to listen and to peer into the darkness for signs of a camp.

"Smell that?" he said to her finally. She nodded. The air was sharp with the smell of wood smoke. Somewhere on the mountain, not far from them, someone was cooking hot food.

"I want you to drop well back and stay out of sight," said Raider. "It may not be Cardenas. Whoever it is, you're my hole card. You and that Winchester. Don't do anything unless you have to. But if I pull off my hat, start shooting."

She nodded.

Raider moved on, walking in a crouch, slowly. In a minute he saw a man a hundred yards away, standing impatiently, shuffling his feet, conspicuously a sentry; the man smoked a small cigar and shifted his rifle from hand to hand.

A minute later Raider stood before him, revolver in hand. The man had turned to find the American standing there, and he dropped his rifle and slowly raised his hands.

Raider looked at him. He wore not even a piece of a uniform—though not all the president's soldiers did, either. He was dressed in white. His sombrero was broad and ragged.

"You follow Juan Cardenas?" Raider asked in Spanish.

The man nodded.

"Where is he?"

The man tipped his head back.

"I want to talk with him. Bring him here. Pick up your rifle and take it with you. Tell him Raider wants to see him. Remember, I could have killed you. Remember, I didn't."

Raider stood his ground. Others, alerted, appeared around him. He stood, casually taking a sip from his canteen. Shortly Juan Cardenas strode up the mountainside, smoking a cigar.

"The Don is alive and well and sends his regards," said Raider.

"You tax the strength of that old man," said Juan Cardenas.

"No I don't. That's why I don't travel faster."

Juan Cardenas smiled faintly. "That's why you are in a trap."

Raider nodded. "That's why you are going to help me out of it."

Cardenas put his cigar between his lips and thoughtfully drew smoke. "You lost a man last night. Now there are only four of you," he said as the stream of smoke escaped with his words.

"If the soldiers capture Don Miguel, they will take him to Mexico City," said Raider. "It will be a long time before President Díaz decides what to do with him. While he lives, he will still have the power you crave for yourself."

"I know," interrupted Juan Cardenas.

"Then it is you who are in a trap," said Raider. "If you try to take him away from me, I will kill him. If you don't and the soldiers capture us, you will suffer worse. As I told you before, if I cross the border safely, I will return him safely to you."

Cardenas again drew thoughtfully on his cigar. "I suppose you have a proposition. Or demands."

Raider nodded. "I need food and water, to begin with. Then I want to return south a few miles and cut east for the border. You can help with the deception, by sending a party of five to the pass and the arroyo. By the time the soldiers find out that party is not us, we will be off the mountain and on our way to Rio Sabinas. The Don says we can lose ourselves in the country east of Sabinas. You can interpose yourself between us and the troops. You have enough men to hold them back. The soldiers are not well disciplined. I'm sure you know better than I."

"This exposes Don Miguel to new dangers," said Cardenas.

"It offers us a chance to escape," said Raider. "The alternatives are no more attractive for the Don than they are for me."

Cardenas shook his head. "Someday, Mr. Raider," he muttered bitterly. "Someday . . . In the meantime, I will do as you say."

CHAPTER SIXTEEN

They broke camp at midnight. Cardenas had sent six men with them—five to continue north along the ridge, descending into the pass to deceive the soldiers in the valleys; one to speak with Don Miguel and report back to Juan Cardenas that the Don was actually alive and well. All six men stared curiously at Ellen. They had heard of her, apparently. Raider could not help wondering what they had heard.

With the five men moving on north as agreed, Raider led his party to the south. They rode in a tight group, surrounding the Don. Raider wanted to be sure against a sudden attack to rescue the old man. He wanted, too, to be sure the Don would not try to gallop off. He had trusted him until now, but now the Don knew he was riding through his son-in-law's troop of horsemen, and the temptation might be great.

Cardenas kept his agreed distance as they passed through. They saw nothing of his horsemen, but they could hear them all around as they crept south in the darkness.

At dawn, Raider saw Cardenas. He stood on a promontory, now to the north of them, watching them through his brass telescope. Raider told the Don to turn and wave. The Don did. They rode on south, and by mid-morning they had passed over more mountain ridge than they had covered the day before. At noon Raider turned east, and they began their descent from the mountain. It was his intention to look for a decent place to camp on the lower slopes of the mountain, with water if possible, where maybe he could wash off the dust and sweat. He meant to rest his party during the afternoon, to reconnoiter the land a bit, then make a quick ride off the mountain after dark, to be miles away in the flat country before the soldiers discovered they had escaped the cul de sac.

He was lucky. He found what he wanted. They dismounted, and Ellen began to prepare their food. He led the horses one by one to the tiny pool fed by a trickle of water running through the rocks, and he let them drink. He replenished their canteens. Then he splashed water on his head and face.

"It is unfortunate," said Don Miguel as they ate. "You are now a part of the bitter struggle between the government at Mexico City and those of us here in the north of Mexico who wish to remain free of that government. You have heard of General Francisco Álvarez? A cruel, wicked man. He commands the troops that are hunting me. They are bringing up more men. In time they may be a regiment. Álvarez is an intelligent man. When he learns of your ruse, he will know where you are going. We cannot move fast enough to evade him long."

"Once we are across the Rio Sabinas," said Raider, "we can move any way we want. To catch us, he has to find us."

"If you would free me—free me, that is, into the hands of my son-in-law—he and I would retreat as rapidly as possible toward my lands, where even a regiment will find all the fighting it wants and more, and the soldiers would all follow us. You, with your people and the gold, would travel on unmolested."

"Juan Cardeñas has sworn to kill me," said Raider.

"When I rejoin him, I am in command," said the Don. "We will go home."

"I'll keep it in mind, Don Miguel," said Raider. "For now . . . well, we are not yet out of the trap."

He returned to their tiny pool of water—it was no

bigger than a washtub—after they had eaten. He soaped his face and began to shave. Ellen left the camp and came to sit beside him.

"Don't trust him," she said. "Don't trust Cardenas. In fact, don't trust no greasers."

"I trusted Perfecto," said Raider without looking at her.

"Sorry," she said quietly.

He went on shaving, and for two or three minutes neither of them spoke. She raised herself to her knees, took off her white Mexican shirt, dipped it in the water, and began to scrub her face and neck and body with the cold water. He looked at her breasts. Her nipples were erect from the touch of the water.

She saw him looking. "Anytime you say," she said.

He wiped the soap from his face. "What will you do when you get home, Ellen?" he asked.

"When I get back to my family—if I ever do—I'll say I was sold to be a maid in a fine Mexican house, worked there and was treated good. I'll never say I was used like an animal. I'll never show the scars on my back. I couldn't live with the shame."

He reconnoitered. Scrambling around among the rocks and brush, he found vantage points from which he could survey the flat valley between them and a range of lower hills to the east. He saw no soldiers. He saw no big dust clouds. He did see carts moving on a road and two villages, three miles or so apart. They would be moving now into land where people lived, and it would be so, Don Miguel said, until they crossed the Sabinas.

At dark they started down. As before, he rode ahead a hundred yards, Jack Foster rode the same distance behind, and Ellen and William guarded the Don.

Within two hours they had reached the bottom of the mountain and had begun to move east across the flat valley. Although he saw lights and twice crossed roads, Raider neither saw nor heard anyone. Yet he was troubled and tense. If Cardenas had decided to betray them . . . maybe they were riding into an army trap.

They were making good progress. Not long after midnight they began to climb a hill that lay to the east of the mountain they had just descended. Half an hour's ride up the hill and he was high enough to stop and look back. He saw nothing, no one, not even Juan Cardenas. He turned south and rode along the flank of the hill for an hour. His idea was that anyone scheming to ambush them would expect them to cross the hill directly east of where they had come down from the mountain and had crossed the valley. A southward diversion might throw them off. Following the flank of the hill, he discovered that the hill did not extend far south. They could ride around it. The slope was wooded in places. He began to think of a place where they could spend the day. A camp in the woods, in the cool shade, would be heaven. It might also be where anyone would look for them.

The moon set. It was not pitch dark, even so. He could see the bulk of the hill above, outlined against the stars. He could see Ellen and William and the Don, following. He wished the night would last, so they could cover more miles before dawn.

He heard hoofbeats, a single horse galloping. It was behind, and he turned and cocked the Winchester.

"Raider! Raider!" It was Jack Foster, hurrying past the three others and coming up to him. Foster reined up. "We've got three men behind us. Comin' up in no big hurry, but comin' up for sure."

Raider turned and rode back with Foster beside him. He told William and Ellen to ride on ahead with the Don and wait. He took a stand with the Winchester in his hands. Jack did the same.

Three riders came toward them. They were Mexes, from the look of them—Mexes dressed like cowboys, not in the whites and sombreros most of them wore. One of them rode in the middle and a little ahead. He was a slight man, his face half hidden behind an enormous black mustache. He rode up with his hand raised, nodding to Raider.

"Señores," he said. *"Adonde van ustedes?"* Where are you going?

Raider only shook his head.

The Mexican glanced back and forth at his two companions. "I know who you are, I think," he said. "You should know there are soldiers camped . . . there." He pointed to the south. "If you wish to avoid them, you must go . . . there." He pointed up the hill. "Even there you will be in danger. You must not stop but keep moving. When it is light, they will search."

Raider looked at the top of the hill. It was not a long climb, but if they could not stop, if they had to keep moving, it would tax the strength of the Don.

"The man . . . there," the Mexican said, pointing toward the Don, "is Don Miguel de Melchor, is he not?"

There was no point in denying it. Raider nodded.

"You are the Pinkerton from Texas," said the Mexican.

"The name is Raider."

"Yes. I know. My own name is Diego Quevedo. I should be most distressed if President Díaz should capture Don Miguel. I can help you tonight, if you trust me."

"How will you help us?"

"I will hide you, and tomorrow night I will guide you across the Rio Sabinas."

"It is difficult for me to trust anyone—in the circumstances," said Raider.

"Yes," said Quevedo, nodding. "But if you go on without my help, likely you will blunder into the soldiers."

"I want to speak to the Don," said Raider. He turned and rode back. The Don said he had heard the name Diego Quevedo. The man was a rancher, he said. He was *jefe* here, the Don supposed.

Raider had no choice. If he did not accept Quevedo's

offer, all Quevedo had to do—if his purpose was to betray them—was to send one man to the soldiers with a message and follow with the other. He told Diego Quevedo they would accept his help.

Quevedo led them north along the hillside, then back into the valley. He led them toward a village, which he said was called La Colina Verte. The earliest light of dawn was showing when they rode around the village and approached the square and the church from the rear.

The church here was more elaborate than most that Raider had seen in Mexico. It had two bells, to begin with, hanging in a low tower. It had a garden in the rear, surrounded by a wall. Trees grew, and flowers, as well as some vegetables—all carefully tended, it was apparent. Inside the church a few candles still burned, even at dawn. There were icons, of the Virgin and of some saints that Raider did not recognize, standing in niches in the brick and adobe walls. A young man, not in a cassock, a novice maybe, was on duty in the church, even at this hour. He addressed Diego Quevedo as *jefe,* with low nods, almost bows.

"Your horses and burro will go with me," said Quevedo. "They will appear to be mine. You will spend your day here, in the church. Pepito will bring the priest presently. You need not worry about them. They are loyal to me. But you must not be seen by anyone else. Not everyone is loyal to me."

The priest, who was introduced simply as Padre Enrique, was an elderly man with a thin, ascetic face, a pointed nose, a wispy white goatee, and long, slender hands with purple veins showing in the pale flesh. He was deferential to Don Miguel, condescendingly polite to the others. He led Don Miguel to his own bedroom— a simple whitewashed room dominated by a big black crucifix and a comfortable oversized bed. The others would sleep where they might find space—Ellen in the novice's bed; Raider, William, and Jack on the floor in the priest's parlor. The priest was annoyed when

Raider told him one of them would remain with Don Miguel at all times, in his room, guarding him; but he shrugged and accepted.

"There will be soldiers in the town during the day, you may be sure," said Quevedo. "You need not worry. They will enter the church to pray, perhaps, but they will not come to Padre Enrique's private quarters."

"When will you return?" Raider asked.

"After midnight, when the town is quiet. I will know where all the soldiers are. We will evade them."

Pepito brought food and wine. He was a consumptive youth, small and fragile and somber. Apologetically, but at the order of Padre Enrique, he brought Ellen a dress and a scarf. He told her the priest required her to dress like a woman while she was in the precincts of the church—and that included covering her head. Ellen laughed when she came out of Pepito's room dressed in the ill-fitting, shapeless dress, with the black scarf tied around her head.

William and Jack slept first, and Raider sat inside the priest's room, where Don Miguel slept soundly. Ellen came in. Raider was sitting on the room's single chair, and she sat quickly on the floor.

"The church is through there," she said, nodding toward a door outside the door to the priest's room. "And you can go up in the bell tower—there." She pointed at another door. "They're saying mass now. The village has come to life."

"We may be inside a closed trap, you know," said Raider.

She nodded. "Pepito told me that Diego Quevedo hates President Díaz. The government in Mexico City wants control over Coahuila and Chihuahua. The *jefes* and hidalgos want to go on running things the way they always have."

"Quevedo will try to take the Don away from us," said Raider.

"Let him have him, once he has put us across the

Sabinas. He's no good to us then. We can run for the border without him."

Raider nodded. "Maybe."

"Think about it," she said.

Raider touched her hand. "Get some sleep," he said. "We have a tough night and day ahead."

Jack Foster relieved Raider in mid-morning. Raider stretched out on the floor in the priest's small parlor, on a rug, with a cushion from the priest's chair under his head. He meant to sleep an hour, maybe two. But he was tired, and he had drunk wine, and for the first time in days he slept soundly. When Ellen tugged at his shoulder and whispered at him, he was disoriented and at first had no idea where he was and who she was.

"Raider!" she whispered. "Listen to me!"

He looked at her numbly.

"There's a hell of a commotion outside," she said.

He sat up. Jack was beside her. She was wearing a belt and holster around her dress, and she had a Winchester in her hand. Jack had his Winchester in hand, too.

"I don't know what's going on. . . ."

"Is William with the Don?"

"Yes. Listen!"

He heard drums. The village must be invested with *federales*, not just a few but a marching column of them.

"We can't be sure they won't come in here," said Raider.

"Like as not the greaser's called them in and we've seen our end," said Jack.

"The bell tower," said Raider. "At least it's the easiest place to defend. Get William and the Don."

All five of them crowded onto the narrow, twisting stairway behind the bell tower door. Ellen, who had squeezed in first, climbed ahead. Raider was next, followed by William and the Don, and Jack was nearest the bottom. The tower was not tall. The stairs led up only twenty feet or so. The wooden platform around the two bells was encrusted with bird droppings, as were the bells themselves. Ellen ventured a glimpse over the top, looking down into the street.

"My God!" she whispered to Raider.

He crawled out onto the platform. It was supported by timbers that extended through the wall of the tower. The holes for the timbers had grown larger over the years, through the crumbling of the adobe, and by kneeling and pressing his face to the wall, Raider could peer out at floor level through one of these holes. He did, and Ellen knelt at another.

On the square below, a hundred uniformed soldiers were drawn up in orderly ranks. Their blue and red uniforms were dusty, and some of the soldiers were ragged and barefoot; but they wore uniforms, complete with tall hats. Two officers on horseback moved around the square, sabers in hand.

"If they order a search of the village . . ." Raider whispered to Ellen.

She nodded, and drew the revolver from her holster.

Two drummers resumed their beat. Five more horsemen, two in uniform, entered the square. The officers shouted commands, and the ranks of soldiers reformed. They established a square within the square, and they drove everyone in the village out until there was no one within their square but their mounted officers. Then the square opened at one side, and twenty men, some in uniform, some in white, trotted into the square. Behind them they pulled a cart loaded with timbers. Other, longer timbers they carried in teams. In spite of the confused shouting of the officers, these men seemed to know what they were doing. They began to raise the timbers and to nail others to them, hastily erecting some rude structure.

"What in the name of God . . . ?" Ellen whispered.

"It's a gallows," Raider said. "It could be for us."

The people of the village, stunned and silent, stood

outside the square of soldiers, watching. Many crossed themselves. Raider raised his head so he could look down. Padre Enrique stood on the steps of his church, passively watching. Pepito stood beside him. The gallows went up fast. Plainly it had been erected and torn down many times before. The pieces fit. The men seemed to drive the nails through old holes. In a matter of minutes it stood, ugly and ominous.

"Druther be shot," said Ellen.

Raider nodded.

"Look!"

The square had opened again. A soldier led a horse in, tugging at its bridle. A man sat on the horse, his arms bound behind him. He was bareheaded. He looked up at the gallows and swayed in the saddle. The soldiers had climbed the gallows and were tying the nooses in place.

Padre Enrique walked down from the steps of the church and advanced to the man on the horse. He spoke to the man, and the man nodded.

Another soldier led another horse into the square. The bound rider was Diego Quevedo.

A third horse was led in, carrying another man. Then a soldier led in a horse carrying a woman. She rode with her head hung down and her dark hair hanging around her face, covering it. Astride her horse, with her hands tightly bound, she had been unable to prevent her skirt from climbing all the way to her hips.

"My God!" Ellen muttered aloud.

Yet another bound man on horseback was dragged into the square, and the square closed. This man was Juan Cardenas.

One by one, the horses were lined up under the gallows, and the mounted officers put the nooses around the throats of the five. Diego Quevedo sat impassively, staring at the officer who tightened the noose under his ears. The woman shook her head and wept as the noose was slipped over her head and tightened around her neck. *"Por qué?"* she sobbed. *"Por qué?"* Juan Cardenas was pale and trembling.

Padre Enrique stood before the five horses, holding his pectoral cross above his head. He prayed loudly in Latin, at length. The five horses stood pawing, still held by men at their bridles. Five other men were now behind them, with quirts. The village was silent. One of the bells behind Raider and Ellen squeaked as it swung on its hanger. The clapper struck then. Someone below was pulling the rope, tolling the bell. The priest fell silent.

A drumroll began, and an officer led the priest away. A mounted officer raised his pistol and fired. The soldiers with the quirts lashed the rumps of the horses, and they bolted forward. Jerked from their saddles, the four men and the woman were left hanging by their necks. They did not die easily. They kicked and struggled and groaned and strangled.

The drumroll had stopped when the horses were lashed, but the bell continued to toll.

"My poor people," Padre Enrique intoned, shaking his head. "My poor people. You see? You saw it? Without mercy."

Raider nodded. They were in the priest's little parlor—Padre Enrique and Pepito, Raider and Ellen, William and Jack, Don Miguel.

"Why?" Ellen asked. "Is Díaz . . . ?"

Don Miguel interrupted. "It is not certain that President Díaz even knows. Mexico City is a long way from here. Who can guess what they tell him? Who can guess what he orders? Too many ears, too many mouths between him and us."

"General Álvarez is our Díaz," said the priest.

"Diego Quevedo did not betray us," said Don Miguel. "He could have saved his life by telling where we were."

"They did not know he knew," said Padre Enrique. "But you are right. They would have given him his life for yours, Don Miguel. They are still looking for you. Everywhere."

"Across the Sabinas?" Raider asked.

The priest shook his head. "Not yet. They still think you are in the mountains."

"Then we must cross the river tonight," said Raider.

"Yes," said Padre Enrique. "Pepito will lead you. And you must leave Don Miguel here, señor. You must. We need him. Our *jefe* was hanged today. Who will lead the opposition to General Álvarez? Around whom will our people rally? To whom will President Díaz listen if we have no leader?"

"He is not our security anymore," Ellen said to Raider.

Raider nodded. He rose and extended his hand to Don Miguel. "I am sorry we have been the occasion of your loss, Don Miguel," he said.

Don Miguel stood and shook his hand. "You are a brave and worthy man, señor," he said. "You are all brave. May God go with you and lead you."

CHAPTER SEVENTEEN

Two of Diego Quevedo's men appeared at the church at midnight, with their horses, and they accompanied Pepito and Raider's party—now of four—out of the village and into the country to the east. Raider was relieved to have Bastardo again. The big horse nipped his leg, but Raider could not believe the nip was anything but affectionate.

The two men said the soldiers had appeared and seized Quevedo in the morning, with no reason given. They did not know Quevedo had helped Don Miguel and Raider. They had hanged Quevedo simply to frighten and subdue the region. The woman? They had less reason. She had offended an officer. The men had heard that Juan Cardenas was taken after a short fight in the mountains. The other two men were his.

The hills they had not crossed last night remained to be crossed. Pepito knew a track that led through an arroyo, then up the hill on an easy climb and between two tops, through a sort of pass. Looking back and down, they could see fires burning up and down the valley. Some were not campfires, where the soldiers were cooking; some were houses burning. The military expedition to capture Don Miguel—and if possible to capture the gringos and their gold—had become a campaign to crush resistance to the government at Mexico City.

"It was inevitable, señores," said Pepito. "Sooner or later they would have assembled an army and attacked."

The eastern edge of the little range of hills was marked by another arroyo. They crossed it three hours after they left the village. Pepito said it was ten miles farther to the Sabinas, and they must cross it after the moon had set and before the first light of dawn. By the time the moon had set—and they had had to slow their horses because they were traveling in darkness relieved only by the glow of the stars—Pepito said they were within a mile of the river.

"I must leave you here, señores," he said, reining up. "The river is ahead." He pointed at a star. "Follow that star. The river is not deep. Ride across and do not stop on the other side. Ride another hour. Be on your guard. I think we have escaped the soldiers, but there are Indians and others to fear. May God go with you."

The night was very dark and very quiet, and Raider set off toward the river with a constricting sense of uneasiness and foreboding. They rode as a party now; there was no reason to string out. Their horses stumbled in the darkness, and they made slow progress. Even so, soon they could hear the water. The Sabinas was swift and shallow, and they could hear it moving.

They came out of the desert brush and into a line of willows that grew on the bank. At the water's edge he could see up and down the river for maybe a mile in either direction. A campfire burned to the north.

He urged Bastardo forward, and the big horse put his forelegs cautiously into the water. He found nothing alarming. He put his hooves down on a solid bottom, and he pushed forward willingly then. The water ran swiftly, but it did not reach his belly. He splashed across and reached the eastern bank in a minute. Raider sat there, waiting. He heard Ellen coming. She reached the bank beside him. William and Jack followed. They were across, and no one had moved to stop them.

They let their horses drink, and they filled their canteens before leaving the river.

*   *   *

They hobbled the horses in a draw at dawn. Leaving William as a first guard, stationed well outside the draw, they moved a hundred yards away and made their rude camp. Raider stayed awake while Jack and Ellen slept. He explored the land around and found nothing.

He sat down beside William. "Whose idea was it to run to Mexico?" he asked.

"Jack's."

"You've been lucky. You picked a hell of a place to run to."

"If I'd stayed and tried to face up to it and prove I didn't kill that little girl, I'd have long since been hanged," said William.

"I know you didn't kill her," said Raider. "My partner knows it. Your father knows it. But you still have to face trial and prove it. That's why you're going back, you know."

"Trial? In El Aguila?"

"Not in El Aguila," said Raider. "Before a real judge. In a real court."

"And then I'll hang," said William bluntly.

"We'll give the judge the evidence," said Raider. "The name Pinkerton has some weight, you know."

William nodded. "So will I, at the end of a rope."

Raider slapped his shoulder and stood. "I wouldn't count on that," he said. "I've got a smart partner. No tellin' what more he's come up with back in El Aguila."

"Raider," said William as Raider began to walk away, "I swear before God, there was no more than $7,800 in those saddlebags."

"I never doubted it," said Raider.

Raider slept during the heat of the day. When he woke, the sun was still high and blazing. The desert was quiet. He heard nothing. William, who had slept beside him while it was Jack's and Ellen's turn to guard, was not there. Neither was Jack or Ellen. He sat up.

"Put your hands up, Mr. Raider, and don't do nothin' foolish."

He swung around. It was Jack, sitting a little apart

from the camp, pointing the muzzle of his Winchester
at Raider's belly.

"I'm sorry about this, Mr. Raider," said Jack. He
was not sarcastic. His voice did sound sorry, genuinely.
"But a man has to do what a man has to do."

"Yeah. What does a man have to do, Jack?"

"Unbuckle your gun belt, Mr. Raider, and do it
slow. That's what *you* gotta do. Me, I gotta have the
gold you got in them saddlebags and take it home."

"Home?"

"Never mind where it is," said Jack. "Jake Bridenbaugh'll never miss it. But me . . . He'd never pay me
that much for a lifetime of workin' for him. Not for a
lifetime. A man like me never has no chance . . . not
unless he grabs it when it comes for him. I'm sorry to
have to take it from you, Mr. Raider. You're a good
man."

"What are you gonna do, Jack?" Raider asked. He
had dropped his gun belt and sat with his hands above
his head. "Kill me?"

Jack shook his head. "Naw," he said. He reached
carefully and pulled the gun belt back to himself. He
lifted the Remington out of its holster. "I want you to
sit up on y' knees an' put y' hands down to y' sides."

Raider obeyed, and in a moment Jack dropped the
gun belt over his head and pulled it tight around him,
pinning his arms to his sides. Jack fastened the buckle,
pulling the belt even tighter. He had short lengths of
rope ready, and he used them to tie Raider's wrists to
the belt.

"Git up," he said. "C'mon."

He led Raider to the draw where the horses were
hobbled. William and Ellen were there, both tied hand
and foot. He motioned to Raider to sit, and he tied
his legs together at the ankles and knees.

"I thought you weren't going to kill us," Raider said.
"You might as well shoot us as leave us here like this,
in the sun."

Jack had gathered all their weapons, including

Raider's knife. He was pushing them into the scabbards and lashings on the horses. He tossed two canteens to the ground. "Never knowed nobody couldn't work out of some ropes, given the time," he said.

"You take all the guns, all the horses," said Raider. "What good will two canteens of water do? You know the situation."

Jack had unbuckled the straps on the saddlebags astride Bastardo. He pulled out a handful of gold coins. He tossed two coins in the sand. "You can buy anythin' in Mexico for forty dollars," he said. He swung up on Bastardo. The stallion pawed and twitched but did not try to throw him. He leaned out and pulled together the reins of the other three horses. "I figure you'll make it," he said. "Tough man like you. I also figure I maybe won't if I don't tilt the odds all the way in my favor. I watched you too long, Mr. Raider. I own I'm fear'd o' you."

"Tell me one thing, Jack," he said. "How much did McMullen pay you?"

"Pay him for what?" asked William.

Jack looked down at William. "Never mind, sonny," he said scornfully.

"Jack will do anything for money, as we now see," said Raider. "The banker owed your father $25,000 in gold. He didn't have it. He put less than a third of that in locked saddlebags and turned them over to you. Tell me somethin', William. Whose idea was it to stop by Sister's and have one more fling with Susie Bradford?"

William tugged at his ropes so he could look up at Jack. "It was yours, Jack," he said. "I remember . . ."

"Somebody—Tom McMullen, I imagine—killed Susie just before you got there. Jack had given them the high sign, that you were on your way to Sister Edwards's cathouse. He had helped get you drunk. When you got there . . ."

"I was supposed to bust him loose from them cowboys that grabbed him on the porch," Jack interrupted.

"The cowboys was primed not to put up no fight. But Sam, he drawed on 'em first. Like to scared 'em to death."

"And you're the one whose idea it was to run to Mexico," said William.

Jack nodded. "Right."

"What would have happened if it hadn't worked out?" Raider asked.

Jack's face turned grim. "They would'a laid for us on the road. No way they was gonna let him go home and have his daddy find out them saddlebags didn't have $25,000 in."

"You almost got yourself killed for me, more than once, since we've been in Mexico," William protested.

"For *me*," Jack said, tapping his chest with one finger. "Savin' *my* hide, not yours."

"Why didn't you just take the gold and kill me, weeks ago?"

"We wuz follered," said Jack. "McMullen figgered on gittin' the gold back his own self. He had shootists hired. They'd a got you, sooner or later, if the Don hadn't. They'd a got me fer sure, and if I'd been without you and had the gold . . ." He shook his head. "I couldn't a run fast enough or far enough."

"It's different now?" Raider asked.

"Yeah," said Jack. "I figger you kilt the only ones left, back on that mountain that night, with the knife. Anyways, they're off the track now, and I got a good start on 'em—like I'm goin' to have on you."

"My father trusted you especially," said William quietly.

"Yeah. He trusted Jeff McMullen, too."

There was a way maybe to twist the cap off one of the canteens with their teeth and some way to tip the canteen then and drink the hot water inside. But they would spill it, more than likely, Raider said; and the water, heated by the sun, was not the cool water of their fantasies. They had managed to roll into the shade of some brush, but the sun was hot and the sand was hot, and they lay drenched with sweat in clothes that seemed to have shrunk. Raider had been chewing for an hour on the rope around Ellen's wrists, but he could see no sign he was any closer to freeing her hands.

"I hurt, Raider," she croaked. "I ain't embarrassed to say it. I think I'm goin' to pass out. I was done this way by the Apaches, but never this bad."

William lay watching them. His struggles against his ropes had only pulled the knots tighter. Raider was not sure he was conscious all the time. His face was red and swollen, and his breathing was irregular.

Raider hurt, too. His shoulders throbbed. His hands were numb. The sun had moved, but it would be hours yet before sunset. He was not sure if the night would be better for them, since they would be defenseless against the snakes and Gila monsters that would come out with sunset. Right now he hated Jack Foster more than any other man he had known in his life.

"Raider," said William. It was the first word he had spoken in an hour—or maybe two hours; it was impossible to judge time. "I'm rubbin' my rope on a piece of rock. I'm not sure, but it seems like it's cuttin'."

"Try," said Raider. *"Try."*

Gnawing on Ellen's rope, he could not feel with his tongue that he had broken any of the hemp strands. He was not sure his teeth would not wrench out before the hemp yielded.

Ellen had rolled on her face. She was sobbing. Her hands, cruelly bound, writhed.

"Can you take a look?" asked William. His breath was short. He had little voice left.

Raider rolled and humped painfully until he was behind William. William was rubbing the rope between his wrists convulsively. Raider pushed his face up close and stared.

"You've broken a strand," he whispered hoarsely. *"Go, man, go!"*

William rubbed faster, but his strength was obviously exhausted. He rubbed in short bursts.

"Five more minutes and you get a drink of water," Raider muttered.

William choked and coughed, but he rubbed. The hemp, an infinite bundle of hair-thin, steel-hard threads, yielded grudgingly. They slipped and rolled under the friction, rather than surrendering. When one broke, it snapped back. The strands were woven of these threads. To sever a strand was the work of many minutes of unrelenting friction.

"Up a little. The rock's sharper up higher," Raider said.

William moved. "I gotta rest a minute," he said.

"Just a minute," said Raider firmly. "No more."

Ellen moaned. William began again to rub.

"That's two!" Raider breathed. "Keep at it! Don't give up now. We'll go back to the river when we're loose. It's not far."

Ellen had been silent for some while by the time the last strand broke and William's hands jerked free. "I can't untie . . ." he breathed to Raider, his eyes wide. "They're numb! I'm paralyzed!"

"Rub 'em," Raider muttered. "Check the water. Pour some on 'em. If it ain't too hot, pour some on her."

Awkwardly, William managed to lift one of the canteens and to pull out the stopper. He took a sip of water, then poured water on Ellen's face. She stirred. He held the canteen to her mouth, and she drank. He came then to Raider.

On the river, in the shadow of willows that grew down to the water's edge, they lay naked in the water and let it cool them. Their skins seemed to absorb water. They lay quietly under a bright moon. They did not speak. Their thoughts were the same, and there was nothing to say.

They had no food. They had no horses. They had

no weapons. The border was fifty miles away, across a hostile desert.

"I'll be honest," Raider said after they had been in the water an hour. "I don't know where to start. We can't walk to the border. We've got to have horses."

"Gotta have guns," said Ellen.

"Gotta look around," said Raider. "We've got to look at the territory we're in, see what our chances are. You two stay here and keep out of sight and quiet. I'll do some exploring."

He pulled on his wet clothes and his boots, and stumbled off up the river. Anything good he might find—or anything bad, for that matter—he judged he'd find near the water. He walked upstream for an hour and found nothing, no sign of anyone, neither camp nor house. Even though he had resolved not to recross the Sabinas, he waded across and worked his way south again on the west side of the river. He came on the charred remains of dead campfires, maybe from the night before, but nothing more. When he judged he was well downstream from where he had left William and Ellen, he waded across again. After a weary three-hour trek, he had found nothing they could use.

The sky was turning iron-gray when he began to believe he was in the vicinity of where he had left William and Ellen and ought to be finding them. He became more cautious as he approached where he thought they should be. It was instinct with him to return to his own camp with an excess of caution.

He heard a grunt. He heard a laugh. Frozen quiet, he dropped to the ground and listened. He edged forward, quiet and careful. He heard a horse snort. He heard Ellen's voice. She was sobbing. He edged forward more. The pre-dawn light was reflected off the river, and he saw William first. Then he saw Ellen. . . .

William sat with his face pressed into his hands. Ellen, naked on her back, was sobbing. There were three men. Mexicans. One stood with a gun held on

William. Another was pulling on his pants. It was plain what they were doing.

The one who stepped away from the others to piss was the first to die. Raider's fist snapped his neck as he stood with his cock in his hand, and he fell without a word. Raider took his pistol and worked his way back to the copse of willows. Two Mexicans were still guarding William and Ellen; one carried his rifle loosely. Stepping into the copse, Raider shot them both before they could react.

"I'll get myself raped anytime you ask, for three horses, three revolvers, two rifles, and some grub," said Ellen sullenly as they rode east. She had kept silent for a long time. "It's what I'm for, I guess."

"If I could have helped . . ." said William.

"You'd of got yourself killed trying," she said blankly.

Raider rode ahead, climbing every high ground, looking all around. The men on the river had only chanced on Ellen and William. They had not been looking for the Bridenbaugh gold. Maybe they weren't even bandits—just men who saw the chance to take their pleasure of a woman and had taken it, with no ill will. He was ashamed to have killed them. Maybe it had not been necessary. He wondered what Doc would have done.

The horses were poor, as were the saddles, but they would carry them to the Rio Grande if nothing more happened. Their canteens were full, and they carried the Mexicans' water bottles, also full; and they had a little food. With luck they could reach the border by tomorrow night.

He was sorry to lose the Bridenbaugh gold. He was sorrier to lose Bastardo. He had grown fond of the big, ill-tempered horse. Bastardo had tried to throw him a dozen times, to brush him against walls and fences, to nip him, to step on his feet; but he had carried him to the limit of his strength, too, understanding like a man when it was important to make the last exertion. Perfecto had admired him. . . .

"Raider!" William and Ellen came galloping to catch up. They pointed to their right. They had spotted a wisp of dust on the wind. Now it was here, then it was farther west. Something was moving fast.

"We'll keep away from 'em, whoever they are," Raider said.

He led them into an arroyo, and they waited there, keeping quiet. Two of the horses were mares, and now one of them raised her head and whinnied loudly. She snorted and pawed, and they could not control her. Plainly she had been heard. The wisp of dust rose closer, and they heard hoofbeats. Raider dismounted and took a place at the edge of the arroyo with a rifle. The rifle was a single-shot, worn and loose and unlikely to be accurate. It was the best they had, and William and Ellen crouched beside him with worse weapons.

"One horse," Ellen whispered. "I only hear one horse."

Raider nodded.

That one horse appeared suddenly at the edge of the arroyo. It was a big stallion with a saddle but no rider.

"Bastardo!" Raider yelled.

The gold was still in the saddlebags. Raider's Winchester was in its scabbard. Two canteens hung over the saddle horn.

"He's thrown the son of a bitch," said Ellen grimly.

"Or just run off from him," said William.

"I'd like to have him alive for a witness at William's trial," said Raider.

They did not search for Jack Foster, but as they rode east they kept an eye out for him. An hour later they found another of their horses, wandering without a rider. A little after that they spotted still another one, this one just standing, pawing. Jack lay not far away.

"Jesus!"

He had been thrown by Bastardo, from the look of

him. He had broken his leg or hip. The horses had run away with his canteens. He had crawled a little distance toward a draw with some shade in it, but he had not made it. He was dead. His body was swollen, and insects had already begun to work on it. Raider's Remington was in his holster, and Raider knelt and retrieved it. They had no shovels with which to dig a grave. The earth was rocky and hard, anyway. They left him.

CHAPTER EIGHTEEN

"Miss Crittenden, I—"

"Doctor," the girl interrupted firmly. "I don't care what anyone says. It works. I want you to see. I just had to talk to you before you leave town. I need another bottle of the expander and another jar of the cream."

Charlotte Crittenden continued unbuttoning as she spoke, and in a moment she had bared her breasts.

"Miss Crittenden . . ."

"You see? When my mother brought me to see you, I was hardly symmetrical at all, as you remember. Now . . ." She lifted her breasts in her hands. It was true there had been a noticeable change in the two or three weeks since he had first massaged them and put her on a regimen of daily massage with Fleur de Lis Bust Expander and Seroco Bust Cream or Food. "I am grateful, Dr. Weatherbee."

Doc bowed slightly and smiled. "I am pleased to have been able to help you," he said nervously.

Kathleen was downstairs, ordering a meal to be brought up. He was uneasy when she was out of the room, never being sure someone would not see past the black hair dye and padded corset and realize that "Mrs. Weatherbee" was Kathleen Reilly.

"Now allow me to help *you*, Doctor," said Charlotte. She began rebuttoning her shirtwaist. "I can tell you something you need to know."

"I'll be grateful."

"I think you know my father owns a spread outside

of town, out to the south. As of yesterday we have a houseguest. I think you know him. Mr. Keene. Mr. Douglas Keene."

Doc nodded. "I know him."

"He speaks of you. There are two other men with him: a Mr. Oliver Bodine and a Mr. Lemuel Pickering. Do you know them?"

"No. Who are they?"

She finished buttoning her shirtwaist, reached for her little jacket, and looked up at his face as she spoke. "Mr. Bodine is the president of the San Antonio, Houston & New Orleans Railroad. Mr. Pickering is always with him. He is a bodyguard, I think. A shootist. He always carries a revolver."

" 'Always,' " Doc repeated. "You've seen him before?"

"Several times. Mr. Bodine has stayed in our home before."

"What do they say about me?"

"Well, in the first place they don't think you are a real doctor." She blushed faintly. "I could hardly show them my evidence to the contrary."

"No."

"Mr. Keene speaks of arresting you," she said. "He is a railroad policeman, and he asked Mr. Pickering to help him subdue you and your wife. He speaks of taking both of you to San Antonio in handcuffs."

"He is talking about a kidnapping," said Doc. "He has no reason or authority for arresting either one of us."

"You'll be lucky if that's the worst they do," said Charlotte. "When Keene talked about it, the others told him to wait."

"What others? Wait for what?"

"Mr. McMullen was there. He and Mr. Bodine are close friends. Mr. Bodine told Mr. Keene to wait until the showdown."

"Showdown?"

"When Mr. Bridenbaugh arrives. They say Mr.

Bridenbaugh is coming with his ranch hands and shootists."

"They know better," said Doc.

"They speak of it as a certainty."

"And El Aguila will be ready," he said.

She nodded. "My father is coming into town with ten of our men. Other ranchers are doing the same. They'll be armed."

"Against an attack that isn't coming."

"How can you be so sure? Unless . . ." She put her hand to her mouth. "Unless I've betrayed my father and what they say of you is true."

"What do they say of me?"

"That you work for Jacob Bridenbaugh."

Doc walked to the window and looked down at the street. "Does anyone know you're here?" he asked.

"My mother," said Charlotte. "She believes you're a real doctor and a fine gentleman."

Doc sighed. "When the town is full of armed men . . ."

"You might have an accident," she said blandly.

He turned to face her. "Does your father countenance that?" he asked firmly.

"No. And neither does Mr. Keene, who insists he will take you to San Antonio to face a court, be identified, and be charged with some crime he has in mind—stock manipulation. But the others—McMullen and Bodine and Pickering—just smile and shrug. I think they mean to do you harm."

"It's time for Dr. Weatherbee's traveling medicine show to travel," Doc said to Kathleen as they sat in the room, eating.

"It's not just the town," Kathleen said. "They're gonna put men on the border, to look for Raider coming back with Bridenbaugh. They'll shoot on sight."

"Do they really believe the bullshit that's going around?" Doc asked.

"That's the talk downstairs. McMullen's got 'em

stirred up so they're sure the town's about to be besieged."

"If I could only guess where Raider will come back across the border," said Doc, shaking his head. "If I could only be sure he's not one of the men they hanged at Colina Verte. I've assumed he's coming back, but . . ."

Kathleen put her hand on his cheek. "They couldn't hang Raider," she said. "He was born to be shot by a wronged woman."

"I've got to move out," said Doc. "I'm just sitting here now waiting for someone to try to kill me. And so are you. You don't have to go with me, but you should move out, too."

"I'll stick with you, Doc," she said.

"I'll settle my account with you, Mr. Brady," Doc said to the keeper of the livery stable. He smiled. "While I've still got cash."

The grizzled stableman grinned. "I figger you've got cash enough, Doctor," he said. "Considerin' all the pills and tonics you've sold to folks round here."

Doc watched the old fellow calculate what he owed, adding the figures in his head with lips moving and eyes rolled up. It was Doc's intention to seem casual, to suggest he was just settling his bill because he hadn't settled it for a week or so. He did not want the man to understand he was not bringing Judith back, that Judith and the Studebaker would not be there that night. The more miles he could put between himself and El Aguila before the railroad crowd learned he was gone, the better.

"Seem like thirteen dollar, fifty cents, give or take a quarter," said the old man.

"Fair," said Doc. He handed over a ten-dollar gold piece and four silver dollars.

Mr. Brady took a half dollar from his pocket and handed it to Doc. "She's a good girl," he said, nodding at Judith. "Sound wagon, y' got, too. I enjoys seein' a sound rig."

Doc drove the Studebaker along the street toward the Eagle. He acknowledged the friendly salute of Sheriff Jimmy Tate—one of the few friendly greetings he received in El Aguila. Others—the bulk of the citizens— glanced at him with a mixture of curiosity and amusement. Some of them would stop by his wagon when it was set up before the Eagle, to hear him praise the virtues of homeopathic medicines and, some of them, to buy.

He had never been entirely confident of the power of the homeopathic specifics he sold as a cover for his work as a Pinkerton operative. Wagner and others had assured him that, if they did not always cure, at all events there was no recorded instance of their doing the patient any harm. All of them were taken with huge quantities of water, and, as Wagner had said, people who didn't drink enough water could benefit from that anyway, whether the specifics produced benefit or not.

Among the specifics he carried in the Studebaker were crude antimony, arnica, belladonna, cantharis, digitalis, ipecac, mercury in various forms, nux vomica, phosphoric acid, sulphur, and tartar emetic. The underlying theory of homeopathy was that the curative chemical produced a simulacrum of the symptom of the disease to be cured. So, if nitroglycerine produced headache—which it most surely did—a tiny bit of it taken with much water would cure headache.

Not all the specifics he carried were homeopathic. In his experience he had learned of some effective cures that he carried and prescribed even if homeopathy did not suggest them.

Set up before the Eagle, he made his spiel and began to receive patients.

"Dr. Weatherbee," said a burly man tugging a small boy forward. "This boy of mine cain't git his breath a lot of the time. He like to turn blue . . ."

"Asthma?" asked Doc.

"I've heard it called so," said the man. His son, beside him, was slight, thin, wide-eyed, weak, frightened. "They say he'll grow out of it."

. "I don't know about that," said Doc. "Are the attacks severe?"

The man lowered his voice. "Like to die sometimes," he confided, trusting the boy did not hear.

Doc sighed. He frowned. This was a responsibility he had not reckoned with when he agreed to travel as a homeopath. Many of his patients were fools. Others were sick people.

"Mister," said Doc, "I have something that's helped a lot of patients. Just a minute." He went back in the wagon and returned with a small olive-green and red can. "This is Doctor Schiffman's Asthmador," he said. "It's belladonna mixed with saltpeter. When the boy has an attack, you pour some of this in a pie pan and light it with a match. It'll make clouds of smoke. Make sure the boy breathes that smoke. Make him pull it down in his lungs. He won't want to, but make him do it. It will relieve the attack. I've seen it work for lots of patients. You may have to use it more than once to get the benefit. Asthma is a tough disease to work with. This will help."

The man nodded soberly. "How much does it cost, Doctor?" he asked.

"Uh, ten cents," said Doc.

"Maybe I should buy two, three cans."

"You buy this one. It'll last awhile. If it helps, you can order more by mail. The address is on the can."

The man handed over his dime and took the can, squinting over the label. "I thank y', Doctor," he said. "I do thank y' kindly."

Kathleen had been watching. She squeezed Doc's hand. Her voice was small as she watched the boy and the man walk away, studying their can of medicine. "Weatherbee, you son of a bitch," she said. "Jesus Christ would of been proud of you."

*   *   *

Judith plodded out of town. They had told no one they were leaving. Kathleen had settled their account at the Eagle the same way Doc had settled with the keeper of the livery stable. She had carried a few of their belongings down from the room—including, very carefully, his Pinkerton journal—and had put them in the wagon while he was selling specifics. They let the mule amble westward as if with no particular purpose. If the town understood the traveling doctor was leaving, no one said good-bye.

"What have we got, an hour, before they figure it out?" Kathleen asked. "Then another hour, most of, for someone to run out to Crittenden's ranch and pass the word."

Doc shook his head. "Maybe they come after us, maybe they figure they're well shed of us." He shrugged. "We've got Keene's Iver Johnson and your derringer, plus a double-barreled shotgun under the floorboards in back. What I'd rather do is hide. I plan to get off this road and head south toward the border, cross-country if need be. Get an hour out of town, and we can turn a lot of different ways. We get hard to find."

"You figure to find Raider? That's crazy. The Rio Grande is a thousand miles long, and he can come across anywhere."

"*If* he comes across."

"All right, *if*. But you'll never make a hookup."

" 'Hookup,' " Doc repeated. "Kathleen, can you climb a telegraph pole?"

"Now I know you're crazy."

"You can send a telegram from Laredo to Eagle Pass. I checked that. That means there's a line that runs parallel to the border. There's a line for sure from Laredo to San Antonio, but that's farther. We've got to find a telegraph line and get on the wire to Chicago. I think it's time to call for help."

"That's sense."

They traveled west, toward the Rio Grande, and ten miles out of town he took a south branch, along a rutted dry road that was little more than a track. Judith plodded without complaint, and by sunset they were on the bank of the Rio Grande.

It was wide-open country. As the sun set they saw no sign of mankind, no fire or light, up or down the wide, shallow river. Doc stopped in a thick grove of cacti and desert brush, fifty yards back from the water's edge, unhitched Judith, and led her to the water for a drink. He carried his Diamondback. The same prudence that suggested they should not camp directly on the water's edge also suggested he should carry the revolver. It forbade a fire, too. They didn't need it; they had carried food from the Eagle, with whiskey in plenty.

After dark, Doc sat at the river's edge while Kathleen went in the water and gratefully washed the black dye from her red hair. She tossed the stiff corset far out into the current and laughed as it floated downstream and out of sight.

She came out of the water naked, and they retreated from the river into a sandy depression a few yards away. She spread her skirt on the sand and sat down to let the warm air dry her. Doc sat beside her.

"If I weren't a . . . harlot, would you fall in love with me?" she asked Doc quietly.

"That's no obstacle," he said.

"But would you marry me?"

"How could I marry anybody, Kathleen?" he asked. "You see what I do and how I live. I never stay long anyplace. And there's always the risk . . ,"

"What if a woman didn't care?"

"What if there were a child?" he asked.

She sighed loudly. "Always the answer."

"You chose to be what you are," he said. "I chose to be what I am. It hurts sometimes."

Kathleen nodded. Her eyes filled with tears. "You understanding bastard," she whispered.

"Kathleen . . ."

He reached for her, and she fell into his arms. In a

moment he was as naked as she was, and a moment
later he was in her and their hips were grinding together. He climaxed quick and hard, his penis pumping
into her with electric spasms. She brought him up
again, and they did it again. They lay in the sand until
the stars were overhead in a jet-black sky. Then they
walked naked to the wagon and lay together inside
for the rest of the night.

In the light of dawn he walked up and down the
river, maybe a mile. He saw nothing. He heard nothing.
The Mexican side was as quiet as the Texas side. The
river slid by, the air above it clear, without morning
mist. The red sun burst on the world, promising another day of blistering heat.

Kathleen sat on the wagon box, no longer the cor-
seted "Mrs. Weatherbee." She wore a straight blue skirt
and a white blouse, obviously with nothing beneath,
and she remained barefoot. There was no point, she
said, in suffering the heat any more than necessary.
She was beautiful, more attractive in this natural condition than she had ever been before. She had long ago
forsaken modesty. As he drove the wagon away from
the river, she spread her legs and lifted her skirt, to
let the slight breeze blow across her legs and up to her
hips, and she hummed a small tune.

He had decided to look for the telegraph wire. It
had not been south of the road from El Aguila, so it
had to be north or northeast.

"I hate to cross that road again," he said to Kathleen. "On the other hand, if they're looking for us,
they'll look on the river side as much as anywhere."

"Where'd you say that shotgun was?" she asked.

"Under the floorboards."

They traveled north and crossed the east-west road
from El Aguila, just where they had turned off it the
evening before. He guided Judith off the road, across
the open country. It was flat, hard land. The wagon
wheels did not sink into it. He drove around deep draws

and arroyos, and made slow but steady progress northward.

Kathleen's legs turned pink under the sun, and after a while he suggested she ride inside the wagon. It was hotter there, for lack of air, but the sun did not beat on your bare skin and burn you. For himself, he kept his shirtsleeves buttoned at the cuffs and wore a neckerchief of silk to shield his skin from the sun overhead. His derby shielded his ears. Only his hands burned, and after a while he donned gloves. The sweat poured from him, and he drank water. He stopped from time to time and offered Judith water from one of his canteens. Kathleen dozed fitfully in the wagon.

He turned eastward around three o'clock and had been on an eastward course no more than fifteen minutes when he spied the strand of wire running from pole to pole. He stopped. Prudence dictated he stay away from the wire and the road in the daylight. He turned Judith, meaning to retreat half a mile, when he saw it was too late to retreat.

"Ho!" Two men on horses rode toward him. They had rifles across their saddles, and before he could make a move to defend himself they had the rifles leveled on him. "Ho! Well, if it ain't Dr. Weatherbee! Goddam! Look, Pat, it's the good doctor himself. Looks like he's lost."

They were the Murphy brothers from El Aguila. Their father owned the Murphy Saloon, and both of them had been friends of the Galvin boy as well as of Tom McMullen.

They rode up to the wagon. "People lookin' for you, Doctor," said the bigger one grimly. His name was Jess. "Coincidence, findin' you out here."

"Coincidence?" Doc asked.

"Well, maybe not. Pat 'n' me allowed we'd try the north from town. Where'd you hide overnight?"

"Why you looking for me?"

"Hear tell you work for Bridenbaugh," said Jess. He wiped the sweat from his brow with his sleeve. He was heavyset, flushed, drenched with sweat. "Come out this way to meet him comin' in?"

"I don't work for Bridenbaugh," said Doc.

"No never mind," said Jess. "Hop down from that there wagon box." He lifted the muzzle of his rifle.

Doc had no choice. He jumped down to the sand.

"Let's see what we kin find out, little brother," said Jess to Pat. "Ask the good doctor a few questions."

Pat dismounted. He was smaller than his brother, but he was a solid young man, muscular and lean. He tossed his hat on the ground and grinned at Doc.

"Ask him where Bridenbaugh is," said Jess.

"Hmm?" asked Pat.

Doc shook his head. "I don't know. I told you I don't work for him."

Pat swung with his left and knocked Doc sprawling in the sand with a stinging blow to the jaw.

"Git up, Doctor," said Jess, gesturing with his rifle. "Tell us where that feller Raider and his Mexicans is."

"If I knew, would I be here letting you pound me?"

Pat flattened his nose, probably broke it, with a right, and Doc fell again.

"Git up, Doctor. We got some more questions."

Doc struggled to his feet, his nose streaming blood.

"You wanta go back to town, Doctor?" Jess asked. "I'm of a mind to put a rope round your neck right here."

"That'd be murder," Doc muttered, clutching his nose.

" 'Bout what you got comin'," said Jess. " 'Nother question. Why'd you yell out warnin' the night that Raider kilt Billy Bob?"

Doc shook his head and jumped backward to avoid Pat's next swinging right. Pat laughed.

"Stop it!"

Startled, Jess Murphy looked into the back of the wagon, where Kathleen stood with the double-barreled shotgun from under the wagon floor pointing at him. His first look of fear dissolved into a grin. "Well, Katie

Reilly," he said. "Where'd you come fum? The doctor and the whore, huh? Might've figgered. You another one of Bridenbaugh's people?"

"Drop the gun, Pat," Kathleen snapped at the younger brother, who had reached for his pistol and now stopped as he saw the barrels of the shotgun turned toward him. He let go of the pistol, and it dropped back into his holster.

Jess, at that moment, grabbed for his revolver. The blast from the shotgun lifted him from the saddle and threw the ragged, bloody mess of his carcass on the ground. Pat tried to draw, and the blast from the second barrel took off his head.

Kathleen dropped the shotgun and screamed.

CHAPTER NINETEEN

Without the Don, without the burro—which they had left with Pepito—Raider and William and Ellen rode fast across the last fifty miles to the Rio Grande. They had to ride fast. At least a company of cavalrymen had crossed the Sabinas and was hunting them. Their advantage was that no one knew where they would try to cross the border. They didn't know themselves. The soldiers had given them another advantage. With soldiers conspicuously in the area, Indians and Mexican bandits had run for cover.

On a rise of land, not long after dawn, Raider peered westward and saw mounted soldiers a mile or so away.

"North," he said. "They're moving north, for now anyway."

"The shortest way between the Sabinas and the Rio Grande is northeast," said William.

"They know that," said Raider. "If we cut east a little and make for the border around Hidalgo . . ."

"Might confuse them," said Ellen.

They mounted and turned east. When, after a mile or so, they again topped a rise, no soldiers were in sight. Just ahead of them was a deep arroyo with a few pools of water. They approached all water cautiously. They needed water for their horses, but so did anyone riding here.

William put on Ellen's sombrero and rode first into the arroyo. He looked like a Mexican. If he could water his horse without attracting trouble, then likely they could water theirs.

"He's a good-looking boy," Ellen said quietly as they sat beside some tall cacti, watching William thread his way down into the arroyo. "He's growed up some since I first met him back in the mountains."

Raider nodded. "His daddy may like him better now."

"This morning, while you were taking your turn to sleep, he asked me to lay with him," she said. Her eyes remained fixed on William, and when Raider turned toward her she did not seem to notice.

"Did you?"

She shook her head. "No. But would you care?"

"I have no claim on you, Ellen."

"That's what I thought."

William's horse slid in some loose rock and sand, and abruptly he was in the bed of the arroyo. He dismounted and led the horse to one of the pools of water. He knelt and tasted the water, then let the horse drink. He lowered a canteen into the water and let it fill.

"I'll do it, next time he asks," said Ellen, still staring fixedly at William and holding her eyes away from Raider.

Raider nodded.

They rode east, remaining cautious. On every high ground they paused to survey the land around them. Twice they saw bands of horsemen to the west and north of them—both times too far away to be identified.

"We cross the Rio Grande in the dark?" Ellen asked.

Raider nodded. "Same way we did the Sabinas. And I hope we have better luck."

The land was open and desolate, and the sun was unrelenting. They saw two small herds of sheep but no shepherds, half a dozen stray cows but no one looking for them. They tired, and their horses tired, but they kept going. They had plenty of water to last to the river, and they let the horses drink, and they drank themselves and even poured some on their heads. They did not know how far they were from the river, and by late afternoon they were taken with the illogical notion that they might have ridden all day in the wrong direction. Each time they topped a rise they peered ahead, looking for the Rio Grande, and each time all they saw was more arid land and another rise to climb in the distance.

"All I know is the goddam sun comes up in the east and goes down in the west," Ellen complained. "What I don't know is if the river is for sure east."

"You can count on that," said Raider. "It runs more south than east from Del Rio to Laredo, and if you ride east out of Mexico, you're gonna hit it."

And they did. Coming to the top of a rise in the red sun of late afternoon, they looked down into the wide valley of the Rio Grande. It lay flat between its sandy banks, shallow and rippling, its surface dappled with red light, the reflection of the setting sun.

A mile back from the river they settled down in a sandy draw to rest and wait. As always, they would sleep by turns, but as soon as the sun had set and the sky was black, Raider left the camp on foot to have another look at the river in the moonlight. What he saw was no surprise. There were camps along the river, marked by their fires. They weren't all men out looking for him, of course; but some of them were, and he had no way to know which. The fires burned on both sides of the river. Obviously Texans as well as Mexicans were looking for them. Word of their coming had somehow reached El Aguila.

Returning to William and Ellen, he was glad to find Ellen alert while William slept. He could not have gotten past her.

"Over there, nobody knows who you are," he said to her. "Once we're safe across the river, it might be a good idea for you to take a little money—I'm sure William will give you a little of the gold, say fifty dollars—and go on your own. You could stop at a ranch, buy some woman's clothes . . ."

"No," she said. "William and I talked about it. I'm goin' to the Bridenbaugh ranch."

"I see."

"He says his daddy'll be glad to put me up till I can git in touch with my family."

"You could find your way to Adena by yourself."

She shook her head. "I'll come along with the two of you. Come this far. Might's well go the whole way."

Raider slept an hour or two. They woke him when the moon had set. He had found a draw where they could travel almost to the edge of the water while keeping pretty much below the general level of the ground. They rode into that draw and down it. Halfway down, Raider dismounted. They did the same and followed him, leading their horses. At the end of the draw, he handed Bastardo's reins to Ellen and walked ahead, to have a last look.

The campfires were out up and down the river. It was quiet. The river lapped on the shore. He judged it was shallow enough to cross, though the horses might have to swim a little. There was no way to take horses across water like that without a lot of splashing and snorting.

He heard a voice. Damn! William and Ellen should have enough sense to . . . But it was not William and Ellen!

In a crouch he trotted back into the draw. They had heard the voices, too, and were crouched, alert, their guns ready.

"Shit," said the voice.

"By God, I tell you I seen it," said another voice. "It wuz up this hill, and it turned around and bit its own tail, and it give a flip and wuz up in a hoop before you could guess what happened. Now you tell me you never seen no hoop snake, and I tell you that son of a bitch come rollin' down the hill toward me, lickety-split, hell-bent to stob me with that there fang in its tail. Hoss reared and like to threw me. Last minute that son of a bitch spit out its tail and come out of thet hoop shape and flang itself toward me like a goddam spear, and I'm tellin' you, if that hoss hadn't been rearin' and jumpin', that son of a bitch would have stobbed him right in the side—or would have got me on the leg. As it wuz, he shot on past into the brush there. I looked up the hill, and here comes another'n. I tell you, Ben, I give thet horse the spurs and got out o' there fast as a man could. You tell *me* you never seen the like. By God, *I have*."

The first voice laughed.

They were on horses, riding along the river, north to south. The one with the story was an old man, thin and slight. The other was bigger. They rode casually, as if looking for nothing. But what were they doing riding the riverbank in the middle of the night? Patroling the river. Cowboys. Texans. On the Mexican side.

"The question is," he whispered to William and Ellen, "how much riverbank are they responsible for? How far do they go before they come back?"

"*Do* they come back?" Ellen asked.

"We can't be sure."

Raider walked down to the edge of the water. He wanted to see how far sound carried. For several minutes he could hear the two voices. Then they faded, and he could hear them no more.

"We've got no choice," he told William and Ellen. "We've got to cross. It's going to get too tough on this side."

They mounted their horses and walked them slowly out of the draw to the edge of the water. For a short time they sat there, allowing their horses to drink from the Rio Grande. Then they urged them forward, into the water. Ellen's horse resisted. She did not want to go. Ellen spurred her and whipped her flanks with her sombrero. Reluctantly the horse ventured deeper in the water, frightened and tossing her head. Bastardo plunged forward without hesitation. The noise was considerable, as Raider had feared, but it raised no alarm. They moved toward the center of the river.

The horses had to swim. Their footing gave way as the water rose higher on their flanks, and holding their heads high they swam. The current swept them downstream. The three riders urged them on, slapping their rumps, not spurring them. Raider could see the eyes of Ellen's mare—wide, terrified; she was ready to surrender and sink and drown except for Ellen's constant slapping and urging. Ellen kept the mare's head reined in the right direction, and the little horse almost kept up.

Bastardo's hoofs touched gravel. He extended his legs and pounded the river bottom. In a moment he found a purchase and lunged up onto higher ground, with his flanks out of the water. The other horses saw and struggled frantically to catch him. In another moment they too were out.

Now the horses sensed dry ground ahead, and all three lunged forward, anxious to be out of the tug of the water.

"Hey! Hey, hey!"

Raider heard the shout from the Mexican side, now far behind. Then he heard shots. He looked back and could see no one. The shots were not aimed; they were signals, fired in the air. Ahead, on the Texas bank, men and horses came awake and began to move. He could hear scuffling, yelling, hoofbeats.

"Go!" he yelled to William and Ellen, and he spurred Bastardo to splash out of the water and gallop up the riverbank. William followed, his horse splashing mightily; and after him, Ellen's mare lunged and struggled and nearly threw her. Raider paused to see that she was not thrown. She slapped the mare furiously on the rump, and the mare galloped after the other horses as fast as she could.

Horsemen were coming from both up and down the river, converging on the place where they heard horses splashing out of the Rio Grande. Raider aimed his Winchester at a large flat rock and pulled off one shot. The bullet ricocheted off the rock and whined away.

That would give them pause. There were few men on earth who did not shy at the sound of a bullet whining through the night. He pointed forward, and Ellen and William galloped ahead, up the riverbank to higher ground. Gunfire broke out all along the river. It had to be aimless; no one had seen them yet. Raider ricocheted another bullet off the rock and turned Bastardo to catch up with William and Ellen.

He led them two hundred yards from the river, then turned them upstream, running parallel to the river. Pursuers would expect them to ride away from the river, he supposed, and maybe he could throw them off by following the river a little before he turned away from it.

It was too dark to ride recklessly. They had to go slowly and pick their way among rocks and small trees, over gullies, over loose sand. The whole world was calamity around them—men firing guns, yelling, riding drunkenly. Happily, almost all of them were nearer the river. The three had slipped through.

Raider led William and Ellen parallel to the river for another few minutes. He stopped then. "We'll turn away from the water now," he said. "We—"

Three or four horsemen were coming. Ellen, who had sensed them first, had spurred her mare down into a gully, and with luck she was out of sight.

Raider slapped William on the shoulder, hard. "Throw yourself over your saddle, like you're hurt," he said.

William was still moving when the three horsemen trotted up—three rangy ranchers in tall Stetsons, wearing Peacemakers.

"They're thataway!" Raider shouted, swinging his arm toward the river. "One of 'em shot Charlie here. Where's a doc? Where kin I git help?"

Two of the ranchers yelled something unintelligible and dashed off in the direction he had indicated. The third, a big man with a gray mustache, put his hand on his Peacemaker and edged his horse closer. "Just who you say you wuz, mister?" he asked. He came still closer, squinting in the darkness at Raider's face. "Where you from?"

Raider brought the stock of the Winchester up fast. It struck the rancher under the nose and upset him from his horse. As Raider and William and Ellen galloped into a draw and ran hard from the river, they could hear the man's shots. None of the bullets came close. Maybe he was firing in the air, to call for help.

Reaching high ground half a mile from the river, they paused and looked back. Horsemen were still riding wildly up and down the river, yelling, firing shots. None were coming after them—none they could see, anyway. "That's what you call a posse," said Raider. "Let's move before they figure out that we've left them behind."

Just before dawn they settled into another of their rude camps, to wait quietly during the daylight, getting some rest while they listened and watched. They chose a tight area heavily grown over with tangled brush and cactus—near no water, near no house, no road. They chased out a nest of rattlesnakes that had expected to stay there during the heat of the day. Buzzing fiercely, the rattlers oozed away across the sand. Raider tethered Bastardo and gave him water from a canteen.

"I figure we're six, seven miles from the river now," Raider said. "Maybe more. We made good time. We're loose in big country now. All we have to do is figure where we're going and keep away from Texans while we go there."

He scouted the land around. It was no different from what was on the other side of the river, and it was vacant. All the men who had been yelling and shooting last night had gone some other way. It was like he'd said: It was big country to get lost in.

He let William and Ellen rest two hours, then roused them and moved. The farther into Texas, the bigger the country, he said.

They rode northeast, roughly in the direction of San Antonio, which was 150 miles way, Raider guessed.

"Ought to come to the El Aguila road," he said to William. "We have to be damn careful then. They might be out on it."

"Doesn't look familiar, any of this land," William said.

"Not to me, either. Doesn't look right."

They saw no one, but they rode more cautiously as they guessed they must be approaching the road. The sun was high when finally they came to a sandy track, moving southeast to northwest.

"Got to be the road," said Raider. "But I never been here before. El Aguila . . ."

"That way?" William asked, pointing to their right, southeast.

"I suppose so. But—no, by God! That way's *Laredo!* I just figured it out. El Aguila is *that way.*" He swung his arm to their left, northwest.

"I don't want to go there, Raider," said William solemnly.

Raider looked at him for a moment. "No," he conceded. "Neither do I. We got to find a town where they don't believe everything they hear from El Aguila, where I can identify myself as a Pinkerton and get a telegram off to Chicago. Let Wagner tell me where Doc is—or tell Doc where I am."

"The Nueces River is north," said William. "There are towns along it—"

"Maybe all the way to San Antonio," said Raider. "I got a feeling all this country is crazy."

They struck across the road and rode north. Ten miles more and Raider turned a little to the west. The notion of riding all the way to San Antonio appealed to him more and more. There was law there. And he could send wires. He would wire Chicago and Jacob Bridenbaugh. This far from El Aguila, the road to San Antonio might be safe. No one would guess that was where they were going.

The mid-afternoon sun slowed them. Ellen asked for a rest.

"I'd like to find that goddam road to San Antonio," Raider said to her, shaking his head.

"You found your way better in Mexico."

Raider sighed. "I guess we have to stop."

William had ridden a little ahead. Now he came trotting back. "Hey, Raider!" he called grinning as he rode toward them. "We can drop off these horses and sit a spell. Take a look at what's just up ahead."

"What?" Raider asked wearily.

William's grin spread. "Telegraph wire. San Antonio road."

They dismounted. They had just unsaddled the horses and sat down with hunks of bread and the very last of their cold beans when they heard two shotgun blasts and a woman's agonized scream.

CHAPTER TWENTY

"This is none of our affair," said Raider, "but I'm going to have a look. You two stay back."

He trotted forward in a crouch, pulling the Remington from his holster. Keeping quiet, he worked his way through the brush to the road. There he stopped. He could see no one on the road. He ran across. The scream had come from beyond but not far beyond. It had come from a bit farther north along the road. Out of sight of the road, hiding himself in the brush, he trotted toward the place.

"Doc!"

Doc was lying on his back in the sand, a young woman crouched over him. Blood was streaming from his nose. At first Raider thought she had shot him. Then he saw the two horses and the two bloody corpses.

"Raider!"

It was the young woman who had shouted his name, and she was . . . she was the one who had been with him that last night in El Aguila, the one the punks had claimed was theirs. What was her name? Kathleen.

Raider stepped out of the brush, putting his revolver back in the holster. "Doc," he said. "Kathleen." He nodded toward the two bodies lying on the ground. "What the hell's goin' on?"

"You remember the Murphy brothers," Doc muttered through the handkerchief pressed against his bleeding nose. "Where's William Bridenbaugh?"

Raider planted his hands on his hips. "You're all business, ain't you, Doc? You might have asked—"

"—if you're still alive," Doc interrupted. "I can see you are. A little grubby, but alive for sure. You look like you've had it easier than I have. Your nose is straight."

"So would yours be, if I'd been around to nurse-maid you."

Doc lowered the handkerchief and winced at the sight of the blood it had soaked up. Blood had fallen on his silk shirt, too, and he shook his head. "The story is you stirred up a revolution in Mexico."

"They don't need me for that," said Raider. "What's going on in El Aguila?"

"Every man who can is carrying a gun," said Doc. "The ranchers brought their hands in. The town's full of armed men, just looking for somebody to kill."

"Me, I suppose," said Raider. "They sent fifty or so down to the Rio Grande to welcome me home."

"They think you're bringing back an army. That's the story that's been spread. Seriously, Raider, did you bring back William Bridenbaugh?"

Raider nodded. "Plus a woman that was kidnapped by Apaches and sold as a slave in Mexico five years ago."

"Where are they?"

Raider yelled. "William! Ellen! Bring the horses. We've got friends over here."

"Only after I kin git a bath somewheres," Ellen said to Kathleen. It was her response to Kathleen's offer of a skirt and blouse to replace her dirty white pants and shirt, "Then fer sure, and thank ya."

Doc and Raider sat with William in the shade of the Studebaker wagon, talking. "They think my dad is coming down here with men, huh?" said William. "That can be arranged. When he finds out . . ."

"No," said Doc. "We don't work that way."

"Who don't work that way?"

"Don't forget," Doc said to William, but glancing significantly at Raider, "Raider and I are operatives of the Pinkerton National Detective Agency. We don't settle problems by stirring up a little war. We go to law."

"What law?" William asked. "*I'm* accused of murder. *Raider's* accused of murder. And now . . ." He nodded toward the bodies of the two Murphys. "Who'll they want to hang for those two? You? Or Kathleen? Or both of you? Raider shot Galvin in self-defense. Kathleen shot the Murphys to save you. I didn't shoot Susie Bradford at all. But what difference is any of that going to make if they get their hands on us?"

"They aren't going to get their hands on us," said Doc. "I said we're not going to stir up a big gunfight between Adena and El Aguila. I said we're going to law. But not lynch law."

"What law, then?"

"I'm not sure," said Doc. "I'm going to wire Chicago. I'll ask Wagner to arrange for us to see a judge, maybe a federal judge, maybe in San Antonio. We're Pinkertons. A judge who knows that won't just assume we run around murdering people. Besides, we've got a case against McMullen and one against the railroad. We'll get law. Real law."

"I s'pose you expect me to shinny up that goddam pole," said Raider.

Doc smiled. "If you don't mind," he said.

Raider helped Doc to unpack the apparatus from under the floorboards of the wagon. They left the gravity batteries in place, but Doc wanted the key and sounder out on the wagon box. Raider led Judith a little closer to the pole, so the wires would reach. He stretched the wire and began to climb the pole. Doc sat on the box, with the key and sounder beside him. The two women watched, fascinated.

"Give her a try, Doc," Raider yelled. He had attached Doc's wire to the telegraph line and he wanted to know if the connection was good before he came down.

Doc closed the switch on the key and tapped a short message. The sounder began to click then. The connection was good. Doc waved to Raider and began to tap the signal that this message was to be relayed to Chicago.

"Hey!" yelled Raider from the top of the pole. "Trouble comin'."

Raider slid down. He trotted across the sand to Bastardo and mounted. He drew the Winchester from its scabbard and balanced it across his lap and the saddle. He checked the cartridges in his Remington. William mounted, too. Doc sat on the box. He had not been able to start his message to Chicago. He reloaded the double-barreled shotgun and laid it on the wagon box beside him. Ellen mounted her mare and sat with a Winchester in hand. Kathleen stood on the ground by the wagon—she alone unarmed.

The horsemen might have ridden by without seeing them, but they had seen Raider atop the telegraph pole when they were a quarter of a mile away, and now they slowed and stopped and left the road and approached.

"Watch out for the one in the gray suit," Doc said to Raider.

That one was Douglas Keene, the railroad policeman. He rode beside Jeffrey McMullen. Tom McMullen, his jaw still bound in Dr. Hinkley's wires and tape, rode beside Tod Galvin. Horace Chandler was there. He rode beside the old sheriff, Jimmy Tate. These were the ones Doc recognized. Others he had seen around town—ranchers, ranch foremen, cowboys. There were sixteen men. Two he did not know at all. The railroad men, likely.

"Gawd a'mighty, they've kilt some more!" yelled Chandler. He pointed at the bodies on the ground. "The two Murphy boys!"

"Well, I guess it's all pretty clear now," said Jeffrey McMullen. "You two." He pointed at Doc, then at

Raider. "We guessed you worked together. And Bill Bridenbaugh. Well, well."

"We do indeed," said Doc. "Raider and I are operatives of the Pinkerton National Detective Agency."

"I knew you were not a homeopathic physician," said Keene with a cold smile. "It was a clever lie to pose as one. It's not quite as clever to pose as a Pinkerton. I think we are about to learn who you really are."

Sheriff Jimmy Tate pressed his horse forward and stood between the two groups. "Boys," he said. "It ain't gonna do you no good to resist arrest. There's too many of us fer ya, and even if you git away from us, there's others out lookin'. Why don't you jist put your guns down and come back to town with us?"

"If you were the law in El Aguila, Mr. Tate, I'd do that," said Doc. "But your friends would lynch us before any law was done. They have to. They don't dare let the town find out what they've done."

"Whut . . . ?" asked the old sheriff, shaking his head.

"They stole Jacob Bridenbaugh's gold," said Doc. "Or maybe I should say it differently. They stole his land. Jeffrey McMullen handed over the deed to Bridenbaugh's land to the railroad, which he was supposed to do when the railroad paid him $25,000 in gold to Bridenbaugh's account. When Jacob Bridenbaugh sent his son to get the gold, McMullen didn't have it and couldn't pay. If that had gotten out it would have broken his bank, so he arranged the murder of a prostitute and to have William Bridenbaugh accused—"

"Lies!" shouted Jeffrey McMullen. "Despicable lies, told by a man who's just killed two young men and feels the noose around his neck!" The banker shook his head so hard his jowls flapped, and spittle flew from the corners of his mouth.

Some of the ranchers shifted uneasily in their saddles and exchanged glances.

"Mr. Galvin," said Doc. "He couldn't meet your demand for—"

Keene spurred his horse forward a pace and stood in

front of the sheriff. "Enough of this," he snapped coldly. "All of this can be discussed in the courtroom if
it's relevant to the murder trials—which it isn't. You
men—and your two . . . women—are all under lawful
arrest. Put down your weapons. *Now.*"

Keene was wearing his revolver—a Colt Peacemaker
that replaced the Iver Johnson Doc and Kathleen had
taken from him—in a holster outside his gray suit. Now,
in a fast, fluid motion, he drew it. Raider's bullet caught
him in the shoulder. He dropped his pistol and bent
over in pain, until his head touched his horse's neck.
Raider sat with the Remington in his hand, glaring
at the McMullens, Chandler, and some of the others
who were poised as if they meant to draw. All of them
cautiously put their hands to their horses' reins. Raider
returned the Remington to its holster.

"I may not be a real doctor, Mr. Keene," said Doc.
"But if people will let me, I can do something for you."

Tod Galvin dismounted and helped Keene down
from his horse. Doc leaned back into the Studebaker
and pulled out his medical kit. Galvin laid Keene out
on the sand by the wagon. Kathleen bent over him.

"Search him for another gun," Doc said quietly to
her. He jumped down from the wagon box and knelt
beside Keene.

"Where's your daddy's men?" the sheriff asked William.

"They're not comin'," said William. "They never
were. 'Course, if there's a lynchin', that might be somethin' else."

"Let 'em come," growled Tom McMullen. "I'm for
havin' it out, once and for all."

"Where's all the Mexicans I'm supposed to be leading across the border?" Raider asked. He spoke past
the sheriff and the McMullens. "Don't you men see
how this man's been lying to you?"

"You brought twenty men over the Rio Grande last
night," one of the ranchers to the rear said. "I was
there, heard the shootin'."

"I brought two, besides myself," said Raider. "You men were shooting at each other. Somebody got a crack on the snoot with my Winchester. Is he here?"

"That wuz Willard," said a man. "He says there wuz jus' three."

"Have you killed Keene, too?" the banker asked.

Doc looked up from Keene, whose coat and shirt he had cut away to expose the bullet wound. "Look for yourself," he said. "It's in his shoulder."

"What're you doin' to him?" asked the sheriff.

"The bullet's in him," said Doc. "Dr. Hinkley can take it out. For now, I'm putting arnicated carbolic salve on the wound, and I'm giving him some laudanum. He'll be all right."

"He better be," said Horace Chandler.

"Right, he better," muttered Tom McMullen.

Kathleen held Keene's head in her lap, and Doc climbed back to the wagon box. "Mr. Galvin," he said. "You told me Mr. McMullen asked you not to withdraw a large amount of money from the McMullen Bank, because it would inconvenience the bank."

"Sure it would, after I handed over $25,000 in gold to the Bridenbaugh lad," said McMullen.

"Jeff . . ." said Galvin. He shook his head. "It was *before* you paid Bridenbaugh that you asked me not to withdraw money."

"Besides," said Doc, "your bank only acted as escrow agent for the money you were supposed to pay William Bridenbaugh. You were supposed to receive $25,000 in gold from the railroad and pay it over to Bridenbaugh. That would have had no effect on the bank's condition."

"That's right, Jeff," said one of the ranchers.

"This is crazy!" McMullen protested loudly. "We're sittin' here talking bank business with three . . ." He choked. He pointed at Raider. "Some of us *saw* him shoot your son, Tod. We all just saw him shoot Mr. Keene, who is a lifelong peace officer and now a bona fide railroad police officer. We're lookin' down on the bodies of two more of our citizens, the Murphy brothers. The word is up from Mexico that these men killed God knows how many men down there. The Bridenbaugh boy here killed a whore at Sister Edwards's place. There were witnesses to that. If any depositor wants to look into the condition of the McMullen Bank, he's entitled. But I'm lookin' at three murderers. It's obvious that this one's fast with a gun, but it won't make any difference if we all have the courage to move at once. We've got to take 'em in custody. We've *got* to."

Raider tensed. Some of the ranchers and their men had begun to fill with breath, to stiffen, to set their faces grim. He could not open fire on them, even if they drew their guns. They were wrong but they were innocent. He would have to submit to their arrest.

Sheriff Jimmy Tate scratched his beard and asked, "Whut you been doin' to the telegraph line?"

"Reporting to the Pinkerton office in Chicago," said Doc. "Whatever you do with us, the Pinkerton Agency has a full report of everything that's happened here. There'll be other Pinkertons after us. There's no way you can cover yourselves now."

Raider glanced hard at William, then at Ellen and Kathleen. Doc had not transmitted a word, and they must not betray that.

"Let me see that apparatus," a man at the rear of the group said. He rode forward. He was a man fifty years old, gray and thin, with thick gray whiskers. When he rode forward, another man from the rear came with him, keeping to his side. "I want to look at that telegraph apparatus."

"May I assume you are Mr. Bodine?" Doc asked.

The man nodded. "President of the San Antonio, Houston & New Orleans Railroad."

"Company" said Doc.

"What's that?"

"You are president of a railroad company, not a railroad," said Doc. "You haven't laid a foot of track."

"Matter of time," said Bodine casually. His attention

was riveted to the telegraph key. "Where's the batteries?"

Doc tipped his head toward the batteries in the wagon. "Gravity batteries," he said. "It's a twenty-ohm circuit. Western Union standard key."

Bodine peered into the wagon. The man beside him craned his neck and peered in, too. He was younger, a heavyset blond man with a fat mustache. The bodyguard. Pickering. Charlotte Crittenden had told Doc about him. Kathleen caught Raider's attention and pointed at Pickering. She touched her hip with her finger. Raider understood. She meant the man was a shootist.

Bodine sighed. "Let's see you raise an operator," he said.

Doc closed the switch on the key and tapped out a call. Bodine frowned, his lips moving. He could read Morse code. In a moment the sounder began to click. The San Antonio telegraph office was responding.

"Let's see if the Pinkerton office responds to you," said Bodine. He sat stiffly on his horse, watching, listening.

"Could take a while," Doc said, but he began to tap a signal:

PINKERTON NATIONAL DETECTIVE AGENCY
CHICAGO
ATTN WAGNER
URGENT YOU CONFIRM IMMEDIATELY I AM PINKERTON OPERATIVE STOP AS CHECK PLEASE CONFIRM NAME MY PARTNER STOP AS FURTHER CHECK WHERE AM I STOP

WEATHERBEE

The party stirred uneasily in their saddles, waiting. Some of them glanced at the sun. Two opened canteens and drank water. One pulled a pint and took a swig of whiskey.

"This is insane," McMullen protested weakly.

Bodine sat erect, staring at the telegraph sounder,

taking his eyes off it only to glance at Pickering. The heavy bodyguard watched Raider.

Five minutes passed.

"How long do we wait?" asked Tod Galvin.

"As long as it takes," said Bodine. He pulled a gold pocket watch from his vest and checked the time. "As much as an hour. We have to know the truth of this matter. This is real telegraph apparatus, and he does have contact. If he's telegraphed what he says he has to Chicago . . . We'll wait."

Five more minutes passed. Keene stood and asked for water. The laudanum made him reel as he stood. It also made him thirsty.

The sounder began to click. Bodine leaned forward and listened.

PINKERTON NATIONAL DETECTIVE AGENCY CONFIRMS IT HAS TWO AGENTS ASSIGNED EL AGUILA TEXAS AND VICINITY STOP NAMES WEATHERBEE AND RAIDER STOP PLEASE AFFORD EVERY ASSISTANCE AND COOPERATION STOP

    PINKERTON NATIONAL DETECTIVE AGENCY
    BY WAGNER FOR ALLAN PINKERTON

No one but Doc and Bodine could read the code, and Doc wondered if the railroad president would acknowledge the confirmation or tell the others it was a denial and call for a lynching. He looked at Raider and could tell Raider was wondering the same. Raider's attention was mostly on Pickering.

Bodine turned to McMullen. "You're in terrible trouble, Jeff," he said. "They *are* Pinkertons."

"Oliver!" McMullen yelled. "You owe me $25,000!"

"That may be," said Bodine evenly. "I owe a lot of people more than that. But I haven't done what you seem to have done to cover it."

"I ain't done nothin'!" the banker shrieked. "There's no evidence against me, nothin' but the words of—"

"Jeff," said Galvin firmly. "How much of our money have you lost?"

The ranchers began to crowd around McMullen.

"Mr. Bodine," said Doc.

Bodine, who had turned his horse toward McMullen, turned back. "You have it about right, Mr. Weatherbee," he said. "The railroad—railroad *company*—bought land from Mr. Jacob Bridenbaugh, to be paid for with $25,000 in gold. Jeff here, as a banker, was to hold the Bridenbaugh deed until the company paid that money into the bank, after which the company was to receive the deed and Mr. Bridenbaugh was to receive the gold. Jeff is an investor in the railroad. He has his own money in it, and some of the bank's is in it, too. The company didn't have $25,000 in gold. We couldn't come up with it. But if we could sell the Bridenbaugh land, we would have—not only the $25,000 in gold but a nice profit to boot. Making that profit would have protected Jeff's and the bank's investment. If we only had the Bridenbaugh deed, we could sell the land, pay off Bridenbaugh, and put the profit in the railroad company to help it over its financial difficulties. So . . . Need I say more?"

"So McMullen gave you the deed without receiving the gold," said Doc.

"Yes," said Bodine. "Then Bridenbaugh wanted his money immediately. That was what Jeff hadn't expected. He thought Jacob Bridenbaugh would leave the money on deposit in the McMullen Bank, at least long enough for us to sell the land and come up with the money. Instead, Jacob Bridenbaugh telegraphed that he was sending his son to pick up the gold."

"So someone was going to kill William Bridenbaugh or arrange to have him look like a murderer and a thief, to cover the fact that the bank had betrayed its trust."

Bodine smiled. "Well, I wouldn't know about that part."

"The hell you wouldn't!" shouted Tom McMullen. "You was a part of everything! You—"

Tom McMullen stopped. Pickering had drawn his

pistol and had it pointed at him. Pickering's face was cruelly hard, coldly threatening.

"You pointed that gun at the wrong man," Raider said to Pickering. He had raised the muzzle of his Winchester. "If you don't drop that gun in about two seconds, your head comes off."

Bodine reached for a pistol. "Careful," said Ellen. She had her Winchester leveled at him.

"Somebody had better disarm Horace Chandler, too," said Doc. "He's part of it."

"Me?" yelled Chandler. "What'd I have to do with anything?"

"Tom McMullen killed Susie Bradford," said Doc. "You're the deputy. You came out to the whorehouse and announced that William Bridenbaugh had done it. If you had believed that, you could have captured William. This town can raise quite a posse when it wants to. You could have caught William before he crossed the Rio Grande—or even after. But you didn't want to. The plan was for him to be killed in Mexico. You sent men after him, to kill him over there and bring back the gold he was carrying—$7,800, all the bank could raise, I suppose."

"If all this is true, why would McMullen send William Bridenbaugh to Mexico with that much gold?" asked one of the ranchers.

"It's right, that was all I could raise," said Jeffrey McMullen weakly. He swayed in his saddle. "There was so much at risk. If someone besides my men got to him, I wanted them to find a lot of gold on him. They could fight about what had happened to the rest of it."

"You admit all this, Jeff?" asked Tod Galvin.

The banker nodded. "The bank is bust," he said sadly. "The railroad busted it. I thought we'd all get rich off the railroad comin' through, but the San Antonio, Houston & New Orleans Railroad is a fraud."

"It's not a fraud!" snapped Bodine.

"But it's bust, too," said McMullen.

"Any question now, boys?" asked Tod Galvin.

"Sheriff, it's your duty to arrest Jeff and Tom McMullen, Bodine and Pickering, and Horace Chandler."

The ranchers moved fast. In a minute they had bound the hands of all five men.

"How 'bout Keene?" Galvin asked.

"I don't think he knew what they were up to," said Doc.

"What 'bout the Murphys?"

"Kathleen shot them," said Doc. "Uh . . . you recognize Kathleen, Mr. Galvin?"

The big rancher grinned and touched his tall Stetson. "Sure," he said. "How do, Miz Weatherbee?"

"We were alone, she and I," said Doc. "The Murphys came riding in. They were going to kill me. They broke my nose, as you can see. Kathleen shot them. She saved my life."

Galvin nodded. "Your nose *is* broke," he said.

"Keene is bleeding," said Ellen. "Better put him in the back of the wagon."

"I can ride," said Keene. He faced his horse for a moment, gathering strength, then swung up into the saddle. He blinked at Doc. "I *knew* you weren't no doctor."

"I knowed they was somethin' wrong," said Jimmy Tate.

"We're all bust if that bank is," said Galvin. "We got a hell of a job ahead of us, tryin' to save somethin'."

"It ain't all that bust," said Jeffrey McMullen. He twisted his shoulders, trying to relieve some of the strain on his bound arms. "Treat me easy, boys," he pleaded. "It ain't busted completely. It'll pay fifty cents on the dollar maybe."

"After you hang," growled one of the ranchers.

"Ahh, no, boys," he whined. "You don't want to hang me. You got no call. I was only tryin' to protect your deposits."

"You'll be comin' into town," Galvin said to Doc and Raider. "We've got a lot to straighten out." He glanced at the two women. "You're all welcome to be guests at my ranch while we do it."

"I'm the one who shot your son, Mr. Galvin," said Raider.

"Did he draw on you, Mr. Raider?" asked Galvin solemnly.

"Yes, sir. He did."

Galvin nodded. "So Dr. Weatherbee told me. And so have others. I don't know what else you could have done. A man has to defend himself. You're welcome in my house, Mr. Raider."

Doc sat on the wagon box, telegraphing a long report to Wagner. They were alone—he and Raider, William and Kathleen and Ellen. The men from town had loaded the Murphy brothers' bodies on their horses and taken them down the road. Doc and Raider had promised to follow as soon as Doc had telegraphed Chicago.

"You'll get that bath you've been wanting, Ellen," Raider said. "And not in a river or a mountain pond, either. I bet that ranch house has a tub and hot water and soap. Then you can put on women's clothes again, and we'll set to work to find your family."

"She'll be comin' home with me," said William.

Raider nodded. "Good. Doc and I will have a new assignment right off. You get no time off when you work for Allan Pinkerton."

"You're going to get a lot of thanks in El Aguila," said Kathleen. "You're some kind of heroes, you two."

Raider grinned. He looked up. The sounder was clicking, and Doc was taking down a reply from Chicago.

"I figure there's congratulations for a job well done comin' in on that wire," he said. "We don't get bonuses, but I bet we get some thanks."

"You have it coming," said Kathleen.

The sounder stopped. Doc tore a piece of paper off

his pad. "This part of the message is for you," he said, and he handed the paper down to Raider.

Raider read it. "Well, I be . . . I be . . . *Damn!* That does it, Doc. I quit. Send 'em a wire right now. Tell Wagner and Allan Pinkerton they can both go to hell. I quit. Goddam! Send it, Doc. Send it!"

Doc disconnected the key from the wire. "Will you be so kind as to go up the pole and disconnect from the line?"

"No, by God! That wire will hang there till buzzards peck it off before I climb another pole for the Pinkerton National Detective Agency."

"Our pay's waiting for us in Abilene," said Doc. "You'll stick with me that far, won't you?"

"Well . . ."

"So I've got to unhook from the line," said Doc.

Raider shot him a glance of contempt and disgust. As he strode to the pole he wadded up his message and tossed the paper at Bastardo.

The message read:

HAVE RECEIVED FROM JACOB BRIDENBAUGH A STATEMENT FOR ONE HUNDRED DOLLARS FOR HORSE FURNISHED YOU STOP EXPENSE UNAUTHORIZED BUT WILL PAY FIFTY DOLLARS STOP REMAINDER EXCEEDS AMOUNT THIS AGENCY ALLOWS FOR SUCH PURCHASE STOP WILL DEDUCT BALANCE FROM YOUR SALARY STOP

WAGNER

J.D. HARDIN

"THE MOST EXCITING WESTERN WRITER SINCE LOUIS L'AMOUR"

—JAKE LOGAN

_____	16840 BLOOD SWEAT AND GOLD	$1.95
_____	16842 BLOODY SANDS	$1.95
_____	16882 BULLETS BUZZARDS, BOXES OF PINE	$1.95
_____	16877 COLDHEARTED LADY	$1.95
_____	16911 DEATH LODE	$1.95
_____	16843 FACE DOWN IN A COFFIN	$1.95
_____	16844 THE GOOD THE BAD AND THE DEADLY	$1.95
_____	21002 GUNFIRE AT SPANISH ROCK	$1.95
_____	16799 HARD CHAINS SOFT WOMEN	$1.95
_____	16881 THE MAN WHO BIT SNAKES	$1.95
_____	16861 RAIDER S GOLD	$1.95
_____	16883 RAIDER S HELL	$1.95
_____	16767 RAIDER S REVENGE	$1.95
_____	16555 THE SLICK AND THE DEAD	$1.50
_____	16839 SILVER TOMBSTONES	$1.95
_____	16869 THE SPIRIT AND THE FLESH	$1.95

1081-13

 PLAYBOY PAPERBACKS
Book Mailing Service
P.O. Box 690 Rockville Centre, New York 11571

NAME_____

ADDRESS_____

CITY_____STATE_____ZIP_____

Please enclose 50¢ for postage and handling if one book is ordered;
25¢ for each additional book. $1.50 maximum postage and handling
charge. No cash, CODs or stamps. Send check or money order.

Total amount enclosed: $_____